PRAISE FOR *THE GOOD LUCK CHARM*

"Fabulously fun! Lilah and Ethan's second-chance romance charmed me from the first page to the swoon-worthy end."

—Jill Shalvis, *New York Times* bestselling author

"If you love rom-coms, don't miss this second-chance romance novel."

—*Hello Giggles*

"I couldn't stop turning the pages of this sexy, second-chance romance. After reading, you'll want to be Ethan's good luck charm, too."

—Amy E. Reichert, author of *The Coincidence of Coconut Cake* and *The Optimist's Guide to Letting Go*

"*The Good Luck Charm* is an absolute delight. Helena Hunting delivered banter, heat, humor, and family as Ethan tries to earn back the one thing he needs. Ms. Hunting crafted an entertaining and sexy story with a relatable cast of characters. Fans of Emma Chase, Christina Lauren, and Jaci Burton will love The Good

Junkie

WALTHAM FOREST LIBRARIES

D0302334

"Hockey talk, more than one steamy scene, and a hero and heroine who have a genuine respect as well as a fiery passion for each other make this romance an all-around winner."

—*BookPage*

"Writing with a deliciously sharp humor, Hunting shoots and scores in this exceptionally entertaining contemporary romance."

—*Booklist*

"Hunting sparkles in this well-plotted contemporary...She imbues her characters, especially Lilah, with quick wit and enjoyable depth, and the curveball she throws into the plot at the end is truly surprising, yet believable."

—*Publishers Weekly*

"Cute and sexy and fun."

—Girly Book Club

"*The Good Luck Charm* was a delightful gem of a second-chance romance, a sweet and swoony love story that I just adored."

—Angie & Jessica's Dreamy Reads

"A great summer/beach read. The characters had depth and a wonderful connection."

—*Naughty Moms' Story Time*

MEET CUTE

ALSO BY HELENA HUNTING

The Good Luck Charm

MEET CUTE

HELENA HUNTING

piatkus

PIATKUS

First published in the US in 2019 by Forever,
an imprint of Grand Central Publishing, a division of Hachette Book Group, Inc

First published in Great Britain in 2019 by Piatkus

1 3 5 7 9 10 8 6 4 2

Copyright © 2019 by Helena Hunting

The moral right of the author has been asserted.

*All characters and events in this publication, other than those
clearly in the public domain, are fictitious and any resemblance
to real persons, living or dead, is purely coincidental.*

All rights reserved.
No part of this publication may be reproduced, stored in a
retrieval system, or transmitted in any form or by any means, without
the prior permission in writing of the publisher, nor be otherwise circulated
in any form of binding or cover other than that in which it is published
and without a similar condition including this condition being
imposed on the subsequent purchaser.

A CIP catalogue record for this book
is available from the British Library.

ISBN 978-0-349-42358-6

Printed and bound in Great Britain by
Clays Ltd, Elcograf S.p.A.

Papers used by Piatkus are from well-managed forests
and other responsible sources.

Waltham Forest Libraries	C
904 000 00642709	
Askews & Holts	30-Apr-2019
	£8.99
6024507	

For every brother who's ever gone a
round for his sister

prologue

FANGIRL DOWN

Kailyn

Eight Years Ago

"The key to success is to visualize it." The soothing voice commands my attention, mostly because I'm wearing earbuds and it blocks everything else out. I resist the urge to check my schedule again—I know exactly where my class is since I walked the route yesterday and focus on the podcast. It's my first day of law school and I'm determined to go in with a clear mind. "Close your eyes and visualize what your success looks like. Visualize success."

"Visualize success," I murmur, and close my eyes as I cut across the open field. It's a shortcut and also a place where students hang out between classes.

"Exhale your anxiety," the motivational podcast woman exhales into my ear. "And breathe in success." Podcast Woman sucks in a windy breath.

"Inhale success." The fresh scent of grass and trees tickles my nose, and I think maybe someone nearby might be wearing cologne, because I get a whiff of that, too.

I crack a lid, just to make sure I'm not wandering off course.

"What does your success look like? Visualize that success. Say it with me..."

I close my eyes and repeat it, visualizing finals and graduation and getting the best possible internships, having the best average in the class, getting the best job. I repeat the mantra as I continue across the open green space, more and more excited for my first class. I'm going to kick all the asses this year. I'm going to beat every single one of my classmates and climb my way to the very top. Like Mount Everest, except not terrifyingly dangerous.

I'm in the middle of visualizing winning my first case when I'm startled by a loud shout. I open my eyes to find a Frisbee hurtling toward me. Worse than the Frisbee, though, is the huge guy jumping to catch it—the air he gets is rather extraordinary—unfortunately, it's sending him on a collision course, and I'm the object he's due to hit.

My knapsack slips from my shoulder, and I trip over it as I try to avoid either the Frisbee or the guy. The mantra in my ears silences as the headphones pull free.

"Watch out!" someone yells.

I spin around, disoriented, and am slammed into by the guy with the amazing vertical.

"Oh shit!" he yells.

I grab on to his shoulders as I stumble over my stupid knapsack and pull him down with me. We land on the ground with an *oomph*. I'm still gripping his shirt, trying to figure out how this happened, and thinking about how much this is *not* how I visualize success at all.

"I'm so sorry. Are you okay?" He braces himself on his forearms, pretty much doing a push-up on top of me. I'd be impressed if I wasn't so embarrassed.

"I'd be a lot better if people watched where they were going," I mutter as I try to extract my limbs from his without doing any damage to either of us. He's straddling my leg, so any sudden movements and my knee and his man parts will meet in an unfriendly way. I note that he smells like fresh laundry, deodorant, and a hint of cologne, accented by watermelon gum.

His face is only about six inches from mine, so his frown is up close and rather personal. "You walked through the middle of our game."

I glance toward the group of Frisbee players, realizing he's right. I was so busy visualizing my own success that I totally screwed up their game.

"I'm so sorry. I was listening to a podca—" I look back up at him, and my explanation gets stuck in my throat when I stop to really take him in.

I recognize his face as one I've had endless fantasies about all through my teen years. And into my adult ones. As recently as last week, even.

His slightly annoyed expression shifts into amusement as I stare up at him, slack jawed. I'm still fisting his shirt. He's still doing a push-up on top of me. *Daxton Hughes's thigh is between my legs.*

"Holy crap!" My voice is too high and far too loud, especially considering my face is less than six inches from his. In fact, it's a full-on shriek. As if I'm an eleven-year-old girl again. "You're Daxton Hughes! I love you!" I take him totally off guard when I throw my arms around him, setting him off balance so that he lands on top of me. He's remarkably heavy, but I don't care because our bodies are flush against each other. I will never forget this moment for as long as I live. *Daxton Hughes is lying on top of me!* Too bad we're not at the beach and both in bathing suits. Or in bed. Naked.

I'm still hugging him as he drags me up into a sitting position. It's super awkward with the way we both have a knee perilously close to each other's crotch. I also register how stiff he is, and exactly what I've just said and what I'm currently doing. We're in the middle of an open expanse of field, and there are people everywhere.

Horrified, I release him and crabwalk backward, almost kneeing him in the man jewels. I clamber to my feet, taking a step back as he pushes up, rising to his full height. My God he's tall, taller than I expected, and broad. But I suppose he's grown into his body since he starred in my favorite TV show. My hands are flapping. *Why are my hands flapping?* I need to make my body stop doing weird things, but I'm out of control and my nervousness takes over, sending me careening into the land of insanely embarrassing behavior. There are too many witnesses.

His blue-green eyes, the color of a tropical ocean, are wide, and that momentary gorgeous smile falters. Which I understand, because I'm being *that girl*. I am never that girl. Except in this moment.

I gain semicontrol of my hands, toning down the flap to an uncoordinated wave of dismissal, in an attempt to erase those last words. But it's too late to take them back. I also seem unable to do anything apart from spew embarrassing, nonsensical word vomit all over him. "I mean, I loved your show. Like, so much. It was my favorite, like, ever. I watched it every Tuesday night for years. All through junior high and then by high school they had these *It's My Life* weekend marathons and me and my girlfriends would have sleepovers and stay up all night. You were amazing as Dustin. I think season three was my favorite, or maybe season four. Oh my God. I can't believe you're standing here. I can't believe I'm meeting you." *I can't believe my mouth keeps running.*

With every overly loud admission, his jaw tics. I can't tell if he's embarrassed or irritated. Probably both. I wish someone would club me over the head and knock me out so I could stop this train wreck. I'm 100 percent starstruck, and even though I know I'm making an absolute fool out of myself, I'm unable to stop.

"Can I get your autograph? Maybe you can sign my schedule. Or my map. Oh! You can sign me!" I pick my knapsack up, along with my phone and earbuds, shoving those into my jeans pocket. I jam my hand in the front pocket of my knapsack, grasping for any kind of writing implement. I come up with a fistful of options, including a hot-pink highlighter. "Do you think this color will show up on my arm? Oh! How about my shirt? I mean, the pink doesn't really match but whatevs, right?"

He covers my hand with his. *He's touching me again. On purpose!* His eyes dart around, and he leans in close. "I'll sign anything you want, but as much as I love your enthusiasm, and I really do, I'm trying to go under the radar, and you've got some cheerleader lungs on you." His voice is much lower than mine, and I realize it's an attempt to get me to quiet down.

I cover my mouth with my palm. "Right. Sorry. Oh my God. I'm so sorry. This is so embarrassing. I just...you have no idea. Or you probably do. I didn't think you'd be so tall. And you're even better looking up close. I always thought you must wear contacts. Your eyes are so pretty." I squeeze my eyes shut. "I really need to shut up."

He chuckles. "Your eyes are pretty, too."

I crack a lid, and he gives me a lopsided smile as he plucks a Sharpie from my hand and scribbles on my knapsack. I'm never throwing it out, ever.

"Hughes, we gotta roll out," someone calls.

He holds up a finger, then caps the Sharpie and passes it back. "I gotta get to class, but maybe I'll see you around." He winks and turns away, breaking into a jog as he catches a bag from one of his friends.

"I just met Daxton Hughes and he told me I have pretty eyes," I say as I continue across the quad. A couple of girls sitting under a tree give me a weird look, but I don't care. This is the best first day of law school ever. Embarrassment hits as I make a quick stop in the bathroom to prevent hyperventilating due to excessive excitement. I fangirled so hard, and he was so nice. And he touched me.

I always imagined that if I met one of my favorite celebrities, I'd act cool, be all casual about it, treat them like a regular person. Obviously I was very wrong about that.

I spend too much time in the bathroom making sure I look half-decent, and I'm forced to speed walk all the way to my building. By the time I arrive I have only two minutes to spare. So much for getting a good seat. It's fine. *Visualize success.*

I enter the lecture hall through the back door, so I don't have to pass the professor on my way in. I'm sweaty and disheveled as I scan the room. Only a few empty seats remain. I murmur *excuse me* as I shimmy down the aisle, forcing people to move their feet and bags. As I close in on the open seat, I approach a set of outstretched legs and mutter another *excuse me.* I'm so high on the awesomeness of my morning that I don't see the messenger bag strap. I trip *again*, and end up sprawled over the set of legs.

"What the fu—" A takeout cup lands on the floor, and

coffee splatters my face and shirt, a puddle forming under the seat I planned to take.

I struggle to right myself without putting my hand in the puddle of coffee. "Oh my God, I'm so sor—" For the second time in the past twenty minutes, I look up into familiar eyes. "This is like that episode from season two!" I'm careful to keep my voice down this time.

Daxton smirks, maybe remembering the episode I'm referring to. The one where the girl trips and falls into his lap and then they end up dating for the next three seasons.

Before he can say anything, the guy beside him pipes up. "Jesus, Hughes, can't take you anywhere without some fangirl throwing herself at you, can we?"

They all burst into laughter, but Daxton rolls his eyes. "Don't be a dick, McQueen, and move your damn bag. It's your fault she tripped."

He rearranges his legs and helps me right myself. I drop into the empty one beside him, throat tight and cheeks heating with embarrassment thanks to his friend's comments. It's too late to find another seat, and I've already drawn enough attention. People are staring and snickering. I have to adjust my feet and keep my knapsack in my lap so I don't step in the spilled coffee. I'm so glad my hair is down today, because my face is on fire.

"Should we put bets on how many restraining orders you're going to have to file this year?" one of his friends asks loudly.

My stomach twists and my skin feels hot and damp. My

eyes threaten to water, so I dig my nails into my palms. The incident in the quad was one thing, but now there are all these eyes I can't escape for the next hour.

Thankfully, the professor calls the class to order, and the snickering beside me quiets. At the end of class I keep my eyes on my bag as I shove my books back inside. A folded piece of paper drops onto my desk.

"See ya next week." Daxton gives me a half grin and shoulders his knapsack, following his friends down the aisle.

I wait until they're gone before I flip it open.

Exactly like season two ;)

Like a love-struck idiot, I carry that note around with me for the rest of the year and then tuck it away in my underwear drawer for safekeeping. Every time he says hello to me I practically swoon. When he arrives to class after me he sits behind me, and he smiles when he passes me on campus. And when the mock trials start up in class, we're always against each other. It feels a lot like flirting.

But when it comes down to it, regardless of how friendly the competition seems, we're all looking out for ourselves. So in our final year of law school when I go to him for help, I shouldn't be surprised that he screws me over so he can have the thing I worked so hard for.

Fat lot of good all the visualizing success does for me in the end.

chapter one

BLAST FROM THE PAST

Kailyn

Present Day

The problem with temp assistants is that they don't know the rules. Such as rule number one: Take down the name of the client before you book them an appointment. My regular assistant, Cara, is on vacation and I miss her so much right now. The only thing I know about my mystery client is that they're a couple looking to set up a trust for their daughter. Pretty freaking broad. And I have zero time to call for details because they'll be here any minute.

My mug is halfway to my mouth when my temp assistant throws my door open. "Your next client is here!"

Half a second later she's ushering in a couple who look to be in their mid- to late fifties. A few steps behind them is a much younger man. A man I recognize.

The same man whose teenage self is forever immortalized on my *It's My Life* mug. The mug isn't particularly flattering, boasting an image of Daxton sobbing with the hashtag #mondayforever stamped under his tear-stained face.

I almost lose my grip on the mug. As it is, the liquid sloshes over the side and runs down my hand. Thankfully, it's just water—yes, I drink it out of a mug. I like cups with handles. I rush to set the mug on my desk and wipe my wet hands on my skirt.

I guess my clients are no longer a mystery. "Mr. and Mrs. Hughes, it's so lovely to meet you!" Shit. My voice is so pitchy.

I shake their hands as they introduce themselves as Craig and Evelyn, and then turn to Daxton, who's only half paying attention since he has a phone in his hand and he's clicking away on it. Probably plotting to take down another friend.

He's still ridiculously gorgeous, possibly even better looking than he was five years ago. He's filled out, the lankiness of his twenties giving way to a physique I'm sure he spends many hours a week staring at in a mirror while he lifts weights.

Beyond being attractive he has that magnetic appeal so many actors possess. It makes him the perfect lawyer. His beautiful face and commanding presence scream *trust me*. But I know better.

I hate that I can still appreciate how nice he is to look at. I wear a tight, practiced smile as I hold out a hand even though the last thing I want to do is touch him—okay, that's a lie, I actually have a nervous flutter in my stomach. It's annoying.

I wait for him to recognize me as his eyes move over me in a slow sweep. They linger on my legs for a few seconds, probably because of my patterned hose—it's how I spice up my business wardrobe. When his eyes finally return to my face, his brow furrows slightly while he shakes my hand. "Daxton Hughes. Nice to meet you." His eyes drift to the mug on my desk, and a smirk tugs at the corner of his mouth. Motherfucker. He doesn't even remember me.

I pull my hand from his grasp, frustrated by the tingles shooting down my arm into inappropriate places thanks to a freaking handshake. "Why don't we all have a seat?" I better not sound breathy to anyone but myself.

They settle into the chairs around the table in my office. I wish I could hide the mug, but the image is on both sides.

Dax stretches out his long legs and slips his phone into his pocket, muffling the constant buzzing of messages.

"My assistant, Laura, indicated that you're interested in setting up a trust for your daughter." I flip open my laptop, and the theme song to *It's My Life* fills the room. The timing couldn't be worse. My best friend Holly regularly sends me memes and video clips as a joke. Normally it's not embarrassing because the guy who starred in the show isn't sitting across from me, with his parents.

I slam my fingers on the keyboard, aiming for the Mute button, but all I succeed in doing is making it louder for a few painfully awkward seconds. "So sorry about that."

Daxton wears an amused smile. Maybe it's not the worst thing in the world that he doesn't seem to remember me. I fold my hands on the table and focus my attention on his parents.

The back of my neck is damp and my face is on fire. "The trust for your daughter. How can I be of assistance?"

Mrs. Hughes smiles kindly. Her graying hair is cut into a short, stylish bob. Her makeup is light and carefully applied. She's not flashy, but she's dressed nicely. She looks so sweet. It's too bad she birthed a gorgeous asshole. I hope her daughter is nicer.

"We'd like to secure Emme's savings, and Daxton wanted to join us." She pats his hand.

Daxton smiles at his mother. "I thought it might be a good idea to tag along since the trust lawyer at my firm is on leave and they didn't want to wait."

"Whitman and Flood is one of the best firms in the city. You'll be in good hands here," I say proudly.

Evelyn nods her agreement. "I keep thinking she's just a baby, but she'll be thirteen soon enough and then eighteen is around the corner and the next thing you know they're moving out." She smiles fondly at her son. "Anyway, we didn't set up a trust for Daxton when he was Emme's age, and it probably would've been a lot easier on everyone if we had."

"Daxton was always very responsible with his money, except for his first year of college," Mr. Hughes says.

"You could hardly blame him for that. Daxton used to star on a TV show when he was Emme's age." Her gaze darts to my mug for a second.

Daxton's cheeks flush a little. "Mom, we're not really here to ta—"

"I'm sure Miss Flowers knows what it's like to have braggy parents," Mr. Hughes breaks in.

I smile but the comment makes my heart twinge. It's been a long time since someone bragged about my accomplishments, and the man who stole my biggest one is sitting on the other side of the table, and apparently doesn't remember the way he screwed me. Not literally, thank God.

"Please, call me Kailyn," I say through a granite smile.

Daxton's brows pull down and he tips his head to the side, inspecting me.

"Where did you go to law school, Kailyn?" Evelyn asks.

"UCLA."

"Really? Daxton went to law school there, too! What year did you graduate? It couldn't have been that long ago, you're so young."

I fight with my hands to stay folded on the table rather than allow them to flutter around. "It's been five years."

"Oh my goodness! Daxton!" She grabs his arm. "You went to law school at the same time! Did you know each other?"

"We might've run into each other once or twice on campus." I look to Daxton, waiting for him to acknowledge, to remember. Waiting for a sign that he feels some kind of remorse over what he did. While we never hung out, we were always competing with each other. We bantered in class, especially during debates, sometimes to the point where the professor would have to put a stop to it. It felt a little like verbal foreplay at the time. It kept us both entertained, or so I'd thought.

Daxton's eyebrows shoot up. "Holy shit!"

"Daxton!" His mother slaps his arm.

"Sorry. Wow. Kailyn. I didn't recognize you." He rubs his fingers over his bottom lip, eyes moving over my face again in a way that reminds me a lot of how he looked at me in law school. "You, uh...look so different. Good. You look good."

I give him a tight smile and adjust my glasses, wishing I'd worn contact lenses today. "Yes, well, T-shirts and jeans don't quite cut it in the business world, as I'm sure you know."

His eyes drift down. "I liked you in jeans and T-shirts."

"Did you have classes together? Were you friends?" His mother seems oblivious to the tension flaring between us.

"We had a lot of classes together," Daxton replies, gaze locking on mine.

Why is it so hot in here all of a sudden? "But we weren't exactly friends." I pick up my pen and flip it between my fingers to avoid pulling at the collar of my blouse, which feels too tight.

He tips his head to the side, his expression curious. "We were friendly rivals, though, weren't we? You kept me on my toes, always two steps ahead of everyone else, me included most of the time. It was hard to compete with beauty and brains."

I bark out a laugh. At one time I'd almost believed we were friends, but he'd proved me wrong. "Rivals, sure. Friends don't generally screw each other over by stealing the top spot in the class, do they?"

"Stealing... what?" His brow pulls down. "I worked my ass off for that. You can't be mad about that after five years."

I sure as hell can still be mad about it, especially when he's acting like he earned it fairly. As we stare each other down, I briefly wish I'd pursued criminal law instead of trust law as a career. Then I would have much better knowledge of how to get away with murder.

At the clearing of a throat, I'm suddenly aware that I'm being completely unprofessional, and this juvenile battle is being witnessed by my potential clients, who are also his parents.

"Well, you two are certainly full of fire, aren't you?" his mother chuckles.

I don't want to let it go, but if I push this further, I'm at risk of embarrassing myself, and I don't want to give Daxton the satisfaction of seeing how much he gets to me. Still. But this is the first opportunity I've had to confront him in five years, so it takes an infinite amount of grace to stow the anger and fix my face with a fake smile. "Daxton and I were always competing for head of the class. In the end I came in second. Anyway, you're not here to talk about law school. Let's discuss Emme's trust and how you'd like the funds allocated. I'm sure we can set up a great plan that will help her manage her money responsibly as she grows."

I spend the next hour reviewing the insane amount of money this almost-thirteen-year-old girl has amassed from six years' worth of commercials. It makes me wish for the briefest moment that my parents had been more Hollywood. And then I take a look at Dax and remember why it's good not to fall into the trap of believing you're above reproach. So much so that he's convinced himself he earned something he stole.

Once we've addressed the major concerns, I inform his parents that I'll have papers for them to review in a couple of weeks.

As I usher them out the door, Daxton snags a card. "It looks likes you've really got it together here." He scans my office.

"It's a great firm." Hints of my personality bleed through in the quirky memorabilia and trinkets I keep on my desk and that hang from the wall.

"It was nice to see you again, Kailyn," he says, but this time his eyes aren't on the walls. Once again he's checking out my legs as he does another slow sweep of my funky patterned hose.

"Likewise," I reply, but my tone sounds a lot more like *fuck you.*

He has the nerve to wink as he slips the card into his breast pocket and follows his parents out of my office. Once he's gone I flip the double bird at the wall and mouth all sorts of profanity. It's highly immature. That man brings out the worst in me. I wish I'd had five minutes alone with him so I could finally confront him about what he did and rip him a nice new asshole.

I glance at the clock and realize I'm running late for lunch. Normally that wouldn't be a problem since I often skip real food in lieu of a bag of Sour Patch Kids, or whatever candy I have stashed in my desk—not particularly health conscious of me, but it gets me through when I don't feel like taking a break.

Today my best friend and I have a lunch date at our favorite bistro and I have a full schedule this afternoon, so being late means less time with her, and I now need to vent post–Hughes meeting. I shoot her a message to let her know I'm on my way. Holly's already seated on the patio when I arrive. She pushes away from the table and pulls me in for a tight hug. "Thanks for making time for me."

Holly is a compulsive hugger, and even though I expect the affection from her, it still takes a moment before I remember to return the gesture. "Of course. Anything for you."

Holly and I have been friends since I moved next door to her at the age of three. Apart from when she went to college in Santa Barbara, we've always lived in the same city.

"So you'll never believe who came by my office this morning," I say as we drop into the chairs across from each other.

"Does that mean you want me to guess?" Holly half smiles and raises her eyebrows.

"You can try, but I doubt you'll get it right."

"Oooh, now I'm really intrigued. Was it that guy from that law conference last month, the one who wanted to see your not-so-legal briefs?"

I roll my eyes. "Oh my God, no, and that was literally the worst line in the history of lines. Try again."

"Just tell me. You're all worked up about it with the way you're fidgeting, so it's got to be good." She motions to my hands.

I'm twisting my napkin into what could approximate a sword, or a knife.

Before I can respond the server comes by. Neither of us needs to open our menu. We come here so often we could practically recite it to each other.

Once our server has taken our order, Holly makes a go-ahead motion with her hand and props her chin on her fist.

"Daxton Hughes." When she does nothing but blink at me, I add, "You know, the guy from *It's My Life*. The show we watched like it was our religion every Tuesday for years."

"Oh, I know who Daxton Hughes is. You pretty much talked about him nonstop for the entire three years you were in law school, and the ten years before that, too."

"Well, he turned out to be asshole, in the end, didn't he?" I mutter. "And that hasn't changed at all in the last five years, either."

"Oh? What happened? What was he there for? Oooh! Does he have an illegitimate love child he's trying to keep secret?"

I glance around the restaurant and make a *keep it down* gesture. The meeting wasn't really about him, so telling Holly isn't a big deal, but I don't need to broadcast it. "No, he was with his parents and they're setting up a family trust."

"That's way less exciting than an illegitimate love child." Holly frowns. "It's actually sweet that he would help his parents do that."

"Do not call Daxton Hughes sweet! He is the opposite of sweet."

Holly bites back a smile. "Let it all out. You know you want to."

I glare, but she's right. I'm so agitated now. "You know what's even worse? He didn't even recognize me at first." I start flailing, as is typical when I'm edgy. "We went to law school together for three years."

"Five years ago."

"Still, you'd think he'd remember the person he intentionally screwed over." I grip the edge of the table and lean forward. "He couldn't believe that I was still angry that he stole the top spot!"

The corner of Holly's mouth twitches. "Pretty sure you'd get the top spot for holding a grudge."

"It's not funny! You're supposed to be sympathetic!"

"I am sympathetic. But from what I remember, you two were always in competition with each other."

"He handed in my paper late!"

"Why didn't you just email it?"

"My professor was old-school and shunned technology. If he'd handed it in on time like he said he would, late marks wouldn't have been deducted and my GPA would've been higher than his. I even went to the professor about it and he said there was nothing he could do." I lean back as the server sets our plates in front of us. I unwrap my silverware and aggressively stab a sweet potato fry.

"You know, Kay, maybe you should pull out one of those *It's My Life* Daxton Barbie dolls you have and perform some voodoo. It might make you feel better."

I roll my eyes. "I didn't expect to see him, like, ever

again, and he was so smirky and smug and kind of flirty and just . . . gah! And he's still hot, and he still has all his hair. I just hate him!"

"So does that mean we're not having that *It's My Life* rerun marathon this weekend?"

I shoot her a dirty look. "That show is banned for life. Oh, and thanks so much for that clip you sent me this morning. It just happened to pop up right as the Hugheses came into my office."

"Oh my God! What are the chances of that happening at that exact moment?"

I shoot anger beams at her from my eyes. "I almost died of embarrassment."

"Are you sure you don't want to have a rerun marathon? It might be cathartic to yell at him, even if it's just on a TV screen."

"Har har, Holly, har har." I exhale a long slow breath and run my hands over my thighs. I really need to calm down. "Okay, I think I'm done venting. Sorry. That man just riles me up in the worst way. Let's change the subject. How's work? How's that adoption case you were dealing with? Is everything okay there?"

Holly smiles, but it's sad. "Physically, Hope is thriving."

"Uh-oh. It sounds like there's a 'but' in there." This is what I need, a distraction from Daxton Hughes and his gorgeous smirk and asshole attitude.

"Unfortunately the birth mother has had a change of heart and there's a problem with the adoption paperwork."

That makes me sit up straighter. Holly is a social worker and often deals with custody issues. "What kind of problem?"

"The lawyer who drew up the contracts was sloppy about it, and the adoptive parents, the Lipsons, didn't see the loopholes. It looks like the birth mom might be able to take custody of Hope."

My stomach sinks. Her mother is a recovering addict, and while she was clean through the pregnancy, past behavior has had her falling into old patterns when the stress gets to be too much. Sadly, retaining custody of Hope is more about the government check than being able to raise her.

I tap on the edge of the table, considering the options for the Lipsons. As someone who was adopted at the age of three and removed from a home where love was only shown to the public assistance check that came on a monthly basis, I found the travesty in this a particularly difficult pill to swallow. "What if I could take on the case pro bono?"

Holly shakes her head. "You're working toward a partnership. You don't have time to take on something like this. Besides, it's so close to your own experience."

"Which is exactly why I *should* take it on. Who better to fight for these parents than someone who's experienced the flaws in the system? It might actually help me earn the partnership in the long run. I'll talk to Beverly, but I think she'll see the benefit."

"Are you sure? It's a lot to add to your caseload." Holly's hopeful expression fortifies my resolve. While I've spent the past five years working primarily in trusts, I've always been interested in this side of law. Enough that I've studied adoption contracts and cases outside of work hours. It's sort of a hobby, which is a little sad, I realize, since it's also related to work.

"If it keeps one little girl with a loving family, then it's worth it. I'll just have to cancel all my Friday night dates." I grin cheekily, hoping to lighten the mood.

Holly rolls her eyes. "You can't do that. I'll be lonely."

We both laugh.

Holly pokes at the lemon floating in her glass with the end of her straw. "But seriously, we should probably think about dating actual men one of these days."

I snort. "Boyfriends are too much work. They want things, like time and energy."

"And blow jobs, don't forget those." Holly snickers.

"Yes, all things I don't have to spare or really don't feel like giving freely. Besides, I have cats. They're lower maintenance." Linus and Shirley are my sweet tabbies. The only time they're a problem is when I'm cooking bacon, but otherwise they're incredibly well behaved.

She spears a fry and points it at me. "If you ever run into Daxton again, you could give hate fucking him a try. I hear it's a good way to exorcise a grudge."

"Since I'm not planning on running into him ever again, it looks like I just get to hold on to that grudge."

chapter two

ORPHANS

Daxton

Six Months Later

I'm staring at a stupid meme—of myself. The image is more than a decade and a half old, but it never seems to stop circulating the internet abyss. It's one of those I Hate Monday memes, complete with an ugly cry face.

One of my colleagues and close friends sent it early this morning, so it's the first email I check. Felix McQueen, a defense lawyer at Freeman and Associates, does it at least once a month under the guise of an URGENT email. We've been tight since undergrad, so I put up with his shit.

Also, his emails often *are* urgent, so I rarely hesitate to open them. He thinks he's being funny, but in reality it's another reminder that I will never live down my years as a child TV star, no matter how far I've come since the days of *Teen Beat* magazine spreads.

The knock on my door has me closing the email. Not that it matters. Everyone in the office has seen the same damn meme at some point. Felix has a coffee mug boasting the image, and he loves to drink out of it at meetings. Because he's an asshole. Whatever. At least my humiliation is profitable. And I'm immune to it. Mostly.

I flip Felix off as his head appears in the doorway. "Thanks for being an asshole, asshole."

He makes a face, one I can't really read. "Sorry about the stupid email. I wouldn't have sent it if I'd known."

"Known what?"

He mutters something I don't catch, his expression somber, almost convincing in his remorse. "I gotta talk to you."

I lean back in my chair and cross my arms over my chest, a heavy feeling I can't explain settling in my gut. I brush it off with sarcasm. "I already know there's a twenty-four-hour *It's My Life* marathon this weekend. No, I don't want to watch it with you and let my vagina hang out."

He closes the door behind him and passes a hand over his tie. He seems fidgety, which is unlike him.

"What's wrong? Did you lose the Kent case?" The jury has been deliberating for two days. It's only a matter of time before they make a decision, but it could go either way.

Felix shakes his head, refusing to look me in the eye as he comes around the side of my desk. "It's not about a case."

"Well then, what's it about? What's with this?" I motion to his serious face.

He scrubs at his chin with his palm, expelling a long breath. "Your parents were in a car accident."

Disbelief needles under my skin, but anger is what pushes to the surface. "Don't fuck with me, Felix."

He licks his lips, throat bobbing with a hard swallow. "I wish I was, but I'm not."

My chair flies backward as I push to stand, making the glass rattle when it connects with the windowpane behind me. "Are they okay? Which hospital were they taken to? How bad was the accident?"

The answers I don't want are already written on his face in grief. "It was fatal. I'm so sorry."

His statement ricochets around in my head, the word *fatal* a blow to the heart. "They're . . . dead? Both of them?" I have to strain to hear him over the rush of blood in my ears.

"They were on the freeway. A tractor trailer jackknifed."

"How did you find out? How do you know this?" Everything feels like it's moving in slow motion and fast-forward at the same time. My mind spins with this new, horrifying truth.

"The police are here. I thought it would be better if the news came from someone who gives a shit. I'm so sorry, Dax. The police said they died on impact. Your parents wouldn't have felt anything."

I reach behind me for my chair and drop back into it, my legs suddenly watery. I drag a palm down my face, the news pinging around in my head, unwilling to settle. A crushing realization hammers into me: This loss isn't just mine. This sudden gaping hole in my chest is echoed in another, more fragile body. "Emme?"

"She's at school. She doesn't know yet."

I root around in my desk for my keys. "I have to— I need to get her. I need to be the one who tells her. I don't want anyone else to tell her." Poor Emme. I'm thirty and this is crushing me. How is this going to impact my kid sister? How is she going to survive without parents?

I round my desk only to have Felix step in front of the door. "Whoa, Dax, you can't drive."

I fist the lapels of his suit jacket, anger and grief stealing rationality. "They're her world. I need to get her, and you need to get out of my fucking way."

He puts his hands on my shoulders, none of my aggression echoed in him. "I know, man. I'll take you. You have to keep it together though, okay? You're all she has. If you need to fall apart, do it now, because you have to be in control once you get to her."

He's right. I'm all she has. And now she's all I have, too. I'm not sure which one of us is worse off for it.

Before I can leave the office, I speak with the cops. Felix was right to be the one to tell me. They wear apathetic expressions, so accustomed to delivering bad news in the form of death. I vomit into the wastebasket beside my desk when I find out the tractor trailer was a fuel truck that exploded on impact. Which is also the moment I break down.

I don't remember cleaning myself up in the bathroom after the cops leave. I don't remember getting into the elevator with Felix. I don't remember getting into his car. When I arrive at the school, I tell Felix not to bother waiting. We'll get an Uber or something. I don't know how long this is going to take, and as much as Felix is my best friend, I need to do this with Emme on my own.

My entire body feels as if it's encased in cement. It's so hard to move, to think. The pain in my chest is a vicious, pervasive ache I can barely function around as I climb the stairs to the front doors.

I arrive at the beginning of lunch. I wait in a chair beside a sullen preteen boy who's clearly gotten himself into trouble based on his hunched shoulders, while they retrieve Emme from the cafeteria.

"Daxton? What're you doing here?" I look up to find my aunt Linda, my mother's sister, standing behind the reception desk as grating bells ring through the building. Her questioning smile drops as she takes me in.

I'm sure my eyes are red rimmed and my expression is grim. I push up out of the chair with the half-destroyed armrests and run a heavy hand through my hair. "I need to see Emme."

"Is everything okay?" Linda asks, suddenly on alert.

"No. It's not."

Before I can explain further, Emme's excited voice twists my stomach into a tighter knot. "Dax?"

I turn to find her standing in the middle of the office. I wish I could bottle her happiness at this moment since I'm about to take it all away. Her wide smile lights up her face, dark eyes sparkling with excitement as she practically dances her way to me. She throws her arms around me. "Are you here to take me for lunch?"

It's always something I tell her I'll do when I see her at Sunday lunch, but work makes it difficult to follow through, especially since her school is a good twenty minutes from my office. I worry I've been a shit brother, too focused on my own life to be bothered to be part of hers outside of family events.

I hug her tightly, hating that I'm about to crush her world. The pain is brutally raw, scraping at the inside of my heart.

She pushes away, her smile full of anticipation. I want to preserve this innocence, keep her safe from the harsh realities of the world for a few more moments.

Her expression falls, sharp brown eyes taking me in. "What's wrong?"

I can't protect her from this. Nothing will soften this violent blow. "It's about Mom and Dad."

"What?" She looks around as if she expects them to appear.

My next words will change her entire life. "They were in a car accident."

The color drains from her face. I wish we were somewhere else. Anywhere else. Somewhere without eyes on us. A room with walls and comfort and privacy.

She lifts her purple-painted nails to her lips. "Are they okay?"

My head feels heavy as I give it a slow shake. "I'm sorry. They're gone, Emme."

"Gone?" she echoes.

"They're . . . dead. They died in the accident." The words spit out like sharp gravel popping under tires.

Her hand drops to press against her chest, as if she's trying to keep her heart from cracking open inside. "No." She shakes her head furiously. "They dropped me off this morning. I had a dentist appointment. They were just here. They were *just here*!" Her voice rises, her fear giving way to a rush of anger as I reach out to comfort her.

"No!" She shoves me.

"Emme!" Aunt Linda's eyes are wide with the same shock as my sister's.

I'd forgotten she was here.

"I'm so sorry, Em."

I grab her fists when she tries to pummel me, and I pull her against my chest, wrapping my arms around her. I want to shield her from the agony as the truth sets in and she crumples.

"No, Dax, no." The fight leaves her and she sags against me, breaking into a fit of sobs, the sound full of anguish. "They were just here. They can't be gone."

And all I can do is tell her how sorry I am. Over and over.

chapter three

NUMB

Daxton

The funeral is much like pouring lemon juice on a fresh wound. Emme is a mess. I'm a mess. I act as her anchor to keep us both from drifting away in a stormy sea of raw emotions and we drag ourselves through the day together. We've shaken hundreds of hands, accepted as many hugs and condolences, but it in no way dispels the feeling that we're floating, untethered in the unknown.

I'm slouched in a beanbag chair on the floor, staring at the glow-in-the-dark solar system on Emme's ceiling, wondering how bad the pain will be before it starts to get better. Easier.

Emme rolls onto her side in her girlie double bed, the stuffed llama she grew out of years ago tucked under her chin. "Dax?"

Her bedside lamp casts shadows over her face, making her dark eyes look hollow. She's been sleeping with the light on since Mom and Dad passed.

"What's up, kiddo?"

Her fingers are at her mouth. Her nails are bitten ragged, the skin around them torn and bleeding. She's so anxious and emotional, no wonder she doesn't want to sleep alone.

"Mom had to reschedule my dentist appointment because it was at the same time as my presentation. That's why they drove me to school."

"Ah, kiddo, you can't blame yourself for this."

"But they might still be here. They might not be gone—" She breaks down again, as she's done so many times over the past few days. She uses her stuffed llama's feet to wipe her tears away. She looks so young, like the little girl whose scrapes I sometimes bandaged so many years ago. But I can't cover this wound with a Band-Aid. It's just too deep.

I want to tell her to try not to think about it, to just remember the good things, but Emme is like me in this regard. She can't stop thinking about it, and not talking isn't going to help her. I brush her hair away from her face—something I've seen my mother do a million times. I wish I had the right words and my mother's soft hug to make it better.

"They could've stopped at a coffee shop on the way to the freeway, Em. If they'd been one minute either way, it could've been someone else and not them. It's not your fault."

"I just want them back. I want to wake up and I want them to be here and I want this to just be a really bad dream."

"I know. Me, too."

I let her cry, because I don't know what else to do. When

there are no more tears, she asks in a meek voice if I'll stay until she falls asleep. I pull the beanbag chair next to her bed and settle in.

I wake up at midnight with a stiff back. Emme is fast asleep. Thank God. She's been up the past couple of nights with bad dreams, and I stay with her until she falls asleep again. I tiptoe out of her room and down the hall, desperate not to disturb her.

I'm exhausted, but now that I'm awake, my brain is in motion. Tomorrow the lawyer is coming to read the will. He knew my dad personally, so the house call is out of respect for him and our family. There's so much paperwork to go through, and my mind has been scattered. I decide it might be best to review some of it before Thomas arrives in the morning so that I'm somewhat prepared. Especially where Emme and custody are concerned.

Light seeps out from the crack at the bottom of my dad's office door. I don't remember leaving it on when I was in there earlier. Aunt Linda jumps when I push it open to peek inside. She's been staying with us during the funeral arrangements, which has been helpful, sort of. She has a habit of coming in and taking over, which can be hard to handle.

"Oh! Daxton, you scared me. I didn't realize you were still awake." She puts the files she's holding into the drawer of my dad's desk.

"What're you doing?"

"Just tidying up. There's going to be a lot to sort out in

the next few weeks." Her smile is sympathetic. "It's a big job, going through this house. Craig and Evelyn have been here since before you were born. Have you thought about how you're going to manage that?"

"I guess it all depends on what the will says." I assume the house is going to me or eventually to Emme once she's old enough, but I won't know for sure until tomorrow. So many things are up in the air until then.

"Of course. So much to consider. Well, I should be going to bed. We have an early morning what with reading the will and all." She crosses the room, her hand resting on my shoulder. "You should get some sleep. You'll need a clear head."

She moves to the hall, and turns around again, as if she's waiting for me to leave the office. I'm foggy and suddenly exhausted all over again by the thought of making sense of all this paperwork.

"Yeah, you're right." I close the door to the office and follow her up the stairs, heading down the hall to my teenage bedroom, wondering what tomorrow will look like.

❧

In the morning, I get dressed on autopilot and end up in a suit out of habit. I find Emme in the kitchen, making herself a fruit smoothie—with ice cream. It's early, but I let it slide. Her appetite hasn't been great the past few days, so if she wants ice cream first thing in the morning, she can have it.

Thomas arrives promptly at ten and pulls me into a hug, patting my back and murmuring his condolences. He's far more formal with Linda, but no less pleasant. He turns a soft smile on Emme and comments on how much she looks like our mother, which makes her teary. I put an arm around her and hug her to my side.

"Why don't we do this in the dining room, where we can be comfortable?" I suggest.

I just want to get through this so we can move forward. I feel like we're all trapped in a state of limbo, waiting for our new realities to begin.

We settle in the dining room, and Thomas begins by reviewing the breakdown of assets. The house is mine—which I anticipated, and everything else is split between me and Emme. Financially, my parents' accounts are divided in Emme's favor because I already have a boatload of money that I've managed well so far, thanks to my parents' guidance.

"Dax, you'll have power of attorney over Emme's accounts and the funds your parents have allocated to support her. It appears your parents have given you some leeway so you can make adjustments based on need, but in addition to the social security checks, which should be significant, you'll also get an allowance each month for care and expenses."

"I'm sorry, maybe I'm confused, but how can Daxton have power of attorney if I'm the legal guardian? How effective is that if I have to ask him to approve every single financial decision that might benefit Emme's future?" Linda asks.

I was actually wondering the same thing.

Thomas graces her with one of his polite smiles. "Daxton is Emme's legal guardian, hence he has power of attorney."

In my under-slept, grievous state, it takes several seconds for that information to sink in. I don't have a chance to ask for clarification, or for Thomas to repeat that information, because Linda does it for me. "But Evelyn told me I would be responsible for taking care of Emme should anything happen to her and Craig."

Thomas glances from me to Linda. "According to the will and trust papers, which were signed by both Evelyn and Craig, Daxton has been named Emme's legal guardian." He addresses me. "Were you unaware of this?"

I'm gripping my own armrests, the news slow to sink in. "I was unaware."

Emme sits up straighter, her eyes wide. "I get to live with Dax?"

Thomas smiles softly. "That's right, Emme. Dax is legally responsible for taking care of you."

"So I don't have to move? I can stay right here?"

"Provided Daxton chooses to keep the house, yes." Thomas addresses Linda and me. "Your parents made changes to the will a little over six months ago. Just after your thirtieth birthday, Daxton. Until that point, guardianship had been appointed to Linda and..." He flips through the pages. "Victor. But then I understand you separated from your husband. Is that correct, Linda?"

"Well yes, we separated, but I wasn't aware Evelyn had changed custody." She seems stunned more than anything, which I understand, because I'm just as shocked by the news.

"Linda, you've been granted secondary custody," Thomas says.

"What does that mean? Is that like partial custody?" Linda asks.

"In the event that Daxton is unable to care for Emme for whatever reason, you would step in as guardian." I can read between the lines. He means if something happens to me, God forbid, custody would shift to Linda.

She turns her attention to me, obviously flustered. "Daxton, you have to see how difficult this would be with the hours you work. Taking care of a teenage girl is a huge responsibility. Do you have any idea how much time and energy goes into raising a child?"

The answer to that is no. Not really. But I can guess. "We'll make it work."

Her expression becomes strangely panicked. "You must see that this isn't what's best for Emme. You'll have to be home every night with her. You can't just leave a thirteen-year-old to fend for herself. Your entire life is going to change."

She's right, but the look on Emme's face prevents me from agreeing with her. "My entire life has already changed, and so has Emme's."

"I can provide her with stability that you can't," she counters. There's desperation in her tone and I'm unsure what the cause is. She's not particularly close with Emme that I know of, despite working at her school.

Besides that, I haven't even had a chance to prove I'm capable and already she's telling me I'll fail. "You think your revolving door of husbands is indicative of stability?"

Her expression shutters and she snaps at me, "Far more stable than you and your Tinder dates and sleeping around with whatever woman you pick up from the bar."

I pin Linda with an unimpressed glare. "You don't know the first thing about me or my personal life. Emme is my sister. I'll make whatever lifestyle changes necessary so I can support her and be there for her."

It's not like I have a rotation of women warming my bed all the time. I have an old acting friend I see once in a while when she's in town. It's a no-strings kind of thing because we're both too busy for relationships. Linda's making me sound like a playboy, when in reality, I'm a thirty-year-old with a healthy sex drive, and I like to be safe and smart about my partners. I don't just screw randoms on a whim whenever I feel like it. Not that I need to discuss this, particularly not in front of my sister.

While I'm not sure I'm the best option, I don't want to disrupt Emme's life more than it already is, so if that means I have to move back here, then I'm willing to try to be the parent she needs, even if I have no idea how to do that.

"Maybe we should ask Emme what she wants." Linda smiles encouragingly at her. "Do you think it would be better for you to live with me, honey?"

Emme looks from Linda to me and back again.

"It's okay," I tell her. "You can answer the question honestly,

Em. I only want what's best for you." Although it might literally kill me if she says she'd rather live with our aunt.

"I want to live with Dax," Emme says quietly.

Linda sighs, annoyance pushing through. "Of course she wants to live where there won't be any rules or supervision." She pushes up from the chair. "This is a mistake. You don't have the first clue what it takes to care for a teenage girl, Daxton. I think you should seriously consider the demands and whether this really is best for Emme."

And suddenly I realize I've gone from single to single dad.

*

Once Thomas leaves, Linda packs her things, her frustration at the situation clear in the jerky way she moves around the house. I understand her shock, but I can't quite figure out why she's so upset. It's not like I'm a drug addict or I go partying all the time. I'm more of a workaholic than anything.

After she leaves, I search my dad's office for the trust files, aware it's another thing I'm going to need to go through. It's been months since it was set up, and aside from the initial meeting, I didn't have much to do with it. I find a set of papers tucked into a filing cabinet in my dad's desk. They're a draft and not exactly what I'm looking for, but it's a start and I'm too tired to keep looking. It appears my parents kept every file from birth for both of us, so locating the full trust documents will be like finding a needle in a haystack.

Later in the evening Felix comes by with a six-pack of beer. He was at the funeral yesterday, but I haven't had a chance to talk to him since he delivered the news that my parents were gone. Emme's in her room, exhausted by the whole custody thing and the reading of the will this morning. Frankly, so am I.

I grab the file with the will, and Felix follows me outside to the backyard and drops down in one of the rickety Adirondack chairs my dad and I built together a good decade ago.

"So give me the lowdown. What happened with the will?"

I pass over the documents and give him the abridged version. "I have custody of Emme."

He's silent for a few seconds, leafing through the papers without really reading them before he clears his throat on a low whistle. "So does this make you Daddy Dax?"

"Screw you, asshole." I laugh a little, though.

I need to find humor in something. Felix is a joker and he's good at making light of things. He sort of has to be, seeing as he's a criminal defense attorney and he deals with some messed-up cases. I'm more than happy to spend my days dealing with actor contract negotiations, and the occasional harassment suit, thank you very much.

"Seriously, though, your parents gave you custody of your sister?"

"Apparently they decided to change guardianship from Linda to me when I turned thirty, and didn't tell either of us." I take a sip of my beer.

"What the fuck were they thinking?"

I shoot him a look, although that was pretty much my first thought, too.

"I'm not saying it to be an asshole, well mostly I'm not, but come on, it's not like you're a candidate for the responsibility award."

"I'm responsible."

He snorts. "Remember that time you went to Vegas for the weekend? You forgot to manage the thermostat in your condo and all your tropical fish died."

"That was one time, and it was an accident."

"Accident or not, your condo stunk for weeks. We had to move poker twice until it went away."

"I'm not good with pets."

"Fish are the easiest pets in the world. They require minimal effort to keep alive. You sprinkle food in there and clean their tank, what, once every two months, if that? Teenage girls are like rabid, angry puppies. They're yappy, they want your attention all the time, they make a mess. Take it from someone who grew up with three younger sisters: Even when they're adorable, it doesn't really make up for the rest of the bullshit," Felix says.

I give him a sideways glare. "You should definitely never have kids."

"I'm just saying, this isn't like raising her from birth. You're taking over someone else's job when she's on the downslide, you know? Like you missed all the years when kids actually like you and rely on you, and now you just get to deal with moodiness and fending off boys."

"Has anyone ever told you your pep talks are legendary?"

"I just think you might need to consider what you're getting yourself into."

"My parents gave me custody. It's not like I asked for it."

"What about your aunt? Hasn't she already raised a couple of kids?"

I've thought the same thing more than once today. "Yeah, but if your parents had just died and entrusted you to take care of your thirteen-year-old sister, wouldn't you at least try?"

Felix drums his fingers on the arm of the chair. "I guess. But it's a lot to take on. It changes everything, Dax."

"I know. Linda kept saying that. Talking about what's best for Emme." I rub the back of my neck. "You know what's weird? My parents didn't leave anything to Linda. She's my only aunt, and she and my mom were pretty close. Or at least it seemed that way. They helped her through some rough spots in the past, so I figured she'd get something, you know?"

"Maybe something happened that you don't know about?"

"Maybe, it's just...odd." I scrub a hand over my face. I'm so tired. "I should talk to a custody lawyer so I can get a handle on all of this."

"It's probably a good idea," Felix replies.

"I'm going to have to talk to the lawyer who set up Emme's trust, too, since I can't seem to find anything but the initial draft, which should be fun." I recall the way Kailyn reacted to me the last time I was in her office. She seemed less than excited to see me, which was strange since I'd kind of had a thing for her back then, and I'd thought it was mutual. "My life is so fucked right now."

"It'll get better," he assures me.

I nod, but I have a feeling it's going to get a lot worse before that happens.

chapter four

FANGIRL RESURRECTED

Kailyn

Cara, my regular assistant, who is never allowed to go on vacation on weeks that don't coincide with mine again, knocks on my office door and pops her head in about thirty seconds after I sit down at my desk. I've had a hell of a morning. It's been meeting after meeting and I finally have a breather.

Cara holds a takeout cup from the café down the street and her tablet. "Nonfat, double-espresso, two-pump vanilla latte with extra cinnamon?" It's framed as a question.

I raise a brow. "Is there some kind of emergency you're buttering me up for?"

"I'm so sorry, but there's a drop-in appointment, and Beverly said it was urgent so..."

Beverly is my boss, and she's highly aware my schedule doesn't permit for drop-ins. "I only have an hour until my next meeting."

"I know. I'm so sorry, Kailyn, but she said you would see him—"

"Him who?"

"Beverly wouldn't give me a name." Cara clutches her iPad to her chest and glances over her shoulder, possibly checking for interlopers. "I think it might be someone famous."

"Someone famous?" I parrot. It's LA; there are a lot of famous people in this city.

Cara pushes her glasses up her nose. "I only caught a glimpse of the back of him. She brought him to the conference room about half an hour ago and she won't say anything about who it is. I tried, Kailyn. I know how much you hate surprises."

"I'll just stop by her office before I go in there."

Cara's gaze darts around the room for a second before returning to me. Her cringe isn't reassuring. "She's in a meeting."

"Shit. Okay. I guess I'm going in blind."

"I'm really sorry."

"It's fine." I give her what I hope is a genuine smile. She's a fabulous assistant, and if Beverly is being mysterious, it's certainly not Cara's fault. "I'll just be a minute and then I'll head to the conference room."

"Okay. Great. When you're finished with the mystery client, we can review missed calls, and I've already adjusted your schedule for the afternoon just in case the meeting takes more of your time than you anticipate."

"Perfect, thank you." This is why I love her.

I wait until Cara leaves before I pull my compact out of the drawer and check my reflection, frustrated that I have no idea with whom I'm meeting or why. The last time this happened I embarrassed the hell out of myself. I smooth my hair and reapply my lipstick. Appearance is half the battle in this world. Appear poised and successful, and people will believe you are. *Visualize success.* I smile at my personal mantra. It's gotten me where I am, albeit with a few bumps in the road.

I adjust my glasses one last time and scoop up my tablet but leave the coffee on my desk so as not to appear as though I have time for chitchat. Cara is already behind her desk, typing away frantically. This whole thing has probably stressed her out and understandably so; I'm particular about how things are run, and while unexpected situations arise, this unpreparedness is exactly the kind of thing I prefer to avoid.

I approach the conference room quietly, hoping I'll get a peek at whoever is in there. A man in a slightly rumpled suit stands facing the windows, with his hands shoved in his pockets. I take in the broad shoulders and sandy hair, a little unkempt, and realize Daxton Hughes is back in my office.

I lean against the doorjamb. "To what do I owe the pleasure?" My tone intentionally lacks warmth.

He turns away from the window, eyes slow to follow. I take in his typically gorgeous face with those piercing blue eyes, and the cut jaw with what I would guess is two days' worth of stubble. He looks...rough. Maybe he's been on a bender.

He blinks a few times, like he's clearing his head, and rounds the conference table. He takes my hand in both of his. It's disarming and unexpected. His voice cracks and he turns his head, clearing his throat before he tries again. "Thank you for agreeing to see me without an appointment. I know you must be very busy, so I appreciate you taking the time to speak with me."

I'm not the least bit moved by this show of false sincerity. "Beverly insisted it was rather urgent." And I assume she fell prey to his pretty face; even as rough as he looks, he's still stunning.

"It was. It is." He clears his throat again and motions to the chair across from his. "Can we sit?"

"Of course. I don't have long, though." I drop into the chair and cross my legs, fighting not to do the same with my arms. This man seems to bring out all my worst traits, which includes excessive fidgeting and flailing.

"Right." He runs his palms over his thighs and exhales, eyes moving slowly over my face. It feels intimate and searching. "I have a personal custody issue."

Maybe Holly was right and there *is* an illegitimate love child. I can see the headline now: WASHED-UP FORMER CHILD ACTOR DAXTON HUGHES KNOCKS UP DEBUTANTE. "I don't deal with paternity issues. I deal with trusts."

His brow furrows and he shakes his head. "It's not a paternity issue. And it has to do with a trust, the one you set up for my sister." He rubs his lips with his fingertips, drawing my attention there. "I'm sorry. It's been a difficult week." He rests his elbow on the table and bows his head, squeezing the bridge of his nose. He swallows thickly and his voice cracks again. "My parents..."

I'm thoroughly enjoying his discomfort, and how hard this seems to be for him, until the next words come out of his mouth.

"They were killed in a car accident last week."

It's like being slammed in the chest with a bowling ball and doused in an acid bath of guilt. "Oh my God." I reach out on instinct and cover his hand with mine. It sends an unexpected jolt through my body, so I draw back immediately. "I'm so sorry, Daxton."

His eyes drift closed and a weak smile touches his lips before it falls again. "I don't know when it's going to get easier to say that out loud." He rubs his hands together, as if he's trying to rid himself of that staticky feeling, too, before he lifts his head. "Uh, anyway"—he pushes a set of papers toward me—"I need to review the trust you set up for my sister, and all I can find is the draft form of the contract."

I almost feel bad for assuming the absolute worst about him, but our history doesn't really allow for warm feelings or thoughts. Then I remember that his sister is only thirteen. I press my hand to my heart, as if it will stop the pang that melts a little of my hatred toward this man. My father passed the year after I graduated law school, and I was devastated. I walked around in a fog of grief for months. I can't even fathom how painful this must be for his sister. "She's so young. This must be so hard for you both."

His face crumples and he runs his hands up and down his thighs, as if he's struggling to control his emotions. "It's been a shock, and it's a lot of change very fast."

"Who's caring for her now?" I know what it's like to be orphaned; I've gone through it twice now.

"My parents granted me custody."

I glance at his hands. There's no ring on his finger. He's close to the same age as me. Maybe a year or two older, so thirty at best. What kind of background does he have in raising a child, let alone a teenage girl? "I see. That's a lot of responsibility."

"Well, the alternative is going to live with our aunt, and that's not what Emme wants."

"And what about you? What do you want?"

"I want what's best for Emme."

"And that's you?" I shouldn't be asking such personal, almost needling questions. This kind of antagonism isn't acceptable for someone in a state of grieving. And yet, he's just lost his parents and he's here about a trust, which sends up a red flag—or maybe I'm looking for reasons to doubt his integrity.

He taps his lips, pensive instead of affronted. "Honestly? I don't know. But it's what Emme wants, and my parents seemed to think it would be best for her, so I'm going to try."

He's either being noble or delusional. Taking care of a teenager is no easy task. "And you need my help for what, exactly?"

"I need to make sure Emme's trust documents are up to date. My aunt was supposed to be the custodial guardian when the trust was drafted, and since that's changed, I want to ensure there's no conflict. I'm not sure at this point what that shift in custody means, and if there are any issues with the change that could impact Emme's trust." He rubs the space between his eyes. "Makes me wish I'd gone into family law instead of entertainment law so I'd know what's what. Anyway, I was hoping I could get a copy of the most recent trust documents, and maybe we could set up a meeting to review it, preferably soon."

I flip through the draft in silence. He's also attached a copy of the will stating Emme is in his care, the power of attorney, and the most recent bank statement with the trust funds. His sister will have access to obscene funds when she's an adult. As long as the money stays safe and out of the hands of people looking to cash in on her. And I'm unsure whether Daxton is one of those people or not.

"I'll need to have my assistant pull the original files. She can email you a copy, and in the meantime I can review them and then we can set something up. I have meetings this afternoon, though, so it won't be immediate." I don't know what his angle is. Is he worried about the money disappearing? Has he frittered all of his away on an excessive lifestyle and expensive cars and now he's looking to cash in? I need time to look over everything and do some research.

He gives me an apologetic smile. "I know I just showed up

here today, and to be honest, it's been a tough week. I tried to call early this morning, and then just figured you'd need all this documentation anyway." He motions to the papers spread out between us. "I know you can't drop everything to deal with this, but I'm a little overwhelmed, so if we can meet early next week sometime, that would be great."

Despite my suspicions and questions, I take pity on him. He's lost his parents and is suddenly responsible for a thirteen-year-old. "Why don't you leave your number with my assistant and we can set something up on Monday or Tuesday, when things are a bit more settled?"

"That would be great. Do you have someone here I can talk to about the custody paperwork? My firm doesn't do family law, so I'm at a bit of a disadvantage. Would it be you?" I don't understand why he looks so hopeful about that, maybe because I'm a familiar face?

"I don't work with custody cases, but I'll speak with Beverly and we'll figure that out, as well. Can I keep these, or do you need me to make copies?" I tap the documents under my fingers.

"Those are yours. If you need anything else, let me know. I just want to make sure my sister's future is protected."

He pushes slowly out of the chair, and I rise as well. Even with my heels, the top of my head barely reaches his shoulder.

I hold out a hand but he ignores it, stepping closer until the tips of his polished shoes nearly touch mine. And then he wraps his arms around me.

I'm shocked by the affection, when all I anticipated was a handshake. He's solid muscle, all hard ridges encased in an expensive suit. Even in his slightly disheveled state he smells divine. I'm annoyed that I notice any of these things. And at how nice it feels to be wrapped up in his strong, warm embrace.

It takes me longer than it should to react—to either extract myself or return the comforting gesture. I'm stunned, frozen because the boy I crushed on as a kid is now a man and hugging me, almost exactly like I did to him eight years ago. Except he's not telling me he loves me. Or fangirling all over me like an idiot. I choke back the ancient embarrassment and tentatively pat him on the back.

His shoulders curl forward, arms tightening. A low tremor runs through him and he makes a soft, pained sound. I don't know what to make of this, whether it's authentic or contrived. Against my better judgment, I return the soft squeeze.

He drops his arms and takes a step back, creating distance as he bumps into the chair behind him. "Fuck." He drags a hand through his hair, sending it into further disarray, face turning a bright shade of red, eyes glassy. "I'm so sorry. I'm on autopilot. I think I've hugged five hundred people in the last forty-eight hours."

Right. Of course, he's not thinking clearly. I put on what I hope is an understanding smile. "You're fine. Totally understandable, considering what you've been through this week."

I motion to the door of the conference room. I need some

space from this man. I might loathe him, but his situation pulls at my heartstrings, and he's still hot as sin, which is something I should probably feel bad about noticing considering why he's here.

Daxton shoves his hands in his pockets and walks beside me down the hall, shoulders still hunched, eyes on the floor.

Cara's eyes go wide when she sees him, and she starts to fiddle with the buttons on her blouse and then with her hair. She looks like she's trying not to hyperventilate by the time we reach her desk.

"Cara, this is Mr. Hughes. Can you please take down his contact information? I need all the files pulled on this trust." I hand her the papers. "And I'd like to set up a meeting early next week to go over everything and make sure all the details are clear and in order."

"Yes. Of course." She takes off her glasses and folds them on her desk, then fumbles with her pen. I'll forgive her the nervousness since I can relate. My palms are sweaty. I surreptitiously wipe them on my skirt, in preparation for his departure.

I offer my hand again, along with a polite smile. "I'll speak with you soon."

This time he takes it with a slow nod. His nails are ragged, but his hand is soft and warm, his grip firm. He covers our clasped hands with his free one, holding me captive. I meet his intense gaze; his tired eyes search my face. "Thank you again, Kailyn. I appreciate it. Everything."

"You're very welcome. And I'm so sorry about your parents. We'll make sure your sister's trust is safe and secure, and so is her future." I can be professional and civil with this man.

His smile holds the kind of tension I'm familiar with—full of sadness, each condolence a reminder of the loss and pain that won't dissipate anytime soon. "Thank you."

"I'll be in touch soon." I squeeze his hand and withdraw mine, lest he hugs me again, and in front of an audience this time.

I leave him with Cara and return to my office. I can't believe I have to meet with him *again*. It'll just be to deal with the trust, though, and then I can be done. It should be fairly straightforward. Anything to do with custody is on Beverly. At least it will be when I speak with her.

I dump my cooled latte from the takeout cup into my Daxton meme mug. I'd like to heat it up, but that would mean having to pass him on the way to the break room, so I settle for lukewarm. I try to tune out Cara's conversation with Daxton while I check my email, but it's difficult to focus on anything but his presence outside my office door. Cara's voice is high-pitched and overly sweet, but she manages to keep herself together until he leaves the office. She practically trips over her own shoes and almost face-plants into my desk as soon as he's gone.

"Oh my God. He's so gorgeous. That's so sad about his parents. He's pretty much a single dad now. I think ovaries around the world will explode over this." She drops into the chair on the opposite side of my desk and fans herself with her tablet. She glances pointedly at my mug. "I had such a crush on him as a girl. Or his character, I guess."

"So did every other teenage girl who watched that show." I toss my pen on the desk so I don't chew on the cap. I'm annoyed that I want to share in the freaking fangirling. He really was dreamy back then. Not much has changed, at least in the looks department.

"He seemed to know you," she presses.

"I went to law school with him."

She leans forward, eyes wide, tablet clutched tightly in her hands. "Really? What was he like?"

"He was an asshole."

"Oh, that's . . . disappointing." She fiddles with her glasses. "I wonder why he left acting."

I don't know the answer to the last question, although I assume it was because he decided to go into entertainment law. "I have no idea. What can I do for you, Cara, aside from discuss exploding ovaries? Have you already pulled the Hughes files?" I know she hasn't had time to pull anything. She's still trying to get over meeting Daxton.

She stops slouching and bolts upright. "Oh, Beverly would like to see you in her office."

"Now?"

"Yes. As soon as you have a moment."

"Did she specify what it was about?"

She blinks twice. "Um, no."

I tap my pen on the desk. "Did you even ask?"

She sinks in her chair. I should feel a little bad that I incite this kind of response, but any incompetence on her part directly affects me.

"No," she says meekly. "She called when I was speaking with Mr. Hughes."

"Ah, so you were distracted."

"No. Well, maybe a little." She hangs her head. "Yes. I was distracted."

"It happens to the best of us." I stand and gather my tablet. "Please pull any files related to the Hughes trust right away, and I'd like to email him a copy so he's able to review it over the weekend. Did he provide potential dates and times to meet next week?"

"He said he would make whatever we had available work regardless. I'll pull his files now."

I leave Cara to collect herself, and head for Beverly's office. I dislike going in to see her unprepared, and that's how this situation makes me feel.

As a senior associate I have a good working relationship with Beverly. Whitman and Flood is a small firm, giving me the opportunity to move up quickly. I've proven myself over the past five years, and pushed even harder since my dad passed, hell-bent on making partner before I turn thirty. My dad and I made a bet before he died, and even though he's gone, I don't want to disappoint him. I also like to reach for the top, always, and partner is the next step.

I knock on Beverly's door and wait for her to call me in.

She gestures to the chair across from her desk and tents her fingers, resting her chin on them. "How did everything go with Mr. Hughes?"

"Fine, for being unprepared. I need to review the trust files so we can discuss them next week and make any necessary amendments."

She nods and leans back in her chair. "I apologize for springing this on you without notice, and I appreciate that you were able to carve out some time to meet with him. It's such a shame about his parents, and then having custody of his sister." Her gaze drifts to the window. "I'm sure it's been quite a shock. I can't even imagine."

"It's a lot of responsibility to take on." And so much grief to manage on top of his own. I'm not sure how to feel about any part of this. "His sister's trust is very substantial. He seems rather concerned about it, which makes me question if perhaps he's after it for some reason."

She shifts her gaze away from the window, her expression unreadable. "I'm sure he has his own money."

"Unless he's spent it all."

Beverly smiles. "Always a cynic."

I lift a casual shoulder, trying to keep the bite and skepticism out of my tone. "Well, it would make sense, wouldn't it? He takes custody of his sister, and all that money is available for him to manage."

Beverly tilts her head a fraction, observing me closely. "How well do you know Daxton Hughes?"

I sit up straighter, uncertain as to where the question is coming from. "We went to law school together, but didn't associate with the same people. Why do you ask?"

"He hugged you in the conference room." I try not to show any emotion, but I must frown because her expression is smug. "I wasn't eavesdropping. I was passing by and saw the interaction. I wondered what your relationship was."

"There isn't a relationship. We went to school together, and I worked on his sister's trust fund when his parents set it up months ago. The connection is purely by chance."

Her long nails rap on the arm of her chair. "You're meeting with him again, though? How soon?"

"Early next week. Why?" Where is she going with this? She's the one who sprang him on me; I assumed that means she wants me to deal with him. And it's not like I have an actual choice since I'm responsible for the trust in the first place.

"He seems to trust you, or at least have some kind of connection to you."

"I don't know that he trusts me, he's just grieving." I don't like the look in her eye. She's planning something.

"You might try to persuade him that working here would be beneficial for him when you meet with him next."

I'm at a complete loss for several very long seconds—in that time I consider how much I do *not* want to work in the same office as Daxton Hughes, regardless of whether he's in a state of grieving. "We don't even really know each other, and you want me to convince him to come work here?"

"He felt comfortable enough to hug you."

"He was emotional and under duress. I assure you, he likely would not have hugged me under normal circumstances." There was that one time in second year when we were on the same side for a class debate, and when we won he spontaneously hugged me, but it was excitement, nothing more.

Beverly gives me one of her knowing looks. I hate them, because it means she thinks she has something on me, something she thinks I want. Which is not Daxton Hughes. Maybe once upon a time, when I was young and stupid and easily influenced by a wink and a smile, but not now.

"Regardless, there's a level of comfort and familiarity that you can capitalize on."

Fine. She wants to play this game, well, I can play, too. If I'm going out of my way to bring the traitorous lion into my own den, I better reap the rewards. "What's in it for me if I get him to come to the dark side?"

"The reward of knowing you've strengthened our team."

"If I'm going to persuade Daxton to switch firms, I'd like to pick up another pro bono case."

Beverly purses her lips. "You just took on a pro bono case."

"That was months ago, and it's been resolved." I haven't been able to stop thinking about a foster situation Holly mentioned last week. If I'm going to invite someone I loathe onto our team, I want something in return. This is the perfect opportunity to get what I want without having to fight for it.

"Fine. As long as it doesn't interfere with you convincing

Daxton to work for me, you can take the pro bono case. Any other negotiations?"

I flip my pen between my fingers, considering all the angles. I can't believe I'm entertaining bringing the man who pulled the rug out from under me into my life and my building on a daily basis.

It's not like I'll run into him all the time. Entertainment law is on the opposite end of the floor. Although I may see him occasionally in the break room. I rarely eat lunch in there. I can deal with seeing him across the boardroom for weekly meetings. I think.

"I'll let you know if I have anything to add to the list."

chapter five

LIFE REPACKAGED

Daxton

I have no idea how people single parent without going insane. I don't cook. It's never been my thing. I order groceries from a delivery service and supplement with takeout. I have a menu for every day of the month. Surprisingly, it turns out thirteen-year-olds don't love McDonald's enough to eat it for an entire week. After six days of fast food, Emme boycotts it entirely.

"Well, what do you want for dinner?" I ask after she turns her nose up at every single takeout menu spread over the counter.

She crosses her arms, annoyed. "I don't want takeout."

I mirror her pose, equally annoyed. Since I have no intention of disrupting Emme's life more than it already is, I put my condo up for sale this morning. I spent the rest of the day packing all my stuff, separating it into two stacks of boxes: things that will go into storage and things I'll need. I ended the day by bringing a carload of things home. It's amazing what one person can accumulate over five years. Tomorrow I need to work on getting rid of some of my parents' old things to make room for mine.

"I'm bagged, Emme. I can't do a restaurant tonight." I also need a serious shower after all that packing.

"I want shepherd's pie."

Well, that's rather specific. "Why don't we go to the grocery store to pick one up, then?" That seems like something they'd have in the frozen food section.

"I don't want store-bought shepherd's pie. I want Mom's." Her bottom lip trembles, and I feel like shit for getting snippy with her.

"Why don't we check the freezer and see what's in there?"

She chews on her thumbnail, but nods and follows me to the basement. I'm relieved when I find more than one pan of our mom's homemade shepherd's pie in the chest freezer, and like the amazingly thoughtful mom she was, there are cooking instructions fixed to the lid. "It'll be an hour."

"That's okay. I can wait." She takes it from me, hugging the frozen brick to her chest as she heads back upstairs to the kitchen. She turns on the oven, setting it to convection— which apparently takes the cooking time down by about fifteen minutes.

I pop the cap on a bottle of beer while we wait.

"Can I have a sip?" Emme asks as she chops vegetables to make a salad.

I raise a brow. "A sip?"

"Of your beer." She fidgets with the cuff of her hoodie.

Sometimes at dinner on the weekends my parents would let Emme have a sip out of their wineglass. They'd been the same way with me.

I pass her the bottle and she tips it up. She makes a face and hands it back, wiping her mouth on her sleeve. "That's gross."

"It's an acquired taste." One I'm happy she hasn't acquired yet.

She roots around in the fridge and produces a can of Coke, presumably to wash away the unpleasant flavor. "Are you going to move into Mom and Dad's room?"

"Eventually." I can't sleep in the shrine to my teenage stardom years much longer if I want to keep my sanity. "Are you okay with that? Me taking their room?"

She chews on the inside of her lip for a few seconds, mulling it over. "It's bigger and not filled with all the stuff from ten years ago, so it makes more sense, right?"

I nod, aware this is a conversation we need to have, even if it's difficult.

She rolls the can of Coke between her hands. "Are you going to give away all their clothes?"

"Are there things you want to keep?" I could store some stuff in the basement until she's ready to let go.

"Can I help you clean it out, so I can pick the things I want?"

"Of course, Emme."

When dinner is ready we sit at the island and dig in. The potato topping is a little dark around the edges, but it tastes so much like my childhood. Emme makes it halfway through her meal before she breaks down.

She pushes away from the counter, already out of the room and rushing up the stairs before I can call her name. Her bedroom door slams shut a few seconds later. I stare at my half-eaten meal, no longer hungry. I don't want to waste any of this, because soon all these tangible pieces of my mother will be gone.

"Help me," I mutter to the empty room, looking for the advice I so often sought from my dad on family dinner nights. "Someone tell me how to help her."

No one ever mentions how much harder everything is once the funeral is over, when everyone else goes back to living their lives and we're stuck here, wading through years of memories and trapped in the relentless grip of grief. At thirteen everything is supposed to be fun and friends and what the hell you're going to wear to school the next day, not packing up your parents' things because they're no longer alive.

$\backsim$

The next morning I find my sister already in my parents' room, sorting through our mother's clothes. She has two piles, and they're roughly the same size. I brew a coffee in the Keurig I purchased for them last Christmas. They were a lot better than me, using those recyclable pots that are a huge pain in the ass to clean.

When I return, my sister has moved on to my dad's closet.

"You okay?" I ask, my voice still gravelly.

"Yeah."

"You were pretty upset last night."

She shrugs. "I had a day."

It's hard to argue with that, so I let it go and help her empty out my dad's closet. Once the space is mostly clear, Emme tackles our mother's shoe rack. My mom loved her shoes.

"You can't wear heels until you're eighteen," I say when she comes strutting out in one of our mom's very old sequin dresses and a pair of stilettos.

She props a fist on her hip. Her outfit, combined with her stance, makes her look like a young version of our mother. "That's ridiculous. There are dances in eighth grade, and semi-formals in high school."

"Well, you're sure as hell not wearing those to a school dance, or that dress."

"Why not?"

Because I will have to walk around with a baseball bat and threaten all the boys with it to keep them away from you. "Because you look like a foal, wobbling around. You want to wear heels, you pick ones you're not going to topple over in, and only on special occasions. Heels aren't even comfortable and they ruin your back."

Emme disappears again inside our mother's closet. "You sound exactly like Dad."

I smile at that. I must be doing something right if I'm pissing her off and she's compared me to our father.

Emme carts boxes of shoes to her room—who knows where in the world she's planning to store them—while I start going through my mother's dresser.

I'm halfway through cleaning out the sock drawer when I discover the thing no son ever wants to find. Tucked neatly behind two rows of socks, hidden well enough that they're not noticeable at first but not so far back to make it difficult to access, are sex toys. Plural.

I search the dresser for something I can prod with, uncertain whether it's just perverse curiosity ruling me at this point. Holy hell. It appears my parents were kinky motherfuckers based on the non-sock items taking up space in the drawer. There is a seriously vast array of lace and satin, and *dear fucking God*, there's leather in here, too.

I find a pen and start poking around, appalled to discover my mother had—has—*owned*—several vibrators.

"What's next?" Emme scares the crap out of me when she appears in the doorway.

I slam the drawer shut, smashing my thumb in the process. "Shit!" I shake it out, then put pressure on the nail, hoping it doesn't go black. It's hurts like hell, though.

"Are you okay? I didn't mean to sneak up on you."

"It's fine. We're good." I inspect my thumb and see ice might be necessary. "I think we can be done for today."

"Don't you want to move your bed and stuff in here?"

"There's no rush. Why don't we grab some lunch?"

She shrugs. "Sure."

I push off the dresser, exhaling a relieved breath as I follow my sister down the hall. She's already talking about what she wants to eat and where she wants to go.

Crisis averted. For now.

There are enough shitty things I'm going to have to discuss with her over the next several years; our mother's collection of fake and vibrating dicks is not one of them.

Lunch with Emme is actually pleasant. She talks about what color she wants to paint my old bedroom and making it her "friend hangout room." Mentally I cross all boys off the list of friends allowed up there.

My phone rings in the middle of our meal. I fully intend to ignore the call until the name Spear and Associates flashes across the screen. It's the firm that Beverly at Whitman and Flood recommended. She mentioned it being a potential conflict of interest for her firm to work on the custody case when they were handling Emme's trust. Family law seems significantly more complicated than entertainment law. I spoke to a woman named Trish immediately following my meeting with Kailyn over the trust. She already has a copy of my parents' will, outlining the custody arrangement, and tomorrow morning we're meeting to review everything.

"Sorry, kiddo, give me a second. I need to get this." I give Emme an apologetic smile and bring my phone to my ear. "Hello, Daxton here."

"Daxton, it's Trish. I'm so sorry to call you on a Sunday, but I have bad news."

A cold feeling trickles down my spine. "What kind of bad news?"

"Linda's officially suing for custody."

chapter six

FLIP-FLOP

Kailyn

In light of recent events, I'm appointing you as Emme Hughes's conservator."

I almost fall out of my chair. As it is, I drop the pen I was flipping between my fingers and it rolls under her desk. Dammit. I really liked that one. It had a funky swirl pattern on it. I wait for Beverly to crack a smile. She does not. "You're kidding, right?"

Her foot bobs once. "Have I ever been a kidder, Kailyn?"

I search for some kind of facial tic, anything to indicate she will soon start laughing. But that does not happen. "You're serious."

My morning started out fine. Well, fine-ish. I arrived in the office at seven with the intention of briefing Beverly on the Hughes files—which came home with me this weekend. Instead, I'm being told his aunt is suing for custody. And she has an excellent lawyer. Hopefully Daxton has a better one.

"Who's representing Daxton?"

"Trish Monroe."

I almost heave a sigh of relief. She has an outstanding reputation for winning cases.

"What's the purpose of appointing me as conservator?" I already know the answer to this question, so I'm not sure what the point of asking it is, other than I want to hear Beverly say it.

This time Beverly almost smiles, but manages to keep it to a semi-smirk. "While the custody case is being handled, Emme needs a neutral third party to look after her. Be her voice. You wrote up the trust. It's logical for you to remain involved since your priority is to protect Emme and her finances. And once the court rules on who has custody, the legal guardian will take over control of the trust."

She makes sense, which is frustrating. "Isn't there another family member who can take on this role?"

"No one local. Besides, it will give you a chance to find out exactly what's going on between Daxton and his aunt, and you'll have contact with Emme. Plus, you'll have an opportunity to warm Daxton up to the idea of coming on board here. It's a win all the way around, Kailyn. You must see that."

"I'm legally responsible for the welfare and finances of a girl I don't even know."

"Who has recently lost both her parents, so you understand what she's going through."

It's my turn to be stone-faced. This is unfair leverage she's using against me.

Beverly steeples her hands, meeting my unrelenting glare. "You are the best person to take on this role for a multitude of reasons. Beyond the ones I've already provided, Daxton has a connection with you and he seems to trust you."

"You said I could take on a pro bono case if I brought Daxton to the firm. That isn't going to be enough anymore. This whole thing could get messy, and if it does I'm right in the middle of it. We have no idea what this aunt's angle is. Maybe she's just after the money, or maybe Daxton is. All I've heard so far is his side of the story. He looked like hell last week and I have no idea if it's because he's grieving or because he's been making bad choices recently."

"He works for one of the top firms in the state, so his choices can't be that bad."

"Professionally, who knows about personally?" She has a point, but then, so do I. We have no idea if he wants guardianship of Emme for the right reasons or not. "I need more than one pro bono case and the glory of taking on a challenge."

Beverly considers that for a few seconds before her smile turns into a full-on grin. "What if I make you partner?"

I laugh and then stop immediately when she doesn't join in. "Are you serious?"

"Again, joking is not really my thing."

"You'll make me partner if I agree to be the conservator?"

"If you take on that role *and* manage to do what I haven't been able to for the past five years in bringing him over, I'll most definitely make you partner, Kailyn. I already have the best trust lawyer in the state. Now I'd like the best entertainment lawyer, as well, and this is the perfect opportunity to make it happen. I'll even waive the buy-in."

"The entire buy-in?"

Beverly nods. "The whole thing."

That she's willing to waive the buy-in tells me exactly how much she wants Daxton on our team, which burns my ass a little. But the partnership buy-in can be in excess of a quarter of a million dollars. That's a lot of money I won't have to worry about parting with. Money I'd have to borrow since I'm still paying off my school loans. While I inherited everything when my dad passed, there really wasn't much left after the hospital bills, apart from the house, which I still live in.

Partner before thirty with no buy-in is amazing. It'd be nice to make partner on my own merit, but maybe in some ways this counts. Especially since I'll be working with a man I can't stand on a daily basis, that has to mean something. And I'll be making good on my promise to my dad, another reason to agree.

I should feel bad that I'm considering ways to draw him in, particularly in his vulnerable state. But logistically this is the best time to persuade someone to make a change. Catch a person in a weak moment and offer them something helpful. That actually sounds awful in my head.

"I'll need flexibility with my hours and the cases I'm taking on while I'm acting as conservator."

"Of course, we'll adjust as necessary."

If we're bargaining, I'm putting all my cards on the table. "And if I make partner, I want to be able to pick up a few pro bono cases a year of my choosing."

Beverly gives me a look saying I just stepped over a line, but this is my chance and I'm going to at least ask.

"We'll have to discuss it further."

It's not a no, which coming from Beverly is almost as good as a yes. "It reflects well on the firm."

She taps on the arm of her chair. "You bring Daxton over and we'll negotiate."

I don't know what kind of person it makes me that I'm actually looking forward to the challenge on all levels now. "And if Daxton agrees to come on board, he'll need flexible hours and a reduced caseload, without taking a pay cut." Now that I have my ultimate goal within reach, I'm determined to make it a reality, even if it means giving someone I dislike a whole lot of perks. In this case, I need to remind myself that Emme is the priority, and her needs are paramount.

Beverly smiles. "Look at you, already negotiating his contract."

"Can I get this all in writing?"

She flips her perfect hair over her shoulder. "You have my word. That should suffice."

"I'd prefer your signature in blood, but I guess that'll have to do."

In light of this new development, I call Daxton as soon as I'm back in my office. We need to discuss my role as conservator, and I'd like to meet the girl I'm now legally responsible for.

Daxton felt it would be better to meet outside of the office to avoid causing Emme additional stress. Prior to meeting them for lunch, I review the news articles and footage related to the accident. I want to go into this with a clear understanding of what happened. I run across an amateur video taken with a cell phone and wish I hadn't watched. It's horrifying. So as much as I'm not excited about having to deal with Daxton, possibly on a daily basis eventually, I would be a coldhearted bitch if I didn't feel empathy for him and his sister.

And maybe he's right. Law school was five years ago; I should just get over it. In the grand scheme of things, coming in second hasn't had a negative impact on my career. Besides that, I'm no longer a college girl with a crush on a former star. As an adult, I don't do crushes anymore.

At least that's what I tell myself as I trade my glasses for contacts, check my hair, reapply my lip gloss, and adjust my skirt before I leave the office to meet them for lunch. As soon as I step outside, my phone buzzes with a message from Holly.

Instead of texting back, I call her so I can fill her in. "You'll never believe what happened this morning."

"Jason Momoa appeared shirtless in your office and did triceps dips on the edge of your desk?"

"That's your fantasy, not mine, and no, not even close." I squeeze between an older couple shambling down the street and a woman pushing a stroller while texting. "So you know how I told you about Daxton Hughes showing up in my office last week?"

"Um, how could I forget? You talked about it at least once every hour on Friday and then twice at brunch on Sunday."

I ignore her dig. "Anyway, to make this whole crappy situation worse, I've now been appointed as conservator for his sister."

"Can you speak like a human instead of a lawyer so I can understand what that means?"

I pause at the corner, waiting for the light to change and the walk sign to appear. "Essentially I'm the legal guardian because I'm neutral."

"Whoa. Wait. Does this mean she has to live with you?"

"No, it's more of a formality, but now it means I'm involved and I'll have to speak with him on a regular basis until custody is worked out. But that's not the worst part. Or the best. I don't even know anymore."

"There's a good part to all this?" Holly asks.

"Beverly's offered me partner for taking this on, and she'll waive the buy-in."

"Holy sh—sugar balls!" She's obviously in the office. "That's awesome, Kay! We need to go out and celebrate."

"There's nothing to celebrate yet," I mutter bitterly. "I only make partner *if* I can get Daxton to come over to Whitman, which means I'll have to work with him. Not directly, but I'll be subjected to his face every day."

"It's a nice face, though, right?"

"Unfortunately, yes." I spot the diner about a hundred yards up the street. "I have to go. I'm meeting Daxton and his sister for lunch, but I'll talk to you later. Oh, any recent updates on the Lipsons? I need some good news right now."

"They're fantastic. Little Hope is a crawling machine. I have cute pictures I can show you."

"Excellent." That makes me ridiculously happy. Hope is freaking adorable. "And what about that new foster case?"

"That's a story for another time."

"Uh-oh, well, if you need my help, I've been given permission to take on another pro bono."

"Seriously?"

"Super seriously. What are you doing tonight? Maybe you could fill me in over dinner or something?"

"Or you could come with me to the SPCA. It's kitten adoption day."

"Hit me right in the soft spot, why don't you? I can't bring home another one. Linus has just stopped humping Shirley on a daily basis."

Holly laughs. "I told you to get a girl cat, didn't I?"

"Well, it's too late for that. I'm attached to both of them and I worry adding another one would only give Linus more humping options."

"I'll pick you up at six? You can vent all you want about Daxton Hughes while you snuggle with pussies."

"I knew that was coming. I'll see you tonight." I end the call, slip my phone into my bag, and take a deep breath, buoyed a little by the good news about Hope.

Daxton and Emme are already seated at a booth when I enter Earl's Diner. Since their backs are to me, I take a moment to watch them before I'm spotted. I recognize Daxton's hair and broad shoulders—which is odd, I realize, since I've only seen him twice in the past five years. But then we had multiple classes together for three years. If I made it to class after him, I would sit behind him and his friends, mostly so I could indulge my crush undetected. Which means I still recognize the set of his shoulders and the small cowlick on the right side, which only appeared by his ear when his hair grew too long. I'm so glad I'm not that silly, fawning girl anymore. Mostly.

He's sitting on the inside of the booth with Emme beside him. Both of their heads are bent, so I assume they're looking at the menu. I take a deep breath, preparing myself for the full force of his stupidly gorgeous face, and approach their table hoping to appear open and friendly.

Daxton is first to look up. His smile is warm and makes my scalp prickle, along with other, less appropriate body parts. Freaking teenage crushes die hard.

"Thanks a lot for meeting us here."

"It's really no problem. I needed to break for lunch anyway and they have the best milkshakes." I slide across the bench opposite them and turn what I hope is a warm and welcoming smile to his sister since she's the reason I'm here. Well, that and I want to make partner.

Emme's oversize hoodie is black and frayed at the cuffs. She has the same color hair as Daxton but with brown eyes instead of blue. They also share the same wide mouth and full lips. She's tiny, shorter than me even, and I'm just over five feet tall. Thank God for heels. It would be easy to mistake her for his daughter, despite how young he is, based on her size alone.

Emme's eyes light up. "Oh my God, the milkshakes are the best! They're all so good!"

"Right? How many have you tried? It's my life mission to get through all of them at some point."

"Me, too! I think I'm through half the menu, but then I get stuck on my favorites and it's hard to move on," she admits.

"It happens to me all the time."

"I'm Emme." Her hand shoots out and I take it, my smile growing wider. She's freaking adorable.

"I'm Kailyn. It's nice to meet you."

"Dax said you went to school together."

"We did." I glance his way, wondering what else he's told her about me.

"Dax said he was an idiot in school."

I laugh. "Is that so?"

She nods. "He said all boys are stupid, especially in high school and college, but I think they're all pretty stupid now, and I don't start high school until next year." Her nose wrinkles and she looks at her brother, as if checking to make sure it's okay for her to share.

Dax gives her a solemn nod. "It gets worse before it gets better, kiddo. Might as well stay away from boys altogether until you're closer to thirty."

Emme rolls her eyes. "Anyway, my favorite milkshake is Oreo, but they have a peanut butter chocolate one that's just as good, so I have a hard time deciding."

"Hmm." I tap my lip. "Those both sound amazing. It's going to be a tough decision."

"Yeah, but the good thing is you can't really go wrong. My dad takes me here all—" She jolts as if she's touched a live wire. "I mean, he used to take me here." Her head drops and she brings the sleeve of her hoodie to her mouth. Her thumb pushes through a tear in the fabric.

Daxton puts his arm around her and pulls her into his side. He gives me an apologetic smile as he rubs her shoulder and whispers something to her. Her small frame shakes, and she nods into his chest. After a few more seconds she excuses herself and slips out of the booth.

Daxton watches her disappear into the women's room, worrying his bottom lip before slowly turning back to me. "Sorry about that. It comes in waves, you know? One second she's happy and laughing and the next she's in tears."

"How are you managing?" I ask. Dark circles ring his eyes, and although he's put together, his exhaustion is obvious.

"It's a learning curve. She has to go back to school tomorrow and she's nervous, and frankly, so am I. She's going to have to deal with all her friends and the questions, and of course our aunt works there, so there's added stress. The whole custody thing just threw us for a loop, especially so soon after our parents—" He pauses and clears his throat. "I'm hoping that us talking will alleviate some of her anxiety about possibly having to move."

"How much have you told Emme?"

He fiddles with his napkin, smoothing it out. "That Linda would like her to come live with her, but that I'd like her to stay with me, so we need to figure it out."

"And what did you tell her my role is?"

"I told her you were kind of like a bank manager and referee. You make sure her trust is safe and that she has what she needs while I work on keeping her with me."

I'm about to ask if that's what Emme wants when she returns to the table, effectively shutting down the discussion.

We order our meals and milkshakes when the server comes around. She's a woman in her early twenties, and she makes goo-goo eyes at Daxton whenever he speaks. I get it, he's a hottie, but she needs to tone her simper down a notch. Or ten.

While we wait for the food to arrive I explain the parameters of the trust and my new role in Emme's life.

"But I still get to stay with Dax, right?" She pokes at her milkshake with her straw.

"That's right. Everything stays exactly the way it is for the time being, apart from me being involved in more than just your trust."

"Okay." She nods, as if this makes sense, but then chews on the inside of her lip.

"Do you have any other questions? I know it's a lot of new things happening, so I'm here to help however I can."

Emme looks to Daxton, as if seeking his approval before she speaks. I'm not sure if it's because she's wary of me, or of his reaction to whatever questions she has. At his nod she clears her throat. "So if you're responsible for me, does that mean you have to move in with me and Dax?"

Daxton's eyes go wide and his gaze darts to me. I'm not capable of speaking, though, since I'm coughing up the french fry I almost choked on.

"No, Em, it's not like that. It's still just you and me," he replies.

"Oh. Okay. 'Cause, like, that might be a little weird, but at least you and Dax were, like, friends before, right? And Dax doesn't have a girlfriend or anything, so it wouldn't be *that* weird. Except if Kailyn had to stay in your old room." Emme's eyes light up and she leans in closer, as if she's about to tell a secret. "His bedroom is full of stuff from his old TV show. Posters and everything."

I glance at Daxton and then back at her. "Is that right?"

She nods. "Dax said we can clean it out and I can put all the stuff on eBay and decide what I want to do with the money."

"Oh, really? Is there lots of cool stuff?"

Daxton's face is an interesting shade of red. "It's just memorabilia and crap."

"But some of it might be worth money, so I'm going to see what I can get for it."

What I wouldn't give to help clean out that room. I find myself a little giddy over the thought. I'm a TV memorabilia junkie. I may have boycotted watching the show after law school, and boxed up all my old things, but they're still in my bedroom closet.

A few minutes later Emme slumps back in her seat, rubbing her tummy. "You all right, kiddo?" Daxton eyes her plate. She's barely touched her burger or fries, and only managed to drink about half of her shake.

"Just not really hungry anymore." She fiddles with her napkin and peeks up at him. "I'm sorry. I know it's a waste."

"You want it packed up?"

She shrugs. "Can I go next door to the bookstore and look around while you guys eat and talk about stuff that you don't want to say in front of me?"

Daxton gives her a look. "Em."

"What? I'm not dumb and I'm not trying to be rude and, like, I'm kind of done hearing about Aunt Linda, so can I go?" She gives him sad puppy dog eyes, which I'm sure are at least 50 percent authentic.

"Fine."

Emme slides out of the booth, grinning.

"Hold on." Daxton pulls his wallet from his back pocket, flips it open, and retrieves a twenty.

"What's this for?"

"You're going to a bookstore. This is so you can buy a book."

"Oh." She smiles and pockets the money. "Okay, thanks."

"And you only go to the bookstore. Nowhere else, okay?"

"Okay, Dax."

"And no crossing the street."

She makes a face. "What?"

"Stay on this side of the street."

"I'm not a baby. I don't need someone to hold my hand all the time. I know what the walking guy and the flashing red hand mean." And there's the teen snark I've been waiting for. I fight my own smile because I don't want to encourage the sass, but I'm curious as to how Daxton handles it.

He glares at her until her eyes roll. "If I'm just going to the bookstore, I have no reason to cross the street anyway. Any other rules?"

"I think you're good. You have your phone?"

She pulls it out of her pocket. "Satisfied?"

"Can the attitude."

"If you stopped treating me like a baby, I wouldn't need to pull out the attitude."

Dax raises a brow. "I can take the twenty back."

That changes her tune. "Sorry. Okay. No more attitude. I know you're just trying to, like, show me you care, or whatever. I'll be back in a bit."

"Go look at books and don't cause a riot, or stage a political protest or anything that's going to piss me off."

"Oh my God. You're the worst." She rolls her eyes again, waves at me, does a little bouncy spin, and heads for the door.

Daxton watches her leave. "I'm pretty sure one of these days her eyes are going to roll up into her head and stay there."

He glances at her plate, frown still in place. "She hardly ate a thing."

"She giving you a hard time?" I bite the end of a fry. The portions here are huge. I still have half a sandwich and half my fries, but Emme's plate looks like she mostly pushed the food around.

"Not really. I mean, the spontaneous tears are to be expected. It's just . . . she's a teenager. She's growing. When I was her age, I ate everything in sight."

"Her appetite is off, then?"

He runs his hand through his hair. It falls right back into place, which I find annoying for some reason. "Half the time I just offer her junk food to get some calories in her body. She picks at almost everything."

"Is that abnormal for her?"

He fiddles with his napkin. "I don't really know. I mean, I used to have lunch with Emme and my parents every Sunday, but I never focused on her eating habits. It's just not something I thought about. She's already small, smaller than the other kids her age. She can't afford to lose weight. I don't want to stuff her full of sugar and chocolate because that's not any better." He blows out a breath. "Sorry. I'm unloading on you and that's not what you're here for."

I give him a sympathetic smile. "You're taking on a lot and going through a heavy personal loss. People grieve differently. When my mom passed I didn't have much of an appetite for a while, but it came back eventually."

His eyes soften and his hand slides across the table a few inches in my direction. "I'm so sorry. I didn't know."

"It was during my undergrad, so it was a long time ago."

"That must've been hard."

I swirl a french fry in my ketchup. Maybe Beverly has a valid point, maybe Daxton does feel comfortable with me for some reason—because of our law school connection, probably. It's possible he doesn't remember it the same way I do.

Regardless, right now it's not about what happened five years ago, it's about finding points of connection and this loss is something we share. It's a way for him to relate and for me to gain his trust. "It was difficult, particularly for my dad. I think that was the hardest part, seeing him suffer without her. Kind of like you have to watch Emme go through this while you do, as well. It makes you feel helpless." It's taken me a long time to get over that, and in some ways it's made relationships challenging. I've already suffered hard losses, and I know that pain. I'm not sure my heart is meant for much more breaking.

His eyes are on me, soft, maybe a little relieved, and full of painful sympathy. "That's it exactly. I feel helpless and so . . . out of my depth. Is your dad okay now?"

I focus on the napkin in my lap. "In a way, yes. He's with her now, if you believe in that kind of thing. So I'd like to think he's happy and at peace. That they both are."

This time when Daxton reaches across the table, his fingers slide over mine, eyes full of commiserating despair. "They're gone? You lost them both, too?"

My first instinct is to retract my hand and hide it under the table, away from the man who seems to cause no end of conflict every time he drops into my life.

"Not at the same time, and not in such a..." *Violent, horrific, haunting.* "Difficult way."

"But you're alone. Do you have any brothers or sisters?"

His hand is still covering mine. The contact is unnerving because his warmth seems to seep under my skin and into my veins, radiating through my entire body, inciting a very different set of emotions, ones I haven't felt in a very long time. Ones at war with the sadness of my own loss, of his. Ones that definitely don't fit these circumstances. I shake those off. It's just because we share a similar level of trauma, because his loss makes me remember my own. And he's attractive, which is impossible not to notice when I'm sitting across from him like this, and he's touching me.

I withdraw my hand, severing the contact. "No, I don't have any siblings. I have a very close friend who's pretty much like a sister, though, so it's almost the same thing. I imagine this is hard in a different way for you because you have someone, but she's in your care and needs your guidance."

He stretches his leg out and his foot knocks against mine under the table, but he doesn't seem to notice, or move it away. Maybe he thinks my leg is part of the table. "Does the empty feeling ever go away?"

I think about holidays, my parents' birthdays, my own, and what it's like to be without them when I reach milestones. "I think you learn how to live with holes in your heart. You can't patch them up, or plug them with other people, but you find ways to make it bearable, if that makes sense."

The flicker of hope in his eyes dims.

"It gets easier, Daxton. Not right away, and probably not for a long while, but it will get easier. You adjust." You simply get used to having those empty spaces in your heart. But I leave that part out. His wounds are too fresh to poke at, and this discussion makes mine feel the same.

"You're different than I remember," he says.

His words feel like an electric charge. I give him a questioning smile. "I'm sorry?"

"I wish I would've...I wanted to..." He stumbles over his words. It's strange to see him so uncomposed. "I know you're here for Emme's well-being, but I—"

"Daxton?" A shrill female voice makes us both jolt.

Standing at the end of the table is a tall, very leggy, very stereotypical California female. Her blond hair is almost white—artificially so—and her boobs are fake and there's enough collagen injected into her lips to make her look like she's just finished giving head to an entire football team.

His eyes close for the briefest moment and his fingers tense against the edge of the table. When they open again, he gives me an apologetic look, and then his expression and his body language transform as he directs a warm, welcoming smile at the quasi-human Barbie doll.

He gives her an appraising, visual sweep. "Hi."

"How are you? God, it's been forever. It's Jessie. You remember me, right?" Her nose scrunches. "We met at that party at Justin's a few months back. Everyone was skinny-dipping." She does this flaily thing with her hands, and her eyebrows shoot up, like there's more meaning in that than I'd care to know about.

I crumple up my napkin and toss it on my plate. Gathering the files, I slip them into my briefcase. "I have to head back to the office for afternoon meetings." I pull a twenty from my purse and let it flutter to the table.

"No, no. This is on me." He reaches for the money and tries to give it back, but I'm already out of the booth.

I smooth out my skirt, ignoring him. I feel dowdy next to Jessie.

Daxton tries to follow me, but Jessie is already squeezing in beside him. "I need to—" He points in my direction, and Jessie gives him a blank look.

She glances at me and then back at him, tilting her head to the side. "Oh, are you two..." She motions between us with an expression somewhere between confusion and disbelief. "Together?"

I laugh. "I'm just a lawyer."

"Oh, right. That makes sense." Jessie nods. She puts her hand on Daxton's arm. "Is everything okay?"

I have to fight an eye roll. Emme and I have that particular trait in common, I suppose. The thought of her being raised by someone who's clearly into the party lifestyle gets my back up. "I'll be in touch with Trish this afternoon. Have Emme call me if she needs anything."

"Kailyn—"

"You may want to consider what constitutes positive role-modeling as you move forward." And with that parting comment, I leave him to manage what I assume is one of his many previous conquests.

I'm on my way out the door when Emme walks back into the diner. Her smile falls when she sees me, messenger bag in hand. "You're going?" Her frown deepens when she sees the woman barricading her brother into the booth. "Who's that?"

"A friend of your brother's, I think." I have to work hard to keep the disdain from creeping into my voice. I rearrange my features into a smile. "I have to get back to the office. But it was lovely to meet you, Emme."

"Oh. Right. Okay." She fidgets, fingers tugging on a loose thread. "Um, well, thanks for coming to lunch and explaining all that stuff. I don't really get it, but I'm glad you're helping me and Dax."

Poor baby, she looks so lost. I want to tell her everything is going to be okay, even if it's a lie. "If you have any questions, I'm happy to try to answer them."

She wrings her hands. "So I stay with Dax, and you just make sure my trust is safe and stuff?"

I spend a few minutes explaining again exactly how it all works and hope her nods mean she really does get it, but I suggest exchanging contact information so she can call or text if there's anything else she's unsure of.

Meanwhile Jessie fawns all over Daxton fifteen feet away.

"Maybe next time we can just talk about normal stuff," Emme says as she pockets her phone. And then she hugs me. I wonder if hugging is a family thing and maybe they're all big on affection. It takes me a moment to shake off the awkwardness and react. As soon as I wrap my arms around her tiny frame, she tightens her hold on me. I want to protect her from this pain, even though I know it's impossible. I pat her back and give her a squeeze, remembering how difficult it was when I lost my mom, whose hugs were really the only ones that ever made me feel better when I was sad, and my heart aches even more for this lost girl.

When I return to the office, I have a list of phone calls a mile long. One stands out among them because it's not a client. Linda Thrasher left a message requesting a call back regarding Emme Hughes. I'm unsurprised the aunt has tracked me down.

Now I'll have both sides of the story, so I can form an impartial opinion. Currently I don't have many warm feelings for Daxton, and I would prefer not to let my own biases influence our future interactions.

So I call her back and agree to review some paperwork she has regarding her niece's trust, and some concerns she has about Emme's brother still being the legal guardian. If nothing else, it should help inform the case, one way or the other.

chapter seven

THE MIDDLE WOMAN

Kailyn

It's not even noon and already my day has gone to shit. Half an hour ago I received a call from Emme's school requesting my immediate presence thanks to my new role as conservator.

While I anticipated being involved in any financial decisions on account of the trust, I certainly hadn't considered that I might be called in to deal with a fight. One that Emme apparently started with a boy in the middle of the cafeteria.

I'm currently speaking with the school principal, attempting to explain my relationship to Emme, when an irritated voice comes from behind me. "What're you doing here?"

I turn to find Daxton standing in the middle of the office, gaze homed in on me and the principal, Mr. Proctor. Awesome. This situation has gone from bad to worse. I remind myself that dealing with this is going to get me partner, and when I get back to the office, I'm going to make sure Beverly agrees to the pro bono cases, no more "we'll talk about it" brush-offs. This shit was not in my job description.

"The school is legally obligated to call me," I reply evenly. He should already know this, so his irritation is unwarranted.

"Why didn't you call to tell *me* you'd be here?" he demands, completely ignoring Mr. Proctor. I'm annoyed that his focus is on me, and not the real issue, which is Emme's potential suspension.

"I did. I left a message at your office, and your assistant informed me you were already on your way." I grace Mr. Proctor with a polite smile—his name is so unfortunate, much like his suit. "Can you give us a moment, please?" I grab Daxton by the elbow and guide him toward the front entrance, where there will be less ears and eyes should he decide to raise his voice again.

"We don't need a moment. I need to see Emme. Where is she? I want to know what happened."

"Your aunt is with Emme. We can go and get her now," Mr. Proctor says.

"What? Why the hell is Linda with Emme?"

Jesus. He's coming completely unglued.

Mr. Proctor adjusts his glasses and glances from me to Dax and back again. "She was upset and we felt it better she not be left alone."

"Where are they? I want to see my sister."

I dig my nails into his arm in warning, hoping he can feel the bite through the layers of what feels like a very expensive cashmere and silk suit. "I'd like to speak with you. Privately for a moment before that happens."

"Would you like to use my office?" Mr. Proctor runs his hand over his tie uneasily.

"That would be lovely."

Daxton's eyes flash, but he follows me into the office. As soon as the door closes, he's practically in my face. "What the hell are you doing?"

I put a hand on his chest to prevent him from getting any closer. I'm irritated that I notice how firm his pec is under my palm. "You know, generally when a man is close enough that I feel his breath on my face, he's looking to rip my clothes off, not my head." *Why did I just say that?* I push him back a step and remind myself to remain professional. *And maybe it would be better not to antagonize a frustrated man.* "And since we're not at that place in our relationship, I'm going to need to set a few ground rules. First of all, do not get up in my space and use your size to intimidate me. It's beneath you and absolutely unnecessary. I'm not the enemy here. Secondly, get a handle on your damn self. You have absolutely no reason to be irritated with me, since I've done nothing wrong, so why don't you tell me why your first instinct is to bite my damn head off?"

"I wasn't trying to..." He blinks a few times, smoothing a hand down the front of his suit. It's such a nervous man-tell. He straightens, maybe realizing his behavior is a problem. "I thought you were dealing with the trust. Emme's school issues are my problem, not yours."

He tries to get around me, but I cross my arms over my chest and block his way to the door. "You think I'm happy about this? That I want to be here, apparently acting as your scapegoat because you can't handle yourself or a thirteen-year-old?" Okay, maybe the last part was pushing it a step too far.

He takes a step closer, getting all up in my face. Again.

"You *do not* want to manhandle me. I'm wearing stilettos, and they can cause some damage to parts you may be fond of."

"I need to see my sister and you're preventing that. Aren't you supposed to be protecting her? Instead you're in here lecturing me."

I exhale a long, slow breath and resist the urge to find out if my heel will break through the leather on his shiny black shoe. "Linda is familiar to Emme and she works here. It's in her best interest to be with your sister in a crisis situation. You may not like it, but it's the reality. Acting like a complete asshole isn't going to help your case. Use your head, Daxton. If you walk in confrontational, you're making Linda's case for her. Is that what you want to do?"

He takes a deep breath. "Of course not."

"Do you want to upset Emme more than she already is? Make her feel worse?"

"What kind of asinine question is that?"

At my unimpressed stare he sighs.

"Of course not. I just want to find out what happened and fix it."

"Then act like a lawyer, not a brother. You can be that later, when you're not here dealing with this situation. You must go in with a good argument to get Emme out of whatever shit she's stepped in, instead of throwing insults at the one person who's here to help you. Which is me, by the way."

He runs a frustrated hand through his hair. It stands up on end instead of falling back into place like it usually does. "Fine. Okay. Sorry. Just...fuck. I'm calm."

"Really? You're calm?" I'm still blocking the door.

"Yes. Totally calm," he says through gritted teeth.

"Are you sure you don't need to do a few sun salutations before we go out there again? Some breathing exercises?"

"Neither are necessary." His face isn't quite as red as it was before, but I don't know him well enough to be able to tell one way or another if he's going to go off again.

I'm feeling petty, so I root around in my purse and produce a pack of mints. "Here." I slap them into his palm. "I don't know what you ate for breakfast, or for dinner, but your breath smells like stale coffee and garbage. Are you ready to calmly discuss what happened with Emme?"

He puts his hand in front of his mouth, probably checking to see if I'm right. His breath doesn't smell horrible, yes a bit like coffee, but not like garbage. Still it makes me feel mildly better. Before we leave the office, I reach up and fix his hair, smoothing it out. It's irritatingly soft. I might happen to do a little extra smoothing just so I can keep touching it, but I frown the entire time, as if it's a chore I'm not enjoying.

Mr. Proctor takes us to Emme. She's in a small, windowless

waiting room, a pile of used tissues in her lap, and her shoulders are curled forward, her long hair hanging in her face.

A woman I presume to be Aunt Linda, whom I spoke with briefly, has barricaded her in the corner of the room by pulling a chair up in front of her. I'm not sure if it's meant to be helpful or intimidating. As soon as Emme sees her brother, she shoots out of the chair and rushes over to him, tissues scattering on the floor.

She throws her arms around him. "I thought you weren't coming. It wasn't my fault. I'm sorry."

Daxton freezes for a moment, possibly taken aback, but he quickly wraps his arms around her. "It's okay. I'm here. We'll figure it all out."

While this is happening, Linda skirts around the used tissue bombs. "I need to speak with you, Daxton."

"Yeah, that's not going to happen without our lawyers present." He turns to Mr. Proctor. "Are we having this conversation here or in your office?"

"My office would be better."

I nab a tissue from the box, sweep all the used ones in the garbage can, pick up Emme's bag from the room, and follow them down the hall, Linda on Daxton's heels, trying to find a way to walk beside Emme. This is going to be a tense meeting.

Once the door to Mr. Proctor's office closes, he motions to the small table. "Why don't we all have a seat?"

Daxton tries to position Emme so she's not seated beside Linda. He pulls out a chair for Emme and she drops into it, head bowed, eyes on her hands. I take the seat next to Daxton, prepared to mediate however necessary. I really wish I'd had a minute with Emme, but there's nothing I can do about it now.

"Thank you so much for coming in, Mr. Hughes and Ms. Flowers. I'm aware this is a special situation and a difficult time—"

"Can we skip the formalities and get to why we're here?" Daxton snaps.

I shift my foot under the table until I find the toe of his shoe with my heel. He presses his fingertips against the top of the table, but doesn't look my way.

Mr. Proctor steeples his fingers. "Emme had an altercation in the cafeteria in which she physically assaulted another student."

"I was there. I saw Emme punch Billy." Linda's tone is puzzling. She turns to Daxton and continues, "Until today Emme hasn't had so much as a detention."

"She also lost both of her parents not long ago," Daxton replies.

Fantastic. They're going to attack each other, as if Emme's not sitting right here while they talk about her. Someone needs to keep this meeting on track, and apparently it's going to be me. "Since this is atypical behavior for Emme, it would be helpful to know what events precipitated the violence," I break in.

Mr. Proctor's smile is forced and polite as he addresses Emme. "Would you like to explain what happened in the cafeteria?"

"Billy Horton made a cartoon of the car accident."

"Excuse me?" Daxton frowns and looks to Mr. Proctor.

He smooths his hand down his tie. These men and their fucking tells. What a bunch of amateurs. "Well, that's not exactly accurate."

Emme's fists clench in her lap and her angry, despondent glare darts from Proctor to Daxton. "Yes it is. Billy drew a cartoon about two people being blown up in a car accident and he made Jordan Carpenter give it to me. He's been calling me Orphan Annie all week and then he posted that stupid crying meme of you on Snapchat for everyone to see."

"Emme, you need to calm down," Mr. Proctor says, and Daxton tenses visibly. I like seeing his protectiveness; it makes me second-guess his motives for wanting to keep her in his life. I remove my heel from the tip of his shoe and nudge his knee with mine, hoping he understands what the gesture means.

He clasps his hands on the table. "Why is this the first I'm hearing about this Billy Horton kid?"

"Because he's an idiot and he bullies everyone. Usually I just let it roll off me, but he wouldn't leave me alone today, and everything in the house is changing and I just couldn't take it." She dissolves in a fit of tears.

"So a known bully is targeting my sister and *she's* the one sitting here in the office?"

"Billy is being disciplined for his actions, just as Emme is being disciplined for hers."

"He pulls my hair all the time! And he trips me in the hall!" she shouts.

"Emme, don't yell at Mr. Proctor. He's trying to help you," Linda says.

Before Daxton has a chance to cut in with some scathing, thoughtless remark, I offer my opinion. "Emme, would you like a break from the meeting?" I turn to Mr. Proctor. "I think under the circumstances, it might be best for this to continue with just the adults. If we need Emme for any further questions, we can call her back in."

Emme nods, looking relieved.

"You can have a seat in the front office, unless you'd rather go back to the waiting room," Mr. Proctor offers.

Emme grabs her bag and heads for the door. I wait until it closes behind her before I turn back to Proctor. "Is Billy in Emme's class?"

"He is."

"Then we need an action plan to address how to move forward. Emme has gone through a very traumatic event, and being taunted with drawings that make light of what happened to her is absolutely unacceptable."

"We'll have the seating chart revised."

"I'd like that taken care of before she returns to class tomorrow," Daxton interjects.

Mr. Proctor adjusts his tie nervously. Again. "Emme is not permitted to return to school tomorrow."

Daxton's face goes stony. It's an expression I'm unfamiliar with, and it makes my insides a little zingy.

"Excuse me?"

A bead of sweat works its way down Mr. Proctor's temple. He may be older than Daxton by a good fifteen to twenty years, but when it comes to power dynamics, Daxton wins. I hate that I find that a little hot.

"We have a zero-tolerance policy for violence." He clears his throat before he continues. "Emme has a mandatory three-day suspension."

"I wonder what the superintendent would think about this situation. Especially with how much my family has been in the media. It seems with a little more attention and care, this entire thing could have been avoided. Aside from Linda, who else was on duty in the cafeteria? Surely you have more than one adult supervising all of those students."

And there he is. Daxton the lawyer, using whatever means necessary to get what he needs for his sister. I might be warming to him just a little.

"Mr. Hughes, I assure you, the staff did everything they could to keep things under control."

"Apparently not, since Billy got punched in the face and my sister has been bullied by this boy on several occasions, which brings me back to the issue of the suspension." Daxton taps on the arm of his chair, waiting.

"Protocol deems that there must be a punitive course of action." Before I can cut in, he continues, "However, under these circumstances, Emme could work on projects from home for the next two days, not including this afternoon, without a formal suspension, provided she's willing to talk to her guidance counselor on a weekly basis, as well as the school social worker."

Daxton frowns. "She already speaks with her counselor."

Mr. Proctor rearranges the papers on his desk. This is the fidgetiest man I've ever met. "Well, so far it's been fairly one sided."

"Explain that please?"

"Emme hasn't said very much to her counselor, despite repeated efforts to engage her."

Daxton pushes up from his chair. "You know, for a school that prides itself on elite education, you seem to be failing where my sister is concerned."

"I assure you, we're the doing the best we can."

"You need to do better," I say. "Daxton can't help Emme if he doesn't know what's going on, and if your staff fails to communicate, no one can be proactive. Emme will be back on Monday. In the meantime, I suggest you put together a plan to help Emme and her classmates deal with this tragedy in a sensitive, responsible manner." I push out of my chair, done with the conversation.

"Thank you for your time," Daxton mutters as we show ourselves out of the office, leaving Mr. Proctor sputtering and Linda slack-jawed.

Emme is slouched in a chair in the main office, hugging her knapsack, another girl sitting beside her, the two of them whispering together.

"All right, Emme, let's go," Daxton says, back to being angry.

"Am I still suspended?"

"We'll talk about it in the car. Do you need anything from your locker?"

She roots around in her bag. "My journal."

"Do you need me to come with you to get it?" he asks.

Emme looks horror stricken, maybe at the idea of having a chaperone to her locker. "Uh, no, I can go. I'll be right back."

"You can meet me out front by the car."

She and her friend bolt down the hall, whispering furiously to each other. Her friend throws a glance over her shoulder before they push through the door. She may not recognize Daxton from his TV show, but I'm sure she's noticed he's attractive. As have all the secretaries, who seem to be unable to stop their drool. Emme stops about halfway down the hall, still within view.

"Dax, you must see that I only want what's best for Emme." We both turn to find Linda standing behind us.

"And you think blindsiding me and dragging her through a custody battle right after we've lost our parents is best for her?"

"It doesn't have to be a battle. You can make this easy for all of us."

"Emme wants to stay with me."

"Of course she does. The rules will be lax. Look what's already happened. I know this is difficult, and my intention isn't to cause more stress but to alleviate it, for both of you."

Daxton cuts her off with a wave of his hand. "I don't know what your game is, but I'm not buying this..." He makes a random hand gesture while he searches for the words. "'I'm helping you' act. How does suing me for custody of my sister, who's grieving and in pain, make things better or easier for anyone? If you want to communicate with me, you should do it through your lawyer."

He heads for the front doors and I follow. He's clearly struggling to remain calm as he steps out in the warm afternoon. He runs his hands through his hair, muttering a few choice curse words, and spins around to face the door, nearly slamming into me.

"Shit." He grabs me by the shoulders to prevent me from stumbling back. "Sorry. I didn't realize I wasn't alone."

"It's fine." I glance at his hand, which is still on my shoulder. It's warm and wide, and I would really appreciate it if my body would stop responding to physical contact from Daxton like I actually like him. Although the way he stood up for his sister is one check mark against all the Xs.

He drops his hand and exhales heavily. He looks suddenly exhausted.

"I think it would be a good idea to meet and discuss how we're going to deal with future issues as they arise," I say.

"This won't happen again."

I cross my arms over my chest. It seems to be my go-to move when talking to this man. It prevents me from angry flailing, a habit I seem to be unable to curtail when I'm near him. "Let's be real about this. There are always bullies who prey on people they believe are weak. Normally Emme might not fit into that category, but she's struggling emotionally. Acting out is not uncommon, nor should it be unexpected considering the circumstances."

I take a deep breath before I go on, softening my voice. "I realize I may not be your first choice as conservator, but I'm not going anywhere until the custody issue is resolved. I also think we should meet to discuss how you're planning to move forward. If this goes to trial, I'm going to be involved, whether you like it or not, so it would be good to have some background information so I'm not blindsided like you were."

He exhales a long breath and kneads the back of his neck. "You're right. I get it. When's good for you? Should we meet at that diner again?"

"We can meet at my office. That way we can avoid distractions." I'm referring to his Beach Barbie friend from last time, obviously. "I have time tomorrow between eleven thirty and twelve thirty."

"I'll make it work."

Emme comes out with her knapsack slung over her shoulder. Her eyes are red and still a little teary. Shuffling her feet nervously, she looks between her brother and me. "I'm sorry you had to come to the school today, Kailyn. I didn't mean to get into trouble."

I give her what I hope is a reassuring smile. "I know things are tough right now, and sometimes the emotions are just too much to handle."

She nods and sniffs. "Anyway, I just wanted to thank you, 'cause I know I shouldn't be your problem."

I want to absorb some of her sadness, so I step forward and wrap my arms around her. For a moment I worry I've done the wrong thing, at least until she returns the embrace, squeezing hard as her body shakes with silent sobs. Her grief is so big it chokes out sound.

"I know it hurts." I don't give her false promises. I don't tell her it'll get better, easier, even though in a lot of ways it will. But she will be forever changed by this, and diminishing her anguish isn't going to help.

She clings and cries while I rub slow circles on her back. I glance up to find Daxton watching the exchange, his own sorrow etching lines in his young face. Our gazes meet and I see all of his worries: that he can't do this, that he's not enough, that he's going to fail her. It melts a little more of the ice around my heart.

Eventually she steps back and gives me a small smile. "Thanks for not telling me it's going to be okay."

I return the smile. "That's what people say when they don't know what else to say."

"Or they want you to stop being sad." She adjusts her knapsack and chews on the inside of her lip.

"We should probably go. I'm sure Kailyn has meetings this afternoon." Dax's hands are shoved in his pockets and he looks contrite.

"Oh yeah, right. Are you taking me home?"

"We'll talk about it in the car." He tosses the keys to her and she manages to catch them. "Why don't you pick the music since I know you hate all my presets."

"Okay. Thanks again, Kailyn."

"It's no problem."

She glances over her shoulder as she crosses the lot. The lights flash on a black Audi. Of course Daxton drives a sleek sports car.

Dax rolls back on his heels. "Thank you."

I adjust my purse strap and shrug. "I'm legally obligated to be here, so there's really nothing to thank me for."

"You're not legally obligated to be nice to Emme."

"I'm not going to be hard on a grieving teenager. That's your job, not mine. I won't be an asshole to her just because you were an asshole to me."

"I'm sorry about losing my co—"

I cut him off. "I'm not asking for an apology, nor do I want one."

"But can't I—"

I glance at my watch. "I need to get back to the office. I'll see you tomorrow to discuss moving forward with the custody case and where I need to be involved." I have phone calls and some case notes to review on the new pro bono case Holly sent my way. We're trying to make it possible for this family to formally adopt a seven-year-old who's been bounced around for the past two years.

"Will I be allowed to apologize then?"

He falls into step beside me as I head for the parking lot. I can feel him looking at me. Maybe trying to figure me out. Half of me wants to hug him and tell him it'll get better eventually, and the other half wants an apology, but not for taking out his frustration on me.

"I'll let you know if I feel like hearing it tomorrow."

I stop at my very practical Volvo and unlock the door. Daxton is still standing there, with his hands in his pockets.

"Is there anything else?" I meet his perplexed gaze. I'm sure he's used to people giving in to him all the time, accepting apologies just because he smiles and looks pretty.

He withdraws his hand from his pocket and holds up a small tin. "Here are your mints back."

I wave him off as I open the door and tuck myself into the driver's seat, careful not to let my skirt ride up. When I look up his eyes are on my legs. My hose have a lacy-looking pattern on them. They're sexy, but still professional. "Keep them. Who knows when I'll push your pissed-off button and you'll need them again." I close the door before he can reply, and then put on my seat belt, check the rearview mirror, and back out of the spot.

He's still standing where I left him, mints in one hand, the other tucked into his pocket, a small smile tugging the corners of his mouth.

chapter eight

AUNT FLOW WOES

Daxton

Despite the shitty circumstances, I remember exactly why I was semi-obsessed with Kailyn during college. We used to banter all the time during class discussions, volley comments back and forth with the teacher as the mediator. I very rarely won the arguments, but the challenge and the hard-ons were totally worth it.

She was always a tell-it-like-it-is, no-bullshit girl, and that hasn't changed at all. I've only ever seen her drop that cool, unaffected front once, maybe twice, since I've met her.

I don't know what I did to make her dislike me so much, other than earning the top spot in the class, but she seems to have a pretty serious hate-on for me. That rivalry used to amp me up back then, and apparently it still does.

As soon as she pulls out of the lot, I make a necessary adjustment in my pants and head to my car. I can hear Emme singing from twenty feet away, the bass of whatever song she has on making the windows rattle.

I startle her when I open the door, and she hastily turns down the volume.

"I'm really sorry," she says quietly as I pull out of the lot and head toward my office.

"I know. How long has this Billy kid been bullying you?"

She fidgets with the sleeve of her hoodie. "Like, since sixth grade. It's not new, it's just worse now, or it feels that way. I could've handled the cartoon, but then he had that stupid meme of you—you know, the one where you're crying. I told him to leave me alone and he wouldn't so I punched him. He deserved it, Dax. He was being an ass—jerk!"

If it had been me in her place, if I were closer to her age and some kid did that to her, would I have just let it slide? Probably not. "Violence is never the answer."

She hangs her head. "I know."

"But I'm glad you stood up for yourself and didn't let that punk push you around."

Her head snaps up, eyes wide. "Really?"

"Next time use your words. What he did was wrong, but so was punching him, even if he deserved it."

"I know." After a few beats of silence she asks, "So you're not mad at me?"

"I'm not mad. I can't even say I'm disappointed. I know why you did what you did, but it's not a good way to handle conflict. You need to start talking to me instead of reacting.

Or talking to your guidance counselor, or the school social worker."

"But she'll tell Aunt Linda what I say."

"Why would you think that?"

"Because Aunt Linda's always hanging out after I've been in to see Miss Garrett. I don't want to say anything that's going to get back to Aunt Linda because then she might be able to take me away from you."

I worry that she's acting out when normally she's such a good kid. "You have to talk to me, though, Emme. None of us can help you if you keep it all inside. I'll call your counselor tomorrow, but you have to meet with her, and actually speak. That's part of the deal. It's how I got you out of an official suspension."

"I can go to school tomorrow?" She seems mildly shocked, and maybe just the tiniest bit disappointed.

"No, you have the rest of the week off, but it's not a formal suspension. I'm not leaving you at home alone, though, so you'll be coming to work with me."

"I can stay home by myself."

"And watch TV all day? Not a chance. You punch a kid in the face, there are consequences. Your punishment is boredom. No TV until Sunday night."

"What?" Her pitch is nearly dog-whistle high.

"You heard me. No TV, actually, no electronics period. That includes your phone."

Her eyes are anime wide. "Are you insane?"

Probably. "Consequences, Emme, there are always consequences."

"But you said he deserved it!"

"Doesn't mean that's what you should've done."

"Why are you punishing me for it when I'm already being punished by the school?"

I side-eye her. "Let's be real. Two days off from school is not a punishment. It's a holiday. Do you know what would happen if I punched someone in the face?"

"You'd break their nose," she mutters.

"Possibly, and also my fist, but I'd be charged. I'd have a criminal record. Do you know how hard it is to get a job with a criminal record? Especially one for violent behavior?"

"Okay, okay. I get it! Don't hit people! I just want him to leave me alone, and sometimes I get so mad." Her hands are balled into fists in her lap as we pull into the underground parking lot.

Her voice is quieter when she says, "I miss Mom and Dad. I miss the way Mom smells. I miss her hugs. I miss everything, and stupid Billy Horton thinks it's some big joke that they're gone, but it's not. I just want them back. I keep thinking one day they're going to walk through the door and that it was someone else's family in that accident, not mine."

She dissolves into tears. I have to unbuckle my seat belt and awkwardly side hug her, internally punching my own face for taking it one step too far.

I wish I had someone to bounce this stuff off of. I think

about the way Kailyn hugged her and offered her support today and worry that I'm not going to be enough.

⌁

Word to the wise, instituting an electronics ban on a thirteen-year-old is the worst torture in the world, and not just for her, but for me, too. Because the whining is incessant. I imagine this must be what hell is like.

It hasn't even been a full twenty-four hours yet, but it feels like an eternity. I end up having to suspend the ban the following day because Emme has homework that requires her laptop. I also have to allow her to use her phone because I'm dropping her off at the library while I meet with Kailyn. I would take her with me, but I don't want to create more anxiety for her.

The library is only a block from Kailyn's office, but I don't feel right about not having a way to get in touch with Emme. The ban seemed good in theory, but not so much in practice.

"I suspended the data," I tell her as I pull into the library parking lot.

She gapes at me. "You didn't have to do that. I wouldn't have texted my friends. They're all in class anyway, and I don't want anyone to get in trouble because of me." She stuffs the phone in her pocket, punches the release on her seat belt, and gets out of the car, closing the door harder than necessary.

I arrive at Kailyn's office at 11:25 with coffee in hand. Yesterday wasn't a shining moment for me. I hadn't expected her to be at the school, witnessing what felt like my first failure at parenting.

I have a plan today. And it includes an apology for being a jerk, recently and back in college. Maybe what I perceived as a friendly rivalry, she perceived as something else. My friends were always making comments, so it's possible she took them personally when they weren't meant that way. She proved yesterday that she's trying to help, so I should attempt to be civil even if she's prickly as fuck with me.

Her assistant does that blinking thing women often do when they recognize me. She did it the last time I was here, too. I'm not being an egotistical jerk, it's just a fact. First comes the fast blinks, then the hair and/or clothing adjustments. Then the wide smile and the fidgeting, followed by the high-pitched greeting.

"Mr. Hughes!" And there's the high pitch.

"It's just Dax. How are you this morning, Cara?"

"Great! Fantastic. Let me see if Miss Flowers is ready for you." Instead of picking up the phone, she pushes back her chair. Her skirt today is a little on the short side for office wear, but it's not my office, and she's not my assistant, so maybe it's appropriate here.

She returns a minute later with Kailyn in tow. I do a complete visual sweep, starting at her face and moving slowly— slower than I should, probably—over her. She's wearing another pencil skirt, complete with jacket. It's black today, the jacket buttoned, highlighting the dip in her waist and her hourglass figure. Her legs are encased in black hose with a delicate pattern on them. I don't know why I find them so sexy, but I do.

In law school she used to wear these funny shirts, or funky-colored jeans or shoes. She was always serious in class, but she wore her personality and apparently still does. I keep scanning until I reach her feet. Her heels are fire-engine red. I bet they'd look amazing resting on my shoulders with that skirt pushed up to her waist and that crisp white blouse unbuttoned. I wonder if she's wearing thigh highs and garters. Probably not, I decide.

Shit. I need to get my head out of the gutter. Especially considering this woman barely tolerates me. I bring my gaze back to hers, aware I've just been caught ogling, based on the unimpressed arch of her brow.

I hold out the coffee. "Hi."

"What's this?" She eyes it suspiciously.

"A nonfat, two-pump vanilla latte with extra cinnamon. It's a thank-you for taking time out of your schedule for meeting with me today and for coming to the school yesterday, and for the way you treated Emme."

She shoots a suspicious glare at Cara before giving me one of her cold smiles. "Oh, well, you're a client, so...why don't we go to my office?"

I give Cara a wink—she's the one who gave me the coffee details—and follow Kailyn down the hall to her office, disappointed by the way her jacket hides the curve of her ass.

She moves toward a small table where a pile of highlighted and tabbed documents are spread out neatly. Just like in college, there are a selection of funky pens in a variety of colors beside the documents. Even her organizational skills are a turn-on. I think I really need to get some action. And soon. For a moment I imagine shoving the papers off the desk, laying her out, and just...fucking away the ever-present tension between us.

She motions to the chair in front of me. "Why don't you have a seat and we can go over the details."

Right. We're here to talk about Emme, not get naked. Why is my head so deep in the gutter this morning? "After you." I pull out a chair and wait for her to sit, tucking her into the table before I take the seat next to her. It's overkill, but I'm looking to change her opinion of me, and being chivalrous is a better place to start than what's really going on in my head.

She picks up a document and sets it in front of me. "How's Emme today? Actually, *where* is Emme today?"

"She's down the street at the library working on a school project. I would've brought her here, but I don't want to cause her more stress if I don't need to. Besides, she's mopey and you don't need to be subjected to that."

"Oh? Did something happen?"

"I took away her electronics until Monday."

Kailyn's eyebrows shoot up. "That's like taking a baby's pacifier."

"Yeah. Pretty much."

"I wonder who's more miserable, you or her." She grins a little, like that might make her happy.

"It's probably pretty even, at least for now. I assume it'll be far worse by the end of the weekend."

"Good luck with that." She taps the trust document. "I only have until twelve thirty, so we should get down to it. The trust is safe, and the allocated funds will still be transferred into your account at the beginning of every month to help finance Emme's care."

"An allowance?"

"You can think of it that way if you like, except the money will be transferred into a joint account that I'll have access to until the custody case is resolved, and you'll have to provide me with receipts for all expenses."

"Excuse me?"

She glances up from the document, her expression placid. "I'm legally responsible for tracking the funds and making sure they're actually going toward Emme's care."

"You mean you need to make sure I'm not stealing from my sister," I snap.

"Essentially, yes. And any additional monetary requests have to be approved by me."

"Are you serious with this?"

Kailyn sits back in her chair and crosses her legs. She looks just as annoyed as I do. "My role here is to protect Emme and her finances. I would do exactly the same thing if I was dealing with your aunt or any other guardian. So you can be pissed off about it, but I suggest you reserve your hostility for the person who deserves it, and that isn't me."

As irritated as I am by this whole situation, she has a point. My anger shouldn't be directed at her, again, but I sure as hell can't aim it at the person who's put me in this position. Not to mention it's hot as hell to have Kailyn take me down a peg or two.

"Got it." I tap the arm of my chair. "I need to keep detailed records of receipts and go through you for additional funds. Anything else?"

"Regarding the trust, no." She picks up a pen from the desk and flips it between her fingers, something she used to do in class all the time. "We can't make or implement changes until the custody dispute is settled. So I think the most important thing we can do is discuss my role and how we'll deal with future issues."

I don't like how Kailyn's being dragged into this whole thing with me. The finances I get, but having to involve her in anything else is complicated, especially since the antagonism between us still seems to be an issue. And Emme likes her. "I can deal with future issues. If the school calls you, then you call me and I'll deal with it."

"My role as conservator means I must be directly involved, and I'll need to be present for school meetings, should they occur."

Her tone gets my back up and I lean forward, getting closer. "And you need to remember that I'm her brother and she's my number one priority, not an obligation or a job."

She mirrors my pose, leaning in, except she's much more composed than I am. "How exactly do I know that, Daxton? How do I know that you haven't spent all your savings? Maybe you're on your last dime. Maybe you snorted or gambled all your money away, maybe you spent it all on prostitutes and now you're looking to supplement your income with Emme's trust."

"Do I look like I need to hire a prostitute?"

Her gaze moves over me and she lifts a shoulder. All the while the pen keeps traveling back and forth along her fingers. "I have no idea what your sexual habits are, Daxton. But I can make a guess as to your type based on your friend at the diner the other day."

It takes a second for me to tie together the reference. "Jessie's an attention-seeking star fucker, not a friend. She attended the same charity event as I did and made quite a spectacle."

Surprise crosses Kailyn's face, possibly at my candor or my language, I'm not sure which, and she fumbles her pen.

"Regardless, if there are any pictures floating around the internet with the two of you, be prepared for that to come out. I'm just asking the questions Linda's lawyer will if this goes to trial, so if you have any sordid secrets, you might want to fess up now." She sets something on the table and pushes it toward me with the end of her pen. I glance down at the tin of mints.

It's at that moment I realize I'm only a few inches away from her, eyes locked on hers. She grins and exhales, heavily. I feel her breath on my chin. It's fruity, like she was eating some-thing sweet before I arrived. I wonder what that smart mouth tastes like. I wonder if she kisses like she argues.

"You're having issues with personal space again, Mr. Hughes."

I lean back in my chair and run a hand through my hair. I'm typically so much better at keeping myself in check, but this is personal. Between that and Kailyn, my cool seems to go right out the window. I hadn't exactly forgotten what go-ing head-to-head with Kailyn was like, she was always a force, but this version...I like her even more than I did back then. I wonder if she has any idea how sexy she is. Probably not. Which makes her even hotter. "You always knew how to push my buttons."

"You're going to need to learn how to manage those buttons better." She motions between us. "Think of this as retraining."

I laugh and she smiles, some of the tension easing. "Look, Kailyn, I wanted to apologize yesterday, but you interrupted me."

Her smile becomes tight and she leans back in her chair. "That's because I don't require an apology. Especially not because you want to butter me up. This is me doing my job."

I prop my chin on my fist and wait for her to stop. "Can you just humor me for a minute?"

She crosses her arms over her chest, that hot-pink-patterned pen still clenched in her fist. Her blouse is buttoned almost to the top, so the amount of cleavage is disappointingly minimal.

"Staring at my rack isn't helping win you points, FYI."

Dammit. I just keep digging a bigger hole. I drag my gaze back up to her face. "I know this situation isn't ideal for you, but I'd like to clear the air between us."

Kailyn sweeps her hand out. "I already told you, I won't let the past interfere with Emme's best interests."

I keep pushing, though, because she's obviously flustered. "Back in school, my friends were assholes and I thought we had a friendly rivalry. I didn't stop to think you might take it personally."

She blinks a few times. "That's what you wanted to apologize for?"

"Yeah. Well, that and getting all up in your space yesterday and being a jerk. I didn't expect you to be at the school and I was worried about Emme."

"Right. Of course." Her gaze shifts away. "Well, we're both adults now, and I promise not to throw myself at you like a fangirl again."

I can't get a gauge on her, so I go with a joke. "I don't think I'd mind now."

She huffs a laugh. "Someone needs an ego check." She sets her pen on the desk, arranging it neatly beside the others. "I'm over it, Dax. Just let it go, so I can, too."

I feel like I'm missing something. Like the progress my

apology should've made has somehow done the opposite, and I have no idea why.

❧

In the week that follows, things seems to settle a little. Emme has been toeing the line post-suspension, meeting with her counselor—but only after I assure her their conversations are confidential.

Linda has been unnervingly quiet since the suspension. So much so that it incites paranoia. I don't trust her as far as I can throw her since she sprang the custody lawsuit on me with no warning. I have a feeling she's up to something.

If there's any dirt on Linda, I need to find it so I have ammunition to fight back with, which means digging, and I don't have a lot of time for that. By the time I get home from work and Emme's in bed, I'm exhausted. I know I have to tackle my parents' office at some point, but with everything that's going on, it's low on the list of priorities.

It's a Friday evening—I'm missing drinks with the guys tonight. I told Felix in a few weeks Emme might be up for a sleepover at a friend's and I'll be able to join. Sometimes I miss having a life and freedom, and then I feel guilty because my kid sister has to live the rest of her life without parents. If anyone's getting the shit end of the deal, it's Emme.

She's been in a mood all day, complaining about a stomachache. She cried at dinner over nothing and snapped at me when I asked her to help clear the dishes. I finally let her escape to her room to finish up on my own.

I'm almost done washing dishes when a scream comes from upstairs.

"Em?" The pan clatters in the sink, breaking a glass I hadn't gotten to yet. I take the stairs two at a time. "Are you okay?" I check her room, but it's empty. Her laptop is open on her bed, and homework is strewn across the comforter, along with a tattered notebook with doodles all over the cover.

Her bathroom door is closed. I knock. "Em?"

"Go away!" She's crying, a brief silence punctuated by hiccupping sobs.

"You're freaking me out. Can you open the door so I can talk to you?"

"I can't!" she shouts.

"Are you locked in there? Can you tell me what's going on? Did something happen?" I'm bombarded with a million different fears. Did she hurt herself? Is it that Billy kid, bullying her again? Is he attacking her on social media? Do I need to get my baseball bat out?

Emme throws the door open, and it slams into the wall. Her eyes are red and puffy. "I got my period!"

I take a step back, as if she's carrying an airborne disease, not dealing with the shitty part of being a girl. Which—for future reference to all the men of the world out there dealing with teenage girls and periods—is the wrong thing to do. "Okaaaay. Do you need Advil or something?"

She throws her hands in the air. "I don't know! It's the first time I've ever gotten it! I was just sitting there and my stomach was hurting and then I went to the bathroom and...and..." She motions to the toilet and her face crumples again.

I try to hug her but she pushes me away. "What do you need me to do?"

"How am I supposed to know? I don't have anything to use to..." She flails and then drops her hands dramatically. "...stop it!"

I'm a little slow on the uptake. It's her first period. It takes me several seconds to understand that she doesn't have pads or tampons. Fuck my life. "Let me check my bathroom."

I don't remember seeing any feminine hygiene products when I was cleaning it out, but it doesn't hurt to look. I leave a still-crying Emme—which really sucks—and search all the bathrooms in the house before it becomes apparent I've got nothing. I return to Emme's room, where she's locked herself in the bathroom again.

I knock. "Em?"

She opens the door a crack, her one red eye peeking out at me. She sniffles. "Did you find something?"

"Um, no, but I'm going to run to the drugstore. I'll be back in, like, twenty minutes, 'kay?" I want to ask what exactly I should pick up, but I don't think she knows any better than I do.

The closest pharmacy is a ten-minute walk, but since this is kind of an emergency situation, I drive. Also, carrying a bag of tampons is a little weird. It takes less than two minutes to get to the pharmacy and a minute to find the right aisle. Thankfully it's empty.

I'm not embarrassed about buying tampons or pads, or both, but hanging out in the feminine product aisle like an idiot isn't my idea of Friday-night fun. I scan the aisle. There are so many options. I don't even know where to start. Heavy flow, light flow, medium flow. Panic sets in. I don't have the resources for this.

I can't call Linda because then she'll have yet another reason to tell me I'm unfit to parent Emme.

Which leaves Kailyn.

Kailyn who doesn't like me very much. Kailyn who probably barely tolerates me for reasons I'm still unsure of.

This is way beyond her legal duties. But she's the only person I trust right now to help me with this. I don't even know that she'll answer my call. It's Friday night. She could be out on a date. For some reason I don't like this idea, maybe because she's sort of attached to Emme, which means she's also attached to me—which is not rational at all, but there it is.

Friday nights are meant for dates and boyfriend time. And now I have to wonder just how much of a nuisance Emme and I are to her life. I pull up her contact and hit the Call button. I guess I'm about to find out.

chapter nine

DINNER DATE INTERRUPTIONS

Kailyn

Holly eyes my plate. I nod to my fries. "Go ahead. I can sense your salad remorse."

She nabs one from my plate and dips it in the chipotle mayo. "I have pictures of Hope. She's trying to walk."

She's referring to the pro bono adoption case I took on months ago, around the same time Daxton dropped back into my life. Who knew how deeply involved I'd become in either situation. "Everyone's doing well? Is the birth mother still clean?"

"So far, yes."

"That's good, I hope it stays that way." The Lipsons agreed to an open adoption, and the birth mother has supervised visitations, provided she isn't using. So far it's helped her stay clean.

Holly reaches for another fry. "It's a good arrangement for everyone involved. We couldn't have done it without you."

"Well, I love doing it. It's a lot more rewarding than trusts, if I'm honest. Speaking of, I'd like to set up another meeting with the Wilsons to go through the adoption paperwork for Eli. I figured you might want to be there for that."

Holly nods. "Definitely. Thank you for doing this."

"Of course. Let's figure out a date." We both pull out our phones and check our calendars. These pro bono cases are quickly becoming the favorite part of my job. Knowing I'm giving these kids a chance to grow up in a loving, stable home reminds me of my own adoption. I'd spent the first three years of my life in a state of perpetual uncertainty until my adoptive parents came in and rescued me. After we set up a tentative meeting, we move on to lighter topics.

"Any hot dates lately?" It's mostly a joke; Holly and I spend the majority of our Friday nights together.

"I wish. I don't have time to shave regularly these days, let alone time for hot dates." She sighs. "I hate this whole online generation crap. Why can't I just meet a nice guy in a coffee shop, or the library or something?"

"I think you'd have to frequent coffee shops and libraries for that to happen, wouldn't you?" I ask.

"I guess it would help if I started drinking coffee. What about bookstores? That would work, wouldn't it? I could just sit around and wait for some cute guy with glasses to comment on the book I'm pretending to read, and we could strike up a meaningful philosophical conversation."

"In an ideal world." I understand exactly where she's coming from. As I approach thirty I recognize that what I want in a partner isn't going to be found at a loud bar on cheap draft night. And truthfully, I haven't put much effort into dating since I graduated from law school and my dad passed away. Love can be too painful, especially when you lose it.

"I'd ask if you've had any hot dates, but I think I already know the answer since all you do is work." Holly gives me a wry grin. "Speaking of, how's your teenage crush doing these days?"

I smile a little, thinking about how he reacted in my office the other day. He was certainly riled. "Moody and antagonistic about covers it."

"So he's still wearing his asshole pants?" Holly knows all about our history.

"He apologized for being a jerk, so that's progress."

"Did he apologize for what he did in law school?" Holly does her arched brow thing.

I give my head a slow shake. "Maybe he doesn't remember? Who knows?"

"You think he's conveniently forgotten that he handed in your paper late?" Holly asks.

I stir my drink. "You know how people's memories are, they can alter and shift to suit their own purpose. Besides, it's irrelevant now. I got the job I wanted straight out of law school, so it really shouldn't matter anymore."

"Does that mean you'll be fine working with him?"

"I'll hardly see him. Our departments are on opposite ends of the floor."

"But you *will* see him if he's working for the same firm. Don't think I don't remember for a second how worked up you used to get after you had a class with him."

"He was my competition."

"If that's what you want to call it. Who's going to mediate when you two go head-to-head at your Monday meetings?"

"We're adults. We don't need to be mediated." I'm not sure that's entirely true, because I happen to enjoy those heated moments when I piss him off and he gets all up in my personal space without even realizing it. He has pretty eyes and a gorgeous mouth. And face. And body.

"I predict one of two things will happen." She stuffs another fry in her mouth, chewing slowly to draw out the suspense. "You either murder each other or screw each other's brains out."

"Those are two very extreme options. Both of which will not happen."

"You were in love with him for years."

"Correction. I had a *crush* on the character he portrayed. A fictional character. That is not even remotely the same as being in love with someone."

"I just think you need to seriously consider whether you really want him working at your firm. Is it worth it?"

I'm about to reply, but my phone rings—the only person who calls me outside of work is sitting across from me, which I realize is a little depressing. Work is my vice and my hobby, and possibly my boyfriend.

It's probably a telemarketer or something. I check the caller ID and frown. Daxton is calling me on a Friday night? I hope nothing has happened to Emme.

"I need to take this." Holly nods as I answer the call. "Hello?"

"Kailyn? Hey. Hi. Is this you?"

"It is, yes. Is everything okay?"

I don't quite catch his reply, something about being dizzy or busy. Probably the latter since I can't see him calling me about being dizzy.

The restaurant is loud so it's hard to hear. "I'm sorry?"

"It sounds like you're out somewhere. Are you on a date?" The last part has bite.

I sit up a little straighter. "Did you call to ask about my social life?"

"No, I—I didn't... I'm sorry. I shouldn't have called. I just... so—"

I lean back in my chair, too curious as to why exactly he *has* called to let him flounder for long. "I'm just wrapping up dinner with a friend." It's fairly vague; a friend could be male or female, romantic or not. He can draw whatever conclusion he wants. I glance at Holly, who gives me a questioning look.

"Oh, it's nice that you can do that. Go out with friends."

"Is there something I can help you with?"

He clears his throat. "Um, I'm real sorry for calling out of the blue, but I have a bit of an emergency."

I'm back to being on alert. "What kind of emergency?"

"You get your period, right?"

"Excuse me?" This just got weird. Holly gives me the *what the hell is happening?* hand gesture. I hold up a finger. Not my middle one.

"Sorry, sorry. Fuck. That came out wrong. Emme just got hers, for the first time, and there was nothing in the house and I'm at the pharmacy but there's, like, an entire aisle dedicated to this stuff. I don't even know where to start. I need help and I didn't know who else to go to, so I called you, and that was probably stupid."

His panic is entertaining, so I feel justified in giving him a bit of a hard time. "So just to be clear, you're calling me on Friday night for feminine hygiene product advice?"

"You're laughing at me."

"Yes, I'm laughing at you."

"Well, can you laugh at me *and* help me? Emme's locked herself in her bathroom and she's crying, and I don't have the skill set or the reproductive organs to know how to deal with this."

That sobers me. "She's crying?"

"I guess it's pretty traumatic? I mean, I don't know. But yeah, she's crying and I don't know where to start, so some brand guidance or something would be helpful."

I consider what it would be like to be a thirteen-year-old girl getting her period for the first time after just having lost her mother, and only having a brother to go to for help. No one wins in this situation. I can't leave him to deal with this on his own.

"Which pharmacy did you go to?"

"The one at Ventura and Laurel Canyon. Do you know the layout?"

It's pretty close. "Hold on a second." I press the receiver to my chest. "Are you okay with ending dinner a little early?"

"So you can buy feminine hygiene products? Who is that?" Holly narrows her eyes. "Oh my God. Is that *him*?"

"I'll make it up to you with brunch on Sunday." I bring the phone back to my ear. "Can you hold on for ten minutes?"

"Uh, I guess."

"I'm in the neighborhood. I can meet you there if you'd like."

"Seriously?"

"Unless you want me to walk you through it over the phone."

"No, no. I can wait. I'll wait. I might not wait in this aisle in particular because I feel a little weird about standing here looking at pads and stuff, but I'll be in the CVS. Thank you so much, Kailyn. I really owe you."

"I'll be there shortly." I end the call and meet Holly's not quite approving gaze. "What?"

She crosses her arms over her chest and arches a brow. "I don't know. You tell me."

"Daxton's thirteen-year-old sister has her period for the first time and he needs some help. It's a good opportunity."

"Opportunity for what, exactly?"

"To earn his trust."

"Is this about making partner? Come on, Kailyn, I know you better than that."

"Do you remember the first time you got your period? Imagine how hard this is for both of them. And it'll help me figure out whose best interests he really has in mind. I mean, he's calling me because she got her period and not just sending her to the store on her own. That says something, doesn't it?"

Holly sighs. "Just be careful you don't get yourself in too deep with this one."

"Her world just fell apart."

"I know, but don't make it your job to put it back together."

"I won't. I promise." I don't like how much that feels like a lie.

chapter ten

TAMPONOLOGY 101

Kailyn

True to his word, Daxton is in the store, basket in hand, hovering between the cold and flu medication aisle and the sanitary napkins.

As soon as he spots me, he rushes over and hugs me, catching me off guard. Again. He and Emme sure do like to hug. I wonder if he's going to do this every time he sees me. As I pat him awkwardly on the back, I consider how that might not be a terrible thing. He's just so tall, and broad and muscular, but not in an overly bulky way. He's lean and toned, rather than hulking scary. And he smells good. Too good. I take a step back.

"Thank you so much for coming. I really, really owe you, Kailyn. I'm beyond grateful."

I glance at the contents of his basket. He has chips and chocolate bars in there, a decent start on the unhealthy snack food frontier. I grab for the box that most certainly does not belong and hold it up. "What's this for?"

He blinks at me, eyes wide and slightly afraid. "They looked sturdy, and like they'd catch everything."

"Sure, if you're buying incontinence products for your grandmother." I slap them against his chest and grab his elbow. "Follow me."

He doesn't have a choice but to come along, since I'm pretty much digging my nails into his arm. It's a nice arm. Very firm. I need to stop noticing these things. We make a pit stop at the I-can-no-longer-do-jumping-jacks-without-peeing-my-pants section and return the box before I lead Daxton to the aisle with the right products.

I sweep a hand out. "Welcome to the Aisle of Red."

He glances at me, frowning. "That's awful."

"You have absolutely no idea." I tap my lip and survey the selection. "She'll need a box of these for the last couple of days." I toss in some light days. "And she'll need these for heavier flow." Dax cringes, possibly at my terminology. I roll my eyes and stop in front of the midflow ones.

"What the hell are these?" Dax taps a box of triangular-shaped black pads.

"Those are light days for thongs."

His confusion is almost adorable. "Thongs?"

"Will Emme need those?"

"What?"

"Does Emme wear thongs?"

His expression shifts to horror. "She's thirteen."

I raise a brow. "That doesn't mean anything these days."

"She better not be wearing thongs." His sudden protective rage turns to inquisition as he looks me over. "Do you wear thongs?"

"I own a lot of pencil skirts, Dax. Have you ever seen any lines?" Oh God. I should *not* be entertaining this kind of banter. It's dangerous and it blurs lines that already seemed blurred from day one when he hugged me in the conference room, and my little digs and comments since then.

A smile tugs at the right side of his mouth, and his eyes move over me. I'm wearing purple jeans tonight. Skinny jeans that hug all of my many curves. "I can't say that I have."

"You just admitted to checking out my ass, by the way."

"It's a pretty rockin' ass. You can hardly blame me."

I blush at the compliment and turn back to the products displayed before me. "What about tampons?"

"What about them?"

"Do you think she'll want some?"

Daxton shrugs. "I don't know. Maybe?"

"We'll get them, just to be safe, and we'll get the applicator and non-applicator varieties, just in case."

"Non-applicator?"

"Yeah. One has an applicator, the other you just use your finger."

He makes a gagging sound, and his horrified expression returns. This is far more fun than it should be for a Friday night at the CVS in the Aisle of Red.

He looks around, leans in, and drops his voice to a whisper. "But wouldn't you get...stuff on your finger?"

"Stuff?"

"You know, period stuff."

I grin at how uncomfortable he looks. "Yes, Dax, that would happen. However, most bathrooms come equipped with this magical product called toilet paper, and they have sinks and soap and water so you can wash your hands."

"But why would you want to stick your finger..." He shakes his head, obviously confused.

"I don't think it's about *wanting* to. They're just more compact. Discreet." This is far too much sharing.

"Maybe we can forgo those ones for now."

"Sure. We can come back to those another time." Once we're stocked up on all of the sanitary products, we stop in the painkiller aisle, where I explain what each bottle is for as I throw them into the basket. Then we double back to the candy aisle and toss in some more junk food because periods suck, and cravings are everything.

I stand in line at the checkout with Dax and help him unload the basket. By the time they finish ringing through all his purchases, it's well over a hundred dollars. "It's expensive to be a girl," he mutters, handing over his Amex card. It's one of those black ones, the kind with a high limit.

Once we're in the parking lot, he stops in front of his Audi. He looks a little lost with his armload of menstrual defense. "Thanks a lot for your help. I'm sorry I pulled you away from dinner."

"It's fine. I don't mind." I motion to the store. "That was actually rather entertaining. It pretty much made my week."

He chuckles. "Well, I'm glad it was amusing for you, if nothing else. I should probably get back and give all this stuff to Emme so she can figure out what she wants to use." He holds up the bags: one full of pads and tampons, the other full of junk food.

Before I think too much about it, I blurt, "Do you want me to come back with you and explain it all?"

His eyes go wide with hope, which he tempers quickly. "I couldn't ask you to do that. You've already been more than gracious with your time."

"You're not asking, I'm offering. It might be easier coming from a woman than coming from her clueless brother." I don't mean to sound like a jerk, but that's how it comes out.

He nods. "I really am clueless."

"I'll follow you back to your place."

His house is literally one left at a stoplight and a right-hand turn down a side street from the CVS. It's a sprawling, massive home on a huge lot. I'm really not all that far away from him, although I live in a much more affordable area.

I park behind his Audi, noting the lovely manicured lawns and the very pretty flower beds. Ones I'm certain Daxton doesn't have the time or inclination to manage. "Was this your parents' house?" I ask as we make our way up the front steps.

He nods. "I figured it was best for Emme to keep her in the same school and not change too much on her."

"That was selfless of you. Moving must've been difficult."

He shrugs. "I just want to make things as easy for her as possible, and my condo was too small for the two of us. This made more sense."

"Still, cleaning it out is such a daunting task. I had to do that when my father passed." Holly was there to help, but it was emotional. Packing away his things, sorting through pictures, and of course there were all of my mother's belongings that he'd refused to get rid of when she'd passed years before him. It was almost like losing them both all over again.

"The thing about unexpected death is that sometimes you find things you probably weren't supposed to." He opens the door and ushers me inside.

"Such as?" I glance around the living room, which smells faintly of fresh paint. It's a clean, organized space.

I imagine his childhood was spent living out of a suitcase or on a set. Clutter doesn't seem to be his thing; it's not mine, either. I find hints of his parents lingering in the pictures hung on the walls, and the small out-of-place trinkets on the bookshelves.

"Uh, let's just say my parents had an interesting sex life as evidenced by the contents of my mother's dresser." He gives me a wry smile.

"Oh." I can feel my cheeks heat under his gaze.

"Emme?" he calls out, then turns to me with an apologetic smile. "I'm going to assume she's still hiding out in her bedroom."

"Do you want me to stay here or come with you?"

"Um, you can come with?" Dax drops the bag of treats off in the kitchen, and I follow him to the second floor.

I'm only slightly ashamed to admit I check out his butt. I mean, he already confessed to checking out mine, so it's only fair.

To the right is a set of open double doors leading to the master bedroom. The king platform bed is neatly made, and a simple navy comforter lies smooth across the mattress. I turn away, unable to stop myself from imagining Dax in that bed, wondering if he sleeps in boxers, or maybe nothing at all. Why does my head keep going there tonight?

He stops at a door with a KEEP OUT warning sign hanging from a tack pushed into the wood. It's hot pink and glittering with fake gemstones framing the edge.

"Em?" Dax knocks tentatively.

The music coming from the other side of the door lowers, and we hear the creak of a bed and the padding of feet crossing the room. The door opens a crack and one bleary, red-rimmed eye peeks out. "Did you get the stuff?"

This sounds like a bad drug deal.

"I did. I also came with reinforcements."

Her brows dip. "What?"

"I, uh, I called Kailyn."

"You did what? Why?" Her pitch rises to mortification level.

"Because I needed some help and she's a girl with experience in this area."

She throws the door open, and whatever words are about to come out of her mouth die when she sees me. "You brought her *here*?"

"Don't be rude," Dax snaps.

Emme's anger turns to chagrin and she bows her head a little, peeking up at me. "I'm sorry. I'm just—this is so embarrassing."

I want to alleviate some of the tension my presence seems to have caused. "What's embarrassing is your brother walking around a CVS with adult diapers instead of maxi pads."

Emme looks from Dax to me. "Seriously?"

"Oh, totally. Now everyone in that store thinks he pees his pants."

A small smile appears on Emme's uncertain face and she giggles.

"If you want, we can go through your goodie bag and I can tell you what's what," I offer.

She bites her lip. "Okay."

I skim the back of Dax's hand, encouraging him to relinquish the bag. "We'll be out in a bit."

He seems torn as I enter his sister's room, and my heart softens even more at his forlorn expression when Emme closes the door on him.

Her room is typical teenage girl. Boy band posters and her favorite TV stars are taped to the wall. Books are stacked haphazardly on her dresser, and a journal lies facedown on her bed. She closes it and slips it under her pillow, dropping down on the mattress with a soft bounce. The comforter is wrinkled and the room is lived in.

She pats the mattress, inviting me to join her. I dump out the contents of the bag and her eyes widen. "Oh my God. There's so much stuff."

"We wanted to cover all the bases. How're you feeling?"

"Like crap. My stomach hurts and I just feel . . . yuck."

"Sounds about right." As unconventional as this entire situation is, I'm glad Dax took me up on my offer to come back and explain this all to Emme. Teen years are already hard enough with all the hormones and the changes, never mind going through it without a mother.

I spend the next ten minutes explaining everything in the bag, what to use when, how to use tampons—I can't even imagine Dax attempting that conversation—before I send her into the bathroom and give her some privacy.

I almost collide with Dax when I step out into the hall. Apparently he's been pacing the entire time. Like she's been undergoing major surgery, not learning the ins and outs of tampon and pad usage. He grabs me by the shoulders to keep me from stumbling into the wall. "Is everything okay?"

"She's fine. I explained how it all works and she's doing her thing. She'll be out in a minute. I told her we had treats."

"Right, okay." He's still holding my shoulders, thumbs sweeping slowly back and forth. There's about six inches between our bodies, and I'm forced to tip my head back so I can meet his concerned, still-uncertain gaze. But there's something else there, something that warms my belly and makes my toes curl a little. *What the hell is going on tonight?*

"It would probably be best if we weren't standing out here waiting for her."

He blinks slowly, then seems to come into himself. "Yes. Right. We should go downstairs?"

"That's a great idea." I pat one of his hands.

He finally drops them and motions for me to go ahead of him, which is too bad, because I kind of like his rear view as much as I do the front.

Emme comes down while Dax is unpacking the bag of candy and savory snacks.

"Everything work out okay?" he asks.

Her cheeks flush, but she nods.

"Oh man! These are, like, all my faves!" She spreads her arms and leans over the counter, scooping up the entire pile into a hug. She releases it back into a heap on the counter and turns to her brother, throwing her arms around him. "Thank you."

He returns the embrace, his smile sad. "You're welcome. I had a lot of help. I'm sorry I'm clueless here."

"It's okay," she mumbles against his chest. "I just miss Mom."

"Me, too," he whispers back.

I turn away, not wanting to intrude on their moment. This is the first time I've truly seen his love for her. In the weeks since his parents' passing, he's fully immersed himself in the role of parent, while still trying to hold on to the easier one encompassed in being her brother.

I should leave, but I also don't want to interrupt. I take a few steps backward, toward the living room, where I left my purse on a side table. I could make a quiet exit.

"Can we watch a movie and eat junk food?" Emme asks.

"Whatever you want, kiddo." She ducks out from under his hand when he ruffles her hair, batting it away.

Emme gives me a shy smile. "Can you stay, Kailyn?"

"Oh, uh, I should probably go home." I thumb over my shoulder, feeling suddenly awkward.

"Do you have to?" Emme bites her fingernail.

"You're welcome to stay unless you have other plans." I meet Dax's inquisitive gaze, his head tipped a little to the side.

I see things there. Things I shouldn't be looking for. Things I shouldn't want or like. My focus should be on finding opportunities to ask about work and his firm, not watching movies with him and his sister. But it's an opportunity to get to know them both better. It could be helpful. And more than that, I think I might like the man I never got a chance to know outside of class in law school, or at least, who he's become.

"Sure. I'd love to stay. I want one of those ice cream things, though."

"There's ice cream?" Emme bounces with excitement and then cringes a little.

I mirror Dax's smile as he mouths *thank you*. But my stomach twists with guilt over my motivations for agreeing to stay, and how they're conflicting with what seems to be happening in my chest.

chapter eleven

FIRSTS

Kailyn

We make it halfway through the movie before Emme passes out on Dax's shoulder, snoring softly.

"I'm going to take her up to bed," he whispers.

"Want some help?"

"Please."

I hold her head still while he slips an arm around her back and one under her knees. He grunts when he picks her up. "This was a lot easier when she was smaller." He inclines his head to the stuffed llama on the couch. "Can you grab that?"

I nab it, then rush up the stairs ahead of him so I can open her door and throw back her comforter. I leave Dax to settle her in bed, and wander down the hall in search of a bathroom.

I peek in the next door down, flick on the light, and freeze. It's an *It's My Life* fangirl's dream in there. A barely audible squeal bursts free, and I clamp a hand over my mouth, embarrassed.

I'm standing in Daxton Hughes's childhood bedroom. And it looks like a shrine to his teen years. A poster of him and the cast of *It's My Life* is tacked to the far wall, Daxton front and center because he was the star of the show and the reason every teen girl was glued to her television from nine to ten p.m. every Tuesday night.

I try and fail to keep from bouncing as I cross the room to get a better look. It occurs to me that the cast of the show would've been a lot like his family. I wonder if he's kept in touch with them all these years, and if they have reunions, like high school.

Daxton was such an adorable teenager. My infatuation with him was so consuming. I had all the posters, the DVDs, and of course the album that accompanied the Christmas movie prior to the final season.

I pick up the old DVD case—teenage Dax smirks at me—then exchange it for the Dax Barbie doll perched on a stand, smoothing my thumb over his silky hair. It's a couple of shades darker than it is in real life.

"You found my mother's trophy room."

I gasp and turn, hugging the doll to my chest. "I was looking for a bathroom."

His smile is exactly the same as it was in college, cocky, knowing, and he points to an open door on the other side of the room. "There's one through there, but it hasn't been cleaned in a while."

I glance around again, taking everything in. "There's so much stuff in here."

"That show was my life for a long time." Dax leans against the doorjamb. "No pun intended."

"Was it hard when it ended? You must have spent a lot of time with them." I gesture to the poster of the entire cast.

"I was with them more than my family while the show was in production. Most of us still keep in touch." He looks a little wistful. I wonder what it's like to be the center of so many teenage girls' worlds for such a long time, just to trade it in for some normalcy.

"Why did you stop acting? Was it because *It's My Life* ended?"

"Partly, I guess." He pushes off the jamb and takes a few steps toward me. "After the show, I wasn't sure what I wanted to do anymore."

"You could've taken a new role, though?" I ask.

"Sure. There were options, but it meant committing to a pilot, and if that went well a season, and who knew what would happen after that. It could flop or it could've been something that went on for another five years, and I wasn't convinced I wanted to be locked into that, so my dad suggested I take a year off. Emme had just been born and my parents wanted to travel, so we did some road tripping and I took the time to figure out what I wanted, which was when I decided to go to college."

"But couldn't you have gone to college and still acted?"

"Sure, but I didn't want to spend my life on a set and do everything by independent study. I wanted to sit in a classroom with other kids my own age and learn about stuff I was interested in."

"You wanted to be normal."

"As normal as I could be, anyway." He tips his chin down, noting the way I'm clutching the Dax doll protectively against my chest. "Whatcha got there?"

"Oh, nothing." I reluctantly put the doll back on the shelf where I found it, instead of tucking it under my shirt like I want to. Unfortunately it keeps falling over, so I'm forced to adjust the arms and legs.

"You can have that if you want. You can have anything you want in here, actually. I'm pretty sure we have boxes of the same stuff in the basement. My mom didn't like to throw out the memorabilia."

"It's okay. I probably already have it anyway." I clamp my mouth shut, aware I've said too much.

Daxton's grin widens. "Oh yeah?"

"Probably in a box in my closet with the rest of my high school stuff." The Daxton doll—different from the one I was just hugging—is still in its box, because it's a collector's item. The DVDs sat on my shelf for the longest time. My mom and I used to watch the holiday movie every year when I was a teenager, and after she passed, I kept up the tradition, at least until the end of law school. Then they were all packed away with the memorabilia as well.

"I could sign whatever you have, if you find it, I mean."

"Really?" I cringe at how excited I sound.

Dax's smiles again. "I think it's interesting that you have a thing for the teenage version of me but you're not all that fond of the real, adult version."

"Well, the adult version has been a bit of a jerk, but I'm starting to warm up a little now. Besides, that show brings back good memories. I used to watch it with my parents and my girlfriends. I associate it with a time in my life when things were simple." I'm so defensive. "I should probably get going. It's late."

I try to slip past him to avoid further embarrassment, but he blocks the door. "Wait. I'm sorry. I'm not making fun. Well, I am, but only because I've missed riling you up like I used to in law school. I'll stop. Just stay awhile longer and have a drink with me? Please."

I should leave. His proximity does something to me. But then I remember that I'm trying to get him to come over to our firm and this is the perfect opportunity to have that kind of conversation. "One drink."

I have to look away when he smiles this time, because it's soft and warm, and almost all the ice around my heart seems to have melted tonight.

Dax grabs us both a beer from the fridge and we head outside. An in-ground pool takes up a good portion of the yard—the water glowing pale blue in the warm dark night. It's private here, the gardens surrounding the pool lush and full of pretty flowers.

Dax settles beside me, legs spread wide, head tipped back as he stares up at the stars. I imagine tonight has been hard for him, with so many reminders of what he's lost and how many challenges lie ahead. I have the urge to run my fingers through his wild hair, smooth it away from his forehead, soothe him with a gentle touch, which is not at all why I'm here.

I pull my knees up and turn to face him, propping an elbow on the backrest. "You okay?"

He sighs. "Yeah. Fine. Thank you for everything tonight. I couldn't have done it without you."

"You would've figured it out." Tonight has changed my perspective. Watching him care for his sister like a parent would, toeing that line between brother and father, isn't easy, and it's clear he's trying.

"Maybe, but I don't think it would've gone nearly as well. I don't know how single parents do it, especially single dads. It's fucking exhausting."

"Has it been hard balancing work and adjusting to all of this?" I motion to the house, not needing to explain more.

"The firm's been really good about everything, but it's a struggle to keep up. Emme has a lot of after-school activities and my mom was retired, so she had the time to take her to all of them. Emme took a little break from all of it, but she's back at it now, so managing it has been tricky. She'll be in high school next year, which is another adjustment, so for now . . ." He shakes his head on a heavy exhale.

"It's a lot," I finish for him.

"Too much sometimes," he admits.

"Have you thought about changing firms? Maybe going

somewhere that can be more flexible about your hours and the cases you take on?"

He tips his bottle back as he contemplates this. "Yeah. I have. But putting together a résumé, having to interview, making another change, the thought is enough to give me a panic attack. I'm just so overwhelmed already."

"What if you didn't have to do any of those things? What if the change was the only stressful part?"

"What do you mean?"

"I don't think it's a secret that Beverly would like you over at Whitman and Flood."

His gaze moves over me slowly. "She's expressed interest before, but that was a long time ago. She offered me a position right after I graduated, actually. We could've ended up at the same firm."

"She offered you a position at Whitman?" Beverly failed to mention this.

Daxton nods. "Yeah, I mean, I had a few offers, but there seemed to be more opportunities over at Freeman, and the money was a little better so I went there instead."

"Right, of course." There was only one opening at Whitman back then. I hadn't received a call back for almost a week post-interview, and I'd nearly accepted a different position outside of the city until Beverly called. Whitman had been my first choice and obviously I hadn't been theirs. It seems like I'm always coming in second where Daxton is concerned.

I force the next words out. "Well, you'd only be more of

an asset to the firm now. It's a thought, right? She's progressive. Understanding." I don't want to push too hard. "It's just something to think about, maybe when you're more settled and things calm down for you."

He rubs his lips with his fingertips, as if he's considering it. "I just want this to get easier, and it doesn't feel like it's going to."

I put a hand on his forearm. "The trauma is still fresh, Dax. It's going to take a while for you to get your bearings."

His head drops and he releases another long breath. His next words are barely a whisper. "What if I can't do this? What if Linda's right and I'm not cut out to raise a teenager?"

"Don't sell yourself short. You're doing a great job. Being a parent is never easy, especially when you've been thrown into it without any warning."

He huffs a small, humorless laugh. "I had no idea what to do tonight. All of this is way outside of my wheelhouse. Emme needs women in her life she can rely on who aren't her friends. And I can't go to Linda because she'll use it against me."

"I'm here when Emme needs me." I mean it, even though I worry about the weight it carries, and the deeper implications.

"I shouldn't put that on you." He threads his fingers through mine, curling his over the back of my hand. It's unexpectedly intimate and strange how natural it feels. "But I want to."

I'm already involved, Beverly has made sure of that, and beyond wanting to make partner, it's clear Daxton needs the support, and frankly, so does Emme. I can relate to what they're both going through, and it makes it both easier and more difficult to insert myself into their lives like this. I push aside the worry that I'm crossing lines I shouldn't. "You're not putting anything on me if I'm offering."

"I did tonight." He traces my thumb with his own. "I didn't know who else to turn to."

"I'm glad I was able to help." And I mean it. How sweet he is with his sister, how caring, this is more in line with the person I got bowled over by in the quad that first day at law school. I just don't know which version of him to trust.

"Me, too." His smile softens. "I have a confession to make."

"Oh?" There's a shift in the air. A warm breeze ruffles his hair and sends mine fluttering around my face. I feel ridiculously girlie as I tuck it behind my ear, my skin suddenly hot.

Dax waits until I meet his eyes before he continues. "I had a thing for you in school."

"I'm sorry, what?"

"That day I met you in the quad—"

"As if that wasn't humiliating enough when it happened. I'd prefer to leave that memory buried in the past, thanks." I try to pull my hand free from his again, but he tightens his hold.

"I thought it was pretty great."

I roll my eyes. "Yeah, because I drooled all over you like an idiot."

"If you think about it, it was the perfect meet cute, and if I hadn't had my head up my ass at the time, I would've done something about it."

"The perfect what? Did you just refer to me as cute meat?"

Dax laughs, "No, meet cute, m-e-e-t. It's when the hero and the heroine meet in a movie, or sometimes a book."

"Oh, that's significantly better than being called meat, but it was still embarrassing, and then I fell on you again less than twenty minutes later. I figured you thought I was stalking you, and then your friend made that comment." I duck my head, reliving that humiliation all over again. All my *visualizing success* didn't seem to do much for me back then.

"My friends were assholes."

"I think that's pretty typical for college guys. They're all swagger and balls and zero tact."

"That about covers it." He looks down, playing with my fingers, tracing the curve of my nails with the pad of his thumb. "That first day was the only time I ever saw you like that."

"Like what?"

"Unsure of yourself. It was like I got this peek into who you were that no one else did. But in the classroom you were spectacular." His smile is impish. "I loved debates because I knew you'd have an opinion and it would be grounded in fact and conviction. Watching you in class was…enthralling. You pushed me to work harder. You set the bar and we all had to follow. I just wanted to beat you."

"Well, you got your wish in the end, didn't you?" I don't want to rehash this with him, not when I finally feel like I've been able to let it go.

"If it's any consolation, I was rooting for you." His expression is strangely genuine.

I pull my hand free and shift away, confused. "Oh, come on, Dax." I can't tell if this is all an act, or what. "If you were rooting for me, why did you hand in my paper late?"

"What?"

"Just before finals I ran into you on campus and asked if you'd handed in your term paper yet. It wasn't due until the next day, but I knew you had a habit of handing things in early. I asked if you could hand mine in for me because I had to miss class the next day." I remember how frantic I'd been and how perplexed Daxton looked at the time, much like he is now, likely because most of our conversations took place in the form of classroom debates.

"I handed them both in that afternoon, though."

I remember the day I got the paper back with the late marks taken off. The paper was worth 50 percent of the final mark, so the deductions were a huge blow to my pristine record. I was so confused at first, until I noticed when it had been handed in. "It went in a day late. It was stamped, Dax. There's no point in lying."

"But I—" Daxton's eyes fall closed and his jaw tics. "Fucking Felix."

"Who?"

Daxton rubs the space between his eyes. "My friend Felix McQueen. He was in our class."

I recall the name, but not the face that went with it. "That doesn't really explain anything."

He sighs and looks at the sky. "Not to you, but it does for

me. I remember that day, because I was shocked that you'd ask me for a favor like that, knowing how much your grades meant to you. I was actually hoping to run into you because I'd finally grown some balls and I was going to ask you if you wanted to exchange numbers or go for coffee or something. But you seemed so upset, I figured I'd wait, and then I didn't see you again until I walked into your office with my parents." He huffs a little laugh and grows serious again. "Anyway, after class, Felix said he was handing in his paper, and I had study group at the library. I wanted to get the papers in before the office closed for the day, you know, because of the stamp." He shakes his head a little. "So I gave them to Felix, yours and mine."

"Except mine didn't make it," I supply. I remember the sinking feeling when I got it back, how devastated I was, not just because of the late mark deductions, but because I'd felt betrayed by someone I thought was my friend.

I don't know whether to trust what he's telling me or not. He's an actor by nature. He could be making this up to keep me in his corner. All of this could just be for show. Just as my being here is steeped in ulterior motives, although I'm struggling to keep that in perspective.

"Well, this explains the way you reacted to me when I first saw you again after all these years." He rubs his fingers back and forth across his bottom lip, pensive. "I didn't know, Kailyn. I mean, I guess it all makes sense. After that you just disappeared. I expected I'd see you on campus again, but I never did. Not even at graduation."

"My dad had a heart attack. That's why I couldn't turn in my paper. All I could focus on was getting to the hospital, especially since we'd lost my mom during my undergrad. I was terrified I was going to lose him, too." At Daxton's horror-stricken expression, I continue. "He recovered, but it weakened his heart. He wasn't doing well around graduation so I skipped it. A year later another heart attack took his life."

"I'm so sorry, Kailyn. There aren't even words. If I'd known, I would've said or done something. I would've gone to the professor and explained." Dax reaches out as if he's going to touch me, but I stiffen and he stills. "If I could undo it I would. I'm so sorry I took what you worked so hard for away from you."

"Well, you didn't, Felix did." My GPA had been less than a point below Daxton's at the end of the year, and when I did the calculations, without the late marks, I would've just beaten him. But this puts it all into perspective and once again changes my view of him. Holding a grudge over something like this seems trivial and pointless.

"I will gladly junk punch him for you."

I laugh a little. "I don't need you to do that for me."

"I might actually need to do it for me." He tilts his head. "If I could go back, I would've handed that paper in myself."

"I thought we were kind of friends back then, you know? Like we were competing with each other but still on the same team, if that makes sense." We're both clearly driven and career focused. Or at least Dax was until recently.

"And now?" He stretches his unoccupied arm across the back of the couch and twists a lock of my hair around his finger.

"And now what?" I don't know what's happening here. Or maybe I do, but it doesn't fit with the plan I have. And suddenly the attraction I've been fighting since he dropped back into my life isn't something I feel compelled to deny anymore.

"Are we friends?" Dax leans in closer, dragging his tongue across his bottom lip. I track the movement, wondering what I have a million times as an infatuated girl. Season three, episode two was his first on-screen kiss. I'm sure I watched that episode a thousand times as a teenager. Which is just...mortifying.

It's different now, though. I'm attracted to the man I've gotten to know, the one who clearly loves his sister and will do anything for her. The one who gets riled up and riles me. The same man who knocked me over in the quad all those years ago and who told me I had pretty eyes.

I hitch a casual shoulder, the nonchalant gesture a contradiction to what's happening in my head. I still manage to come up with a saucy reply. "I guess. I mean, I did help you navigate sanitary napkins today, so I suppose that could qualify as friendship."

He keeps leaning in, and I find myself mirroring that movement, as if a magnetic force is pulling us together. "Sometimes when you got to class first, I'd sit behind you on purpose."

"To irritate me?"

"No, because I liked the smell of your body wash, or your

shampoo, whatever it was—it was uniquely you. And whenever I was close to you, you seemed to give the best answers, as if you had something to prove. It made me sharper. We would've made an awesome team."

Mere inches separate us, his fingers laced with mine, my heart beating a staccato, frantic rhythm, while anticipation makes my skin tingle and my mind hum with possibilities.

"When you didn't like what someone had to say on a particular subject, you'd either flip your pen between your fingers or bite the end and leave behind tiny teeth marks. It used to drive me insane. You still do that, by the way." Dax caresses my cheek with gentle fingers. "Tell me we're on the same page, Kailyn."

"I think you need to be a little more specific." I'm not putting myself out there first.

He sweeps his thumb across my bottom lip and edges closer. "You're good at reading body language and situations. What do you think I want right now, Kailyn?"

"To kiss me."

His grin is almost wry as he untwines our fingers and both of his palms smooth up the sides of my neck, thumbs following a slow path along the line of my jaw. My stomach dips and clenches.

How long has it been since I've been kissed? How long since I've been this excited by the prospect?

"And you, what do you want, Kailyn?"

"To be kissed."

His lips brush over mine and I latch on to his wrists, an anchor in a storm I want to be swept up in. The firm press of his mouth against mine fills me with longing. Daxton's low groan follows, and then his tongue sweeps my mouth, soft and searching.

I'm falling and floating. Spinning out of control as he angles my head, deepening the kiss. Desire blossoms and takes hold. I want it. Him. And I'm worried this is only happening because we've slipped into the past, to a time where the biggest complication in life was getting the best mark.

But I don't stop it, even if I should.

I give in to the ache of yearning. The explosion of senses; his smell, his taste, the warmth that grows hotter, igniting embers to flame.

One of his hands drops, taking mine with it. I clutch his thigh as his fingers curl around my hip, urging me closer.

The buzz and ding of a phone pierces the hazy cloud of lust, and I pull back, breaking the connection for a moment, but Daxton is right there, crowding my space, his fingers in my hair, twisting in the strands, tugging gently as his lips meet mine again. He nibbles this time, sucks my bottom lip and groans, tongue sweeping out, again and again and again.

But the *ping, ping, ping* of incoming messages is a bucket of cold water on my sensibility.

I put a palm on his chest, and push. "Is that yours?"

"It's not important. Just ignore it." He lifts my hand and kisses my knuckle, following with a light bite.

I feel it through my entire body, the bolt of lust, the rush of heat between my thighs. Even still, I recognize I've complicated so many things with one act of impulsiveness. One kiss that shouldn't have happened, but did.

And I know I won't be able to forget it. Not with the way my lips still tingle and my body still hums with his touch.

I look to the patio table, where beads of sweat trickle down the sides of our half-consumed beers. His phone lights up with an incoming message and rumbles closer to the bottles. A woman's name flashes on the screen.

My throat tightens. Of course he has women calling him on Friday night. I'm sure they're more than willing to come to him even if he can't go to them. I'm probably convenient because I'm here and still obviously infatuated and willing.

"I should go." I stand, adjusting my glasses, embarrassed once again.

Dax rises with me. "What? Why?"

"It's late. You have other things to do." I gesture to the phone, still buzzing on the table. I try to get around him, but he steps in front of me, blocking my escape. "Dax, please." I don't want to look at him right now. I can't face what I've done. How getting caught up in that kiss compromises this situation in so many ways.

"Kailyn."

"I need to go home."

"I'm sorry, I thought you wanted—" I'm still trying to get around him. "I didn't mean to upset you."

"It's fine. I'm fine, I should just…you're under a lot of stress. It's understandable you'd seek comfort in someone safe."

"That's not what this is about."

I slip around him and head for the door. "I'm glad I could be here to help Emme tonight, and I'm glad I'm a safe person for you, Dax, but this, what just happened, shouldn't have."

He doesn't follow me to the door, but I catch his reflection in the window as I slip my feet into my shoes. One hand is shoved in his pocket while the fingers of his other hand sweep back and forth across his lips, his expression forlorn.

He's seeking refuge in the past, caught up in a possibility that never existed because his present is so tragic right now. It doesn't make this any less of a mistake.

It also doesn't make it any easier for me to get in my car and leave.

chapter twelve

POST-KISS FAVORS

Kailyn

Since Dax has my cell number, he resorts to texting over the weekend. He makes sure I arrived home safely on Friday night after I bolted from his house, apologizes again for upsetting me, thanks me for helping with Emme, and issues yet another apology.

I'm polite and to the point with my replies, and of course I ask how Emme is doing, but I try to maintain a semi-professional boundary. Which is difficult to do when I know what it feels like to have his tongue in my mouth.

On Monday I find a box on my desk. Inside is a note from Dax and a set of multicolored pens, exactly like the ones I always used to set out on my desk in class. Every once in a while, when Daxton was sitting behind me in class, he'd lean forward and whisper that his pen wouldn't work, and he'd ask to borrow one of mine. I always lent him an obnoxious color, like hot pink or lime green. It's a sweet memory and an even sweeter gesture.

The following morning I receive a phone call from Linda. "Hello, Kailyn Flowers speaking."

"Kailyn, hello! I'm so glad I was able to get in touch with you." Her voice has that high, reedy quality that automatically puts me on alert.

"Is everything okay? Is Emme all right?"

"Um, well, that's what I'm calling about."

I'm already reaching for my purse, ready to tell Cara to cancel my meetings for the afternoon. "Do I need to come to the school? Should I call Dax?"

"Oh! Oh no, it's nothing so urgent. It's just, well...I've noticed that Emme's been wearing the same clothes repeatedly and I'm a little concerned about the state of them."

"I'm sorry, I'm not sure I follow."

"It might be nothing, but she's been wearing this very worn-out hoodie almost every day. You know how girls can be at this age, usually they're concerned with fashion, and I understand that Emme's in a difficult place emotionally, but I'm worried."

"About what exactly?"

"She's wearing clothes with holes in them every day, surely Daxton can take her shopping and get her some new things with the allowance he's been provided, things are already difficult enough for her socially at the moment."

I lean back in my chair, trying to figure out her angle, and whether she has information that's valuable in this instance. "Do you mean beyond the incident in the cafeteria?"

"She doesn't have a female role model anymore, and to be honest, I'm concerned that the money that's supposed to be for Emme's care isn't being used appropriately. Surely there must be enough funds to afford a few new hoodies. If I was her guardian, I would certainly be taking her out to get her new things."

"I'll be sure to look into it." I have yet to see receipts, but Dax just bought a hundred dollars worth of feminine hygiene products and treats for Emme, so I'm not too worried about how the funds are being spent. I try to be objective, though, because I'm aware my connection to Dax and Emme skews my perception. I suspect this is a fishing expedition on Linda's part.

"Of course, of course. I just thought it was something you might want to know, especially since she's not coming with a packed lunch like she used to, and I'm afraid she doesn't have adequate funds for lunch. I'm always more than willing to help her out. I'd suggest to Daxton that he leaves money at the office, but we both know how unhappy he is with me at the moment."

"I'll be sure to discuss it with Daxton. Is there anything else?"

"No, no. That's it. I just wanted to bring it to your attention."

"Thank you, Linda. I appreciate your concern. Have a wonderful day."

"You, too, Kailyn."

I end the call and rub my temples. I can't decide if her avoiding Dax is a strategic move or logical. Going through me makes a lot of sense since I'm the conservator, but based on the way she's approached this custody lawsuit, I'm not convinced she's completely aboveboard. And I'm also highly aware my relationship with Dax makes me more susceptible to bias.

The call from Linda weighs heavy on my mind for the rest of the day, distracting me and making it difficult to focus.

It's after five when my cell pings with a message. And then another. Emme's name appears on the screen. She uses typical teen texts with shortened words forms and lots of emojis. The gist seems to be that she's stuck at school and she can't get a hold of Dax. I haven't heard from him all day, either, but he's supposed to be in court, which should be finished for the day by now.

I don't mess around with texting.

Her phone rings once before she answers. "Hello?"

I put on my soft, carefree voice, even though I'm worried. "Hey, Emme, what's going on?"

"J-just a sec." She pulls in an unsteady breath, which makes it sound as if she's crying. There's some muffled noise in the background before she speaks again, and it's a whisper. "D-Dax was supposed to pick me up twenty m-minutes ago after m-music club but he's not here y-yet and all the other parents have already picked everyone up. I s-said I could t-take the bus, but my a-aunt said I need p-p-parental permi-s-sion first and D-Dax isn't answering his ph-phone."

"Don't worry. We'll get it figured out. Have you tried his office?"

"Y-yes. A-and his cell. N-no one is a-answering at his office and h-his ph-phone keeps g-going to voicemail." She hiccups three times in succession.

"Okay. It's okay, sweetie. I can come get you."

"Wh-what if h-he was o-on his way? Wh-what if s-something ha-ha-happened? Wh-what if he was in an ac-ac-accident, too?"

My heart squeezes. "Oh, honey, take a few deep breaths for me. I'm sure he's fine. I bet he got stuck in a meeting and just can't get out. Sometimes that happens with lawyers. He's in court today, right? I'll come get you." He mentioned this week was busy with a hearing when he called me yesterday to ask a question that I was sure he already had the answer to. The conversation was stilted and awkward.

"My a-aunt w-wants to take me to her place. But I don't want to go with her."

"You can tell her your ride is on the way. I'll be there as soon as I can." The school is less than fifteen minutes from my office, thank God.

"O-okay."

"Deep breaths, Emme. Dax is fine. I'll be there soon." I'm already in the process of shutting down my computer as I end the call.

Beverly is standing in my doorway, eyebrows raised. "I was hoping you had a minute to chat, but it looks like you're in a bit of a rush. Everything okay?"

"There's a situation with Emme. I'm going to pick her up from school."

"What kind of situation?"

"Dax must be stuck in court and she can't get a hold of him. She's panicking because she's worried something happened, and the aunt wants to take her home with her."

"Oh, this is perfect."

I pause as I shove my laptop in my messenger bag. "I'm sorry?" I don't see at all how this is perfect in any way. It's a clusterfuck, is what it is.

Beverly waves her hand around. "Not for that little girl or Daxton, obviously, but for us. He's stuck in court because his firm isn't giving him the flexible hours he needs and it's putting him in a precarious situation by making him look incompetent. This problem would be solved if his employer was more understanding of his circumstances."

"I'm working on it," I grit as I brush past her, heading for the elevators.

She falls into step beside me. "I have no doubt you'll make it happen, especially when you make strategic moves such as this. Very smart, Kailyn."

I give her a tight grin as I hammer the elevator button with my thumb, thankful when it's followed immediately by the ping. "That's me, Miss Strategy."

"I look forward to an update in the morning," she says as I step inside the steel box.

"Of course." I push the button for the parking garage and the doors slide closed, cutting off my view of Beverly's approving smile. I sag against the wall and blow out a breath. At no point did I consider making partner when I offered to pick up Emme. I just wanted to erase the panic in her voice and make sure this aunt of hers, who seems to be good at stirring up shit, isn't causing Emme more stress.

I pull up Dax's contact. He hasn't messaged since yesterday, which should be a good thing, but with Emme in a state of panic, it's the opposite. When I call his phone, it goes directly to voicemail. "I need you to call me as soon as you get this message, please. It's urgent." I hang up as the door opens to the parking garage and rush to my car. Anxiety makes my hands shake as I pull up the GPS navigation and buckle myself in.

It seems like I hit every single red light on the way to the school. By the time I get there it's almost six, and the lot is nearly vacant. I pull up to the front doors and park in a bus zone. I still haven't heard from Dax, which concerns me. The last thing I want is to tell Emme everything is okay when it's not, but good God, if Dax isn't okay, I think I might have a mental breakdown.

As soon as I get out of my car, Emme pops up from her spot on the front steps and jogs toward me. "Did you get a hold of Dax?"

Reflexively, I open my arms and she steps right in for the offered hug. "Not yet, sweetie, but I'm sure he's fine."

The door opens again and Linda appears, lips pursed and her hands on her hips. "Emme! You can't just leave the building without telling me where you're going." She comes to an abrupt halt when she notices Emme wrapped around me. Her reaction is in opposition to the maternal front she presented in the principal's office the last time I saw her.

I pat Emme's back and whisper, "You okay?"

She shakes her head against my shoulder.

"Emme, who is this?" Linda's heels click as she descends the steps. "Oh, Kailyn. I didn't realize Emme had called you."

I smile coolly, unimpressed with the way she's dealing with her niece, or this situation. "She called when she couldn't get in touch with Daxton. He's in court. I apologize for not getting here sooner. Daxton had made arrangements for me to pick up Emme, but I had it in my planner as a six o'clock pickup instead of five." The lie is only slightly sour.

"I'm more than happy to take Emme home with me and we can wait for Dax to call."

"But I want to go to my house," Emme says.

"We shouldn't inconvenience Kailyn any more than she already has been," Linda says tightly.

"It's not an inconvenience at all. Why don't you run in and get your bag?" I suggest to Emme. "And you can try Dax again."

Emme seems torn, but at my encouraging nod she drags her feet back up the stairs. As soon as Emme's inside the school, Linda crosses her arms over her chest. "You have to be able to see that I'm right about Daxton's inability to care for Emme. If Daxton wasn't family, child services would've been notified by now."

I lift a brow. "For having a late meeting? I hardly think that constitutes as abuse."

"It's neglectful. He has a history of being irresponsible. He shouldn't be caring for Emme. Did you see how she's dressed? She looks homeless." She takes a few steps closer and rummages around in her purse. "I have copies of the original will. Emails between myself and my sister about me being an ideal guardian. I have documented proof that Dax is unfit to parent Emme."

She pulls out a file folder. It's worn and bent, as if she's been collecting things for a while. "I have copies of everything in here. Take this. You'll see I'm right." She thrusts it at me. "Just take it."

If there's anything incriminating in here, it would be good to have. I stuff the folder in my bag, far too curious about the contents of this so-called incriminating evidence she seems to believe she has. I find it odd that she called me today and then this happens. It seems too convenient to be coincidental.

Before Linda can say anything else, my phone rings. I rush to dig it out of my purse, relieved when I see Daxton's name flash across the screen. "Hi."

"You said it was urgent. Is everything okay? I have calls from Emme. I was supposed to be at the school almost an hour ago. I'm just on my way out of the office now."

A rush of emotion hits me, and I have to clear my throat before I can respond so it doesn't carry to my voice. "I'm at the school. I'm bringing her home now."

"I'm so sorry you had to do that. I really owe you." His voice hitches, his emotions clearly just as out of control.

"It's really no problem at all. I'll have her home shortly."

"I'll explain what happened when you get here. I'm about ten minutes away, so I'll probably beat you there." I end the call and return my attention to Linda just as Emme bursts through the doors.

"Dax texted!"

I smile warmly as she approaches. "I told you he was stuck in court. He'll meet us at home. Come on, let's go."

"I'll be in touch," Linda whispers, eyeing my purse.

Emme links her arm through mine and pulls me toward my car. "Bye, Aunt Linda," she calls over her shoulder. She tosses her backpack on the floor and plops down in the passenger seat, buckling up without my encouragement.

I note the frayed sleeves of her hoodie and the holes in her jeans, fairly typical for a teenager. I'm pretty sure it's the same hoodie she was wearing the time we went to the diner, and I have to wonder if it's a favorite, something she's taken to wearing as if it's become the teenage equivalent of a security blanket. When my mother passed I had a blanket she'd made for me that I would often curl up with, just so I could feel close to her. And there was a necklace she loved that I would wear so I could keep her next to my heart. I wore it for years, and still do on occasion.

She bites her already ragged nails as we pull away from the school. I give her shoulder a little squeeze. "You all right?"

She nods, but her voice is small when she says, "I was so scared."

"I know you were, sweetie, but everything is fine now." That's not entirely true, I don't think, but telling her that isn't going to help the situation.

It surprisingly takes only ten minutes to get to Daxton's. He's sitting on the front steps, suit jacket unbuttoned, tie hanging loose, hair a riotous mess.

He stands up as I pull into the driveway beside his Audi. I don't even have the car in park before Emme throws open the door. Her backpack lands on the driveway, door still wide open as she rushes Dax and launches herself at him. A fresh wave of tears makes her body shake.

He wraps her up in his strong arms and bends to rest his cheek on top of her head, smoothing his hand over her hair. I cut the engine in time to hear him soothe her, "Shh. It's okay, it's okay. I'm right here. Nothing bad happened. We're both fine. You're fine. I'm right here."

I have to take a moment to breathe through my own settling anxiety, my heart aching over her panic, which I felt as my own in that short time between her call and hearing from Dax. It reminds me of my own reaction all those years ago when my father suffered his first heart attack.

His eyes lift as I step out of my car, his expression one of gratitude and so many fleeting emotions, it's impossible to pin them down.

"I th-thought something h-happened to you," Emme sobs into his suit.

I round the front of my car, the clip of my heels a loud

interruption as I pick up her backpack and gently close the passenger side door.

"I'm so sorry I made you worry. I'll try my best not to let that happen again."

I'm glad he doesn't make a promise he can't be sure he can keep like I did today.

It's another half a minute of whispered words before she finally lets him go. "I thought I was going to have to go live with Aunt Linda."

"Oh, kiddo, I'm doing everything in my power to keep you right here, with me, okay?"

She nods, her fingers at her mouth, chewing anxiously at her ruined nails.

"You hungry?"

She sniffs and shrugs. "Can Kailyn stay for dinner?"

Dax gives me a questioning, hopeful smile. "If she'd like."

I should go and let them manage this situation, but Emme's expression is just as hopeful as Dax's, and two sets of puppy dog eyes are impossible to deny. "I can stay."

Emme smiles through her tears. "Do you like sushi? Maybe we can order in?"

"That sounds great."

"Why don't you go in and get the menu so you can pick all the things you like?" Dax says.

"Okay." Emme takes her bag and disappears inside.

As soon as she's out of sight, Dax pulls me into him, head

bowed until I feel his warm breath fanning across my neck. "Thank you." He shudders and his hold tightens.

I smooth a palm up and down his back. "It's okay. She's okay now." I should put some distance between us, but I find I like this too much. It's been a long time since anyone has sought comfort in me. He smells so good, a hint of faded cologne, laundry, and watermelon gum. I feel both protected and needed, something I haven't experienced in ages. It's a dangerous combination.

His lips brush my cheek as he finally pulls away. "Her messages were so frantic. I felt sick."

"She was worried something had happened to you." *So was I.* "What made you so late?"

Dax doesn't have a chance to answer because Emme throws the door open and grabs my hand. "I need you to look at the menu with me so you can pick what you like, too."

Once dinner is finished, Emme excuses herself to her room, apparently recovered from the earlier trauma, giving Dax and me a chance to talk. He told Emme that he got stuck in a meeting and his phone died, but his stiff posture tells me there's more to the story.

He opens the fridge and grabs a couple of bottles of beer. "You want one?"

"I should probably go soon."

"You could just stay for one drink? I can explain what happened this afternoon." He inclines his head toward the backyard.

The last time I sat out there with him he kissed me. The memory haunts me like a ghost, and has evolved into dreams that leave me wet and wanting when I wake. "Uh, the living room might be better. It's starting to cool off tonight."

I have no idea if that's accurate, but I do not want to find myself in that position again, especially since I enjoyed it so much. If I manage to persuade Dax to come to Whitman, I can't indulge in this kind of relationship with him anyway. There's a strict no-fraternization policy in effect, and for good reason. Interoffice romances only cause unnecessary drama and discomfort between colleagues, especially when relationships fail. And at a small firm like Whitman, the awkwardness would be magnified.

A small smile appears as he tips his head to the side. "Okay."

I follow him into the living room. Of course he chooses to sit on the love seat, forcing me into close proximity anyway. I'm still dressed in a pencil skirt and blouse. His gaze roams lower, to my signature patterned hose as I cross my legs. I smooth my skirt down, wishing I were wearing something more comfortable. "So what happened this afternoon, exactly?"

"Court went a little long, and I still had to go back to my office, but even with the stop I only would've been a few minutes late. Except Linda's lawyer ambushed me in the lobby."

"Why?"

"Who the hell knows? I assume Linda sent him to make me late. He had papers I've already seen. Emme stays after school on Tuesdays for music, and Linda knows that. I was in such a rush to get Emme, I left my keys in Felix's car, and I had to wait for him to bring them back. My phone died before I could call Emme to let her know. By that time she must've called you. It was just a shit day."

"I think you need to have a backup plan for nights when you might be late, whether you want Emme to be able to take the bus on her own, or you let me know and I can come get her."

"I don't want to put that on you."

"I have clearance for this kind of thing for a reason, Dax. Let me help when you need it."

He scrubs a palm over his face. "It's all been such a whirlwind, you know? I don't know if I'm coming or going half the time."

I run a soothing hand down his arm. "Have you talked to your boss about your hours? Are they being flexible?"

"They're trying, and I guess so am I. They're so used to me working these long hours, I think they forget sometimes that I have these obligations now that they don't. Most of the guys with families aren't doing this on their own, they have wives and nannies. It's just different."

"There are other options, Dax. Beverly would give you very flexible hours. Emme's school is close to the firm, and the library is right down the street. Some of my colleagues' kids hang out there after school and catch up on homework. It's very family friendly, particularly for someone in your situation." Despite what Beverly wants, it would be so much better for Emme, and likely Dax, to make the switch. They'd have stability. I would be suggesting this even if it wasn't what Beverly wanted.

Daxton sighs. "I'm supposed to make partner at Freeman this year."

"There are a lot of demands with being a partner, though."

He rubs the back of his neck. "I had all these life plans and they've been altered so dramatically."

"They're just on hold. You'd have the same opportunities at Whitman, and you can take your time getting there. You can wait until Emme is done with high school and off to college before you make the push for partner if that's what makes the most sense. You're young, you have time." As much as it might sound like a sales pitch, it's true.

"It's something to think about, especially after today." He stretches his arm across the back of the love seat. "You must be close to making partner at this point."

"My dad and I had bet before he passed that I would make partner by thirty."

"Is that what you want?"

"It's something I've been working toward," I reply. Maybe throwing myself into work isn't the most rational way to deal with loss, but up until now it's how I've managed.

"Is this getting in the way of that?" He motions between us and it takes me a second to understand his meaning.

My stomach knots with guilt that he's become part of what will get me the partnership I've been seeking. "Oh, you mean is being Emme's conservator impacting my cases? No, not at all."

"Okay. That's good. Thank you for what you did. That was way outside of your professional or personal obligation."

"I'm glad I could be there to help."

Dax is silent for a moment, then clears his throat. "About the last time you were here—"

"There's no explanation necessary. We can just let it go." I smile and hope it looks sincere. "It's late. I should really head home."

His face falls a little, but he nods and sets his mostly full beer on the coffee table and walks me to the door. His hands are jammed into his pockets, bottom lip caught between his teeth. He looks so uncertain, despondent even. I feel bad for him for so many reasons, not the least of which are my ulterior motives for helping him. I find myself stepping closer.

Despite the directive from my brain to stop, I wrap my arms around him, my cheek pressing against his chest. My actions seem to have shocked him, because it takes him a moment to return the hug. His shoulders curl in as he embraces me.

"Everything will be okay," I say softly.

"I really want you to be right about that."

His palm smooths up my back until I feel his fingers skim the nape of my neck. I have to remind myself to stay in the lines between potential colleague and friend. But this doesn't feel like friends or colleagues, especially not when he drops his head and his nose sweeps along the side of my neck, or when his lips touch my skin and he whispers my name.

"Dax! Do we have ice cream? Can we make smoothies?" The thud of Emme's feet on the stairs has us pulling away from each other.

Dax clears his throat. "Probably," he shouts, but his voice is gravelly.

He jams his hands into his pockets and coughs as he does some surreptitious rearranging. My ego inflates a little at the possibility that I've affected him in such a way just by hugging him.

Emme comes to an abrupt halt at the bottom of the stairs. "Oh! Are you going, Kailyn?"

"I am. It was nice to see you again."

She looks a little disappointed, but she smiles brightly. "Maybe you can come for dinner again soon? I could cook next time."

"You cook?" I glance at Dax, wondering if it's something they do together.

"My mom taught me. I'm not as good as she was, but I'm okay."

"I would love that."

"Great!" She hugs me, then rushes off to the kitchen.

"Just so you're aware, I have no idea if she can actually cook," Dax says.

"Maybe you should make something with her before we set a dinner date, then?" I wink and then internally chastise myself for the flirtiness. I need to keep my head on straight when it comes to these two.

chapter thirteen

DINNER DATE FOR THREE

Dax

Two weeks after the school pickup fiasco, I get a call from Emme's guidance counselor, Miss Garrett. Midterm report cards are being sent home this week, and she didn't want me to be surprised. Emme's marks have taken a nosedive since the death of our parents, and her usual straight As are now littered with Cs and a few Bs.

While her counselor assures me it isn't unusual, she's worried about Emme. She reports other staff members have also expressed concern. I immediately assume Linda must be involved. Miss Garrett throws out terms like *depression* and *social withdrawal*. Is she engaged in meaningful activities at home? Does she go out with friends? Does she enjoy her favorite hobbies? The answer is I don't really know.

She's gone over to her friend Marnie's house a couple of times after school, but hasn't asked to have friends over in the weeks since our parents passed. Most of the time she's holed up in her room like a normal teenager. Or maybe it's not so normal? She sings in her room a lot, mostly sad, lamenting songs. I kind of figured it was a lot like me running lines in front of the mirror, but maybe not. I don't have a good gauge on it since my childhood wasn't exactly normal.

When the school requests a parent conference to discuss how to best support Emme for the rest of the term, I agree. And I'm grateful, instead of put out, that Kailyn is going to be there with me this time.

Three days later I'm standing outside of Emme's school, waiting for Kailyn. I keep checking my phone for the time, even though she called less than fifteen minutes ago to say she was on her way. I offered to pick her up, but she said it would be easier if she drove on her own since she had a prior engagement. I've invited her for dinner, but haven't mentioned it to Emme. I don't want to disappoint her should Kailyn change her mind.

Even though it's still fifteen minutes before the meeting is supposed to start, panic sets in. It's not that I think she's going to stand me up; if there's one thing I've learned about Kailyn in the past several weeks, it's that she's unwaveringly reliable. My fear has to do with her making it here in one piece.

I understand now why Emme was so rattled when I was over an hour late to pick her up. Kailyn is two minutes later than I expected and I'm already concocting worst-case scenarios. As I'm about to call—which I realize isn't a good idea if she's driving—she pulls into the lot.

My anxiety over the impending meeting and the relief that she's okay collide. Unable to stay where I am, I meet her in the middle of the parking lot.

She's dressed in one of those sexy pencil skirts and a crisp white blouse. Her jacket is blood red, her black hose has a geometric pattern that keeps tugging my eyes down, and she's wearing her glasses—I assume on purpose. Her long dark hair is pulled up in a tight bun. She looks incredibly professional and gorgeous.

Her expression is apologetic as she approaches. "I'm sorry I'm late. I got stuck by a train and I dropped my phone under my seat so I couldn't call to let you know."

"I'm just glad you're safe." I pull her against me and hug her hard.

She gingerly returns the embrace. "Dax? Are you okay?"

"You're never late. I was worried," I mumble.

She gives me a tight squeeze. "Oh, Dax, I'm sorry. I'm right here and fine and so are you."

I drop my head, breathing her in, taking comfort in the smell of her skin and how warm it is against my cheek. I struggle to let her go. I recognize that my panic isn't logical, and that my attempts at keeping this platonic on my side are failing. But I need her help right now, so I have to get a grip and not do anything to jeopardize that.

I release her on a deep inhale. "Sorry. This, uh…" I tap my chest. "This anxiety is new."

She presses her palm to my cheek. "It's okay. Deep breaths. This is all a lot to handle. It's not just Emme who's suffering here. You don't have to be strong every moment of every day."

I close my eyes and place my hand over hers to keep the contact as I breathe through the panic. I don't know how I would do any of this without her, which is a terrifying realization. One I need to keep to myself. I was an actor long enough that I should be able to fake confidence and coolness.

I drop my hand and attempt a smile. "You ready for this?"

She regards me cautiously, her worry obvious. "Sure am."

I hold the door open and motion her inside. We check in at the office and then we're ushered down the hall to wait. I'm antsy as we sit in the itchy chairs. The germs embedded in this fabric could probably be cultured for a science project. I tap on the armrest, watching the clock.

"Just relax," she murmurs.

"Sorry."

"Nothing to be sorry about. This isn't a court case, Dax. They just want to help Emme."

I nod and blow out a breath. "I think I'd be less nervous about a court case. At least with that I know what's coming, and I have some control. It's that it's Emme and I don't know what to expect that's stressing me out." I feel lost in my own head. Anxious that I'm going to say the wrong thing and give Linda ammunition against me. Worse, I'm worried I'm not capable of handling Emme and her needs or my own, and Kailyn's presence confirms that in a way.

"You've got this. I'm right here with you."

A loud, feminine shriek pierces the quiet. "Oh my God! Daxton Hughes." A woman in her early forties comes to a flailing halt in front of us. "Oh! Oh God! I can't even. My daughter loves your show and so do I. I used to watch in college. It was *such* a guilty pleasure."

She holds out her hand, so I take it. Her palm is cold and clammy, or maybe that's mine.

"I'm so glad you enjoyed the show."

"I more than enjoyed it." She gives me an exaggerated wink and pumps my hand vigorously. When she finally releases it, she presses her hand to her heart. "Oh! Can I get your autograph? For my daughter, of course." That gets me another wink. "And maybe a picture, too? Oh my God. You're such a wonderful actor. Or you were. It's really too bad you stopped. Why did you stop?"

"I decided to pursue another career path."

"Of course, of course. Well, it's still too bad. Your face belongs on a screen."

Kailyn coughs beside me.

"Do you have anything you'd like me to sign?" I ask, fighting not to look at Kailyn.

She flails again and spins around. "I'll be right back!"

I don't know whether to laugh or be mortified.

Kailyn leans in close, voice a low whisper meant only for me. "I'm a much better fangirl."

I turn so I can see her expression, one side of her mouth pulled up in a slight smirk. She's temptingly close. "Hands down the best," I murmur.

That smile of hers widens and her eyes glint with a hint of mischief, but we're interrupted again by the subpar fangirl. Kailyn offers to take the picture once I've signed several school-issued pieces of paper and a photocopy of my own face. I'm sure the school would be pleased to find their budget going to such useful resources.

Finally, Emme's guidance counselor arrives to show us into the conference room. "I'm so sorry about that. I didn't realize they'd brought you down here. I would've put you in the conference room right away." She motions to the open door, and I step inside and freeze. I assumed this meeting would consist of her guidance counselor and possibly a teacher and the principal, but that's not what I'm looking at.

The entire table is full, and at the end is Linda, of course.

"Dax?" Kailyn's palm comes to rest on my back. "Should we have a seat?"

I nod and allow her to prompt me forward. I have the wherewithal to pull out her chair before I take my own. She gives my knee a reassuring squeeze under the table.

I'm reeling as the introductions take place. The school social worker, the entire support team, the head of special education, her principal, counselor, two of her teachers, and the drama instructor are all in attendance. I feel completely ambushed. Kailyn introduces herself, because clearly I'm over-whelmed.

"I'm sorry. I thought this was going to be a private meet-ing." I direct the statement at Linda.

Miss Garrett clears her throat. "We thought Linda could provide some valuable insight since she has such a close rela-tionship with Emme."

"Is that so?"

"Emme talks to me. Maybe she doesn't share the same things with you." Linda's hands are clasped in front of her, her smile serene.

Kailyn moves her arm so it's pressed up against mine, and taps her lip with her pen. There are teeth marks in the cap. "In the interest of helping Emme, it would be beneficial to hear from all of the adults who see her regularly. I think we'll have a better sense of the whole picture." She smiles gently at me. "Isn't that right, Dax?"

"Yes. I agree." It's hard not to be defensive or reactive with my aunt sitting across the table from me, looking smug.

I listen to Emme's teachers talk about what an outgoing, vibrant student she was at the beginning of the year, how ex-emplary her marks had been, how wonderful she was to have in the class, but in the weeks since our parents passed, there's been a marked decline. She's withdrawing, she's moody, her temper flares, she's pulling away from her friends. The word *depression* is thrown around, along with *post-traumatic stress dis-order, therapy, grief counseling*.

"I know we all want what's best for her," Linda pipes in, her voice deceptively soft. "She spends a lot of time in the library alone these days. Her English teacher says she's been writing poetry, and when I asked Emme about it, she showed me a few pieces. She seems like a very lost, angry girl. I know you're doing your best, Daxton, but maybe you should consider whether it's enough."

She's baiting me. I know this. But rage flares hot, and I have to bite my tongue to stop from saying something that will make this situation infinitely worse.

Kailyn grips my thigh under the table, possibly as a warning, or maybe she shares my anger. Either way, she's the one who addresses my aunt. "Daxton's ability to care for and provide for Emme is not in question here. Just as Emme lost her parents, so has Dax. I think it's reasonable to expect her marks to drop and for her to withdraw."

A murmur of agreement comes from the social worker.

Kailyn turns her steely gaze on Linda, then slowly looks around the room. "We're not here to put Dax on trial or to debate whether he's fit to parent. He's here because he's looking for support from the people who spend the majority of their day with Emme, five out of seven days a week."

"And we're here to do whatever we can to help Emme adjust," assures her counselor.

"I think what would serve us all best here is to provide a list of resources and services for Daxton and Emme to access. Regular emails and phone calls seem to be the most effective way to communicate concerns and issues as they arise. This term is going to be difficult for Emme. We can't expect her to bounce back from this in a couple of months. If anyone else has something of value to add to this conversation, now would be a good time to do it. The school day is long over, and I'm sure Emme is exhausted and would like to go home."

I can't seem to pull my eyes away from Kailyn, and neither can anyone else. Watching her own the room is captivating. It's exactly what makes her a passionate, articulate, and commanding lawyer. It's also likely the reason she can manage to resolve things before it ever gets to a courtroom. She's incredible, and despite what she'd believed I'd done to her, she never once let it affect how she dealt with Emme or Emme's case.

No one seems to have anything to add, or if they do, they're too intimidated by Kailyn to speak up. Emme's in the waiting room, cheek propped on her chin, writing in a book with her earbuds in.

"Hey, kiddo." When she doesn't respond, I tap her on the shoulder.

I get the briefest glimpse of her writing before she slams it closed with a start. It looks like poetry or stream of consciousness. Is this the stuff she shows Linda? I don't understand why she'd confide in her and not me. Maybe because she's female and family?

"Hey! God, you scared the sh—crap out of me." Her eyes dart past me and she shrieks and pushes her seat back, elbowing me out of the way to get to Kailyn. "I didn't know you were here!"

"I'm guessing I'm a good surprise, then?" Kailyn laughs, but her eyes are on me, questioning and a little unsure.

"The best!" Emme gathers up her things and attaches herself to Kailyn as we head out to the parking lot. "Can you come for dinner tonight? I'm making shepherd's pie. I can still cook, right, Dax?"

I fall into step beside them. "Yeah, of course."

When she realizes we came in separate cars, she asks if she can ride with Kailyn. It gives me some time to digest what happened in the meeting.

I'm mentally exhausted by the time I pull into the driveway, having stopped at the store to pick up a six-pack of beer and a couple of bottles of wine. I don't know what Kailyn's preference is, but I thought it would be good to have options.

Emme and Kailyn are already in the kitchen when I arrive, ingredients spread out over the counter. I lean against the doorjamb. "How's everything going? Can I help?"

"Do you have an apron I can use?" Kailyn smooths her hands over her skirt. She's taken off the jacket and rolled up the sleeves of her blouse, and her heels are gone. It's amazing how someone so tiny can be so intimidating. She's also sexy as hell.

Emme makes a face at Kailyn. "That's not really a great outfit for cooking."

Kailyn laughs. "Not really, no."

"Oh!" Emme's eyes light up. "Wanna borrow something of mine?"

Kailyn looks Emme up and down. "That's really sweet of you, but I don't think we're the same size."

Emme is stuck in that rail-thin stage of puberty, but Kailyn is all lush curves.

"I have loads of leggings. I'm sure I have something." She grabs Kailyn's hand and drags her to the stairs.

Kailyn throws a look over her shoulder as if to say *help me*, but I shrug. I'm sure not opposed to seeing her in a pair of leggings. Typically she's always in business wear, apart from that one time I saw her in jeans. Purple ones at that.

A minute later Emme comes down and puts me to work chopping onions. "Where's Kailyn?"

"Getting changed. She'll be down in a minute."

The patter of feet draws my attention to the stairs. Kailyn points a finger at me. "Keep your opinions to yourself."

I bite my lip and raise my hands in mock surrender. "I didn't say a thing." But I sure as hell want to. She's wearing a pair of galactic cat leggings and one of my old *It's My Life* hoodies they must've snagged from the closet of my old bedroom. She looks a lot like the girl I had a hard-on for all those years ago, and still apparently do considering what's going on in my pants. I have to think about things like dentures and incontinence so I don't embarrass myself.

Kailyn claps enthusiastically while glaring at me. "All right. Let's make shepherd's pie."

Emme's smile is radiant as she and Kailyn work together—ordering me around while they try to teach me how to dice onions, I'm learning slowly here—and I know that, despite today's hellish meeting, we're doing okay. And so much of that has to do with Kailyn. She's effortless with Emme. And when we're not competing with each other, we're a hell of a team.

When the shepherd's pie is ready, Emme pulls it out of the oven, her expression a mixture of excitement and sadness. We set the kitchen island, as it has become our preferred dinner location. The dining room is formal and too big for Emme and me.

Emme serves us, her smile wide as she sets the plates in front of Kailyn and me. It looks and smells amazing, the potato topping crisp, the gravy seeping out to cover the plate. I wait until she's seated before I spear a forkful and take a bite. "This is really great," I say through a full mouth.

"Yeah?"

"Awesome," I mumble.

Kailyn takes her own first bite and moans a contented food sigh. "It's delicious, Emme."

And it is. It almost tastes exactly how I remember. Emme has my mother's talent in the kitchen. My favorite meals were always here, in this house. And I feel like I've just gotten that back.

Emme scoops up a small bite and pops it in her mouth. As she chews her smile fades. She swallows slowly and puts down her fork. "It's not right."

"What do you mean? It's amazing." I shove another forkful into my mouth as if to prove my point.

"It really is, Emme. You did a great job," Kailyn says.

Emme shakes her head, chin trembling with the telltale threat of tears. "It doesn't taste the same. Something's wrong." Emme pushes back her chair aggressively, sending it toppling backward. Tears fill her eyes and spill down her cheeks as she picks up her plate and crosses to the garbage. She stomps on the lever, causing the lid to slam into the wall, and dumps her dinner, plate and all, into it.

"Em." I push back my chair and grab her arm, wanting to fix whatever is upsetting her.

"Just let me go, Dax! I wanna be alone!" She shrugs out of my grasp and runs past me, up the stairs.

At the slam of the door I close my eyes and sigh. "Fuck."

Kailyn runs a soothing hand down my back. "I'm so sorry."

"Everything was going so well. I mean, the meeting was shit, but she seemed so happy for once." I motion to the meal in front of us.

"It's been a hard day for both of you."

"What if Linda is right? What if I'm not the best person to take care of her? What if all I'm going to do is mess her up more?"

"That's not going to happen. You're right here with her, trying to be what she needs. Both of you are figuring out exactly what that is."

I toss my napkin on the table. "I should go up and talk to

her." I don't know what the hell I'm going to say to make this better.

Kailyn slips off her chair as I swivel in mine. Her hands come to rest on my knees, maybe to stop me, comfort me, I don't know. "She asked to be alone. Give her a few minutes before you go up there. I know you want to fix this, but respect her need to process."

I swallow and nod, my eyes on Kailyn's hands with her perfect, manicured nails spread over my knees. It's definitely meant to console, but the contact does something else to me. It's been weeks since I kissed her, and more weeks since I've experienced any kind of physical release apart from on my own. This is different, though. I connect with Kailyn on a level beyond attraction. There's something deeper—or maybe it's all in my head because I'm desperate to have someone to hold on to who understands.

"I don't know what I'm doing." I skim the length of her fingers and circle her wrists as I part my legs, pulling her between them. She doesn't resist. In fact, when I release her wrists, she runs her palms up my chest and over my shoulders.

"It's okay," she soothes.

I tug her closer, until her body is flush with mine. She relaxes against me almost immediately. God, she feels good, warm, soft, feminine. I drop my head, glad her hair is coiled on top of her head so I can breathe her in. She smells like sunshine and solace.

Her fingers slip into the hair at the nape of my neck, kneading gently. "It'll be okay, Dax."

"I want this…" I don't finish that thought because I'm not talking about Emme anymore.

"You want what?" she prompts, nails dragging gently across the back of my scalp.

This isn't fair of me. Kailyn's been such a source of strength and compassion over these last weeks, and I keep seeking her out, pulling her into my downward spiral. But she's here and I don't believe this connection is one-sided, so I turn my head anyway, lips finding the sweet skin in the space between her collarbone and her neck. "You."

She stills for a moment, her gasp soft in my ear. I sweep my lips along the column of her throat, aware that if I do this, if I push like this with her, it could go one of two very different ways.

If I'm reading all the signs wrong—and I very well could be, considering the mess my head is—I could ruin this tentative friendship we've formed. I could take away a slice of stability from Emme. But in this selfish moment, I want to get lost in Kailyn and her quiet beauty. I want her strength and her conviction.

I part my lips and kiss that warm spot just below her ear. "Kailyn."

A tremulous breath leaves her. But she doesn't pull away, and she doesn't stop me when I press my lips to the edge of her jaw. I run my hands along her arms, thumbs sweeping up the side of her neck. Her throat bobs under my touch, and her fingers tighten in my hair.

I don't give her time to reconsider, aware Kailyn is far more logical than me. If I waste these precious moments, I'll lose them. I tip her head, angling my own, and find her mouth.

Her lips are soft, like the rest of her. She may be tough on the outside, but inside she's tender and maybe just a little broken from all of her losses. Like me. I stroke the seam of her lips with my tongue and she parts for me. I sink into her sweet taste and her low moan.

The kiss deepens but doesn't explode like a flash fire. It's a slow burn, a steady flame flickering, growing hotter as she melts into me. I bet she's soft between the sheets. And I desperately want to find out if I'm right, but now probably isn't the best time.

I still allow my hand to drift down and find the dip in her spine, pulling her in tighter against me. She sucks in a breath when she feels me, hard for her. Her tongue meets mine, stroke for bold stroke, and I ease my hand lower until my fingers press into the swell of her ass.

That's the moment that her hands leave my hair and come to rest on my shoulders. Before she can push me away, I release her mouth and cup her face in my palms. I can't meet her gaze yet, afraid I'll be met with rejection I'm not strong enough to accept.

Instead I skim her wet bottom lip with my thumb and come back for an easy, chaste kiss.

"Dax." Her tongue peeks out, then her teeth press into that plush skin.

Slowly, I lift my gaze.

"We can't do this," she whispers, but her eyes say something else, and so does her body.

"I think we are doing this."

"What about Emme?"

I bite my tongue against the things I want to say, like what about me and what I need, but she has a point. "We can keep it between us for now."

She opens her mouth to speak but I stop her again with my lips. And she responds, like I want her to, softening against me, letting me get lost in her. When I pull away this time, I stroke her cheek. "We have something."

"You're looking for comfort," she says softly.

I don't deny it. "I am." A flash of hurt crosses her beautiful face, so I continue. "But that's not all I'm looking for, Kailyn. I like you, I always have."

"Emme needs stability."

"I know. And I won't push you to be that for her or me, just please, think about it before you say no. We can be friends when Emme's around, and when she's not we can see if there's something more." I drag a single finger from her jaw to her collarbone and she shivers. "I think there is and I think you feel it, too."

She looks so uncertain as her fingers drift along the edge of my jaw. "I don't want anyone to get hurt."

"Me, either."

She closes her eyes on a deep inhale. "I need time."

My stomach sinks. "I understand."

When she opens them again, her internal battle is clear. I wish what I was asking of her wasn't weighed down with so much baggage. I wish I was in a position where I could give more than I take. It's not just herself she's worried about, it's Emme, and maybe even me. Which is the exact reason I want her, because she understands, maybe a little too well, the gravity of getting involved with me. And I wouldn't blame her if she said no, but selfishly, I want her to deem me worth the risk.

chapter fourteen

GIRL TIME

Kailyn

I run a finger across the cold smooth stone and bend to place the dahlias in front of my mother's grave and the daisies by my dad's. It's quiet in the cemetery at this hour, the sun dropping lower in the sky and taking some of the heat of the day with it. I sink down between the stones, crossing my legs. It's peaceful here.

I was close with both of my parents, but my dad and I had a special relationship. He was the one I always went to for advice, and in those years after my mother passed, that closeness deepened, and then he was gone, too.

I run my fingers across the petals of the daisies. "I've been taking on pro bono custody cases. I think you'd be proud, Dad. I kept a little girl from being bounced around in the system like I was. She has two amazing parents who love her just like you loved me. And now I'm working with a little boy and his foster family hoping to do the same."

I swallow back the tears, aware I'm stalling and Hope isn't the reason I'm here. If my dad were alive and not just a memory, he'd be waiting patiently for me to get to the damn point with a smile on his face.

"I met someone, but it's complicated. He lost his parents recently, and he has a little sister he has to take care of now. It reminds me a lot of the way we were after Mom passed. Sort of. This is different, though. I think I like him."

I close my eyes, picturing my dad's face, the way his brow would quirk and that small grin he'd wear, as if he knew I was leaving something out before I admitted it.

"No. That's not true. I more than like him. We have something and it scares me. For the first time since I lost you I feel . . . grounded. I mean, you know how much I love hugs." I laugh and roll my eyes. "But with Dax I feel safe. Protected maybe? And I'm needed."

I can hear my dad's *But?* in my head.

"If I bring him over to my firm, I'll make partner before I'm thirty, just like I promised I would, but I'm not sure if I want that anymore, at least not as much as I want to keep this feeling."

I try to get a handle on my emotions as tears slip down my cheeks. "I don't want to disappoint you, but I don't want my job to be the only thing that has meaning for me, and I don't think you'd want me to do that. I'm a little scared of the way I feel about this man. I used to have such a crush on him as a teenager, Dad, and then for the longest time I hated him, or thought I did. But now that I've gotten a chance to really know him, the real him, it's different. He's such an incredible man, although I don't think he realizes it.

"But I worry I'm just a comfort for him and he only wants to be with me because I understand what he's going through. I'm in a lot deeper than I meant to be. I've been so reluctant to let anyone else into my heart because I'm not sure I can handle another big loss. I know how hard it was for you when we lost Mom, and your heart never really recovered from that, did it? Eventually it gave out on us." I consider the truth in that statement. How after my mom passed my dad seemed so lost in life without her, and how awful it was to be unable to find a way to bring his light back. "I think I'm falling for him, for both of them, and the possibility of having that is frightening, but I don't know if I can walk away. I just . . . I want to do the right thing, but I'm not sure what that is anymore. I wish you were still here so you could tell me what to do."

The breeze ruffles the leaves on a nearby tree, and the blossoms float through the air like scented snowflakes, landing in my hair and my lap. Silence and stillness follow.

"I miss you both." I kiss my fingers and touch each stone before I leave, feeling lighter and heavier at the same time.

*

I try to ignore my phone as it buzzes on my desk. If I don't check the messages immediately, I somehow believe I have control over what's happening with Dax.

Holly was right when she said I needed to be careful, that it's not just my heart that could end up broken.

The more I see how difficult his job is, the more convinced I am that coming to Whitman is what's best for him and Emme, regardless of whether I make partner.

The policy on interoffice dating is a problem, though. Even worse, I have no idea how he'd react if he found out about the deal I made with Beverly. My head's a mess, and with everything that's happened, I'm no longer sure what I'm doing. Other than avoiding. Even the moral gray line I'm treading isn't enough of a deterrent, which says a lot about my feelings for him.

The phone buzzes again and I bang on my keyboard, nonsense letters running together. "Hold your ground," I mutter. But it's useless. My fingers are itching to reach out and grab it. I check the clock and force myself to wait two more minutes. When I finally do, I find that the messages aren't from Dax, as I expect, but his sister.

Emme: What ru doin this wknd?
Emme: I have girl prob

I frown as I study the messages, as if looking at them will unveil the issue. My first instinct is to call, but teen girls tend to rely on texting, so I fire off a message instead.

Kailyn: What kind of girl prob?

It takes a few minutes before I get a response.

Emme: I need to go shopping n Dax wont understand.

We message back and forth until I finally get the entire story. There's a dance in a few weeks and she wants new clothes. She's asking me to come shopping with her. Obviously I want to say yes, but I have to talk to Dax first, which means I have to call him.

I haven't had a full conversation with him since we made out in his kitchen two days ago. I've thought about that extended kiss incessantly. I relive it in my head over and over again; the way his hands roamed over my body, the way his lips moved over my skin. I've tried not to think about what it would be like to have sex with him. How attentive he would be, how good it would feel. Obviously, I'm unsuccessful.

All of these thoughts flit through my head as I pull up his contact and hit Call. He picks up halfway through the second ring.

"Hello?"

Everything below and above the waist either clenches or perks up. "Hi. Hey. It's Kailyn."

His voice is soft like silk. "How are you?"

"Fine. Good. How are you?"

"I'm good. I'm glad you called."

I bite my lip so I don't tell him it's nice to hear his voice.

"Kailyn?"

"Still here, sorry." I take a breath, grounding myself. "Emme messaged me."

"Is she okay? Is everything okay?"

"Everything's fine. She's fine. There's a school dance coming up. Did you know about it?"

"Oh. Yeah. She mentioned it a couple of times this week. I told her she could go. I mean, it's good that she wants to do something normal with her friends, right?"

"Yes, definitely, that's very good." Everything between us is a little awkward, probably because of me.

"So Emme texted you to talk about a school dance? Did she want advice on boys or something?" His panic is comical.

"Yes, it was about the dance, no, it wasn't about boy advice. She asked me to take her clothes shopping, and I thought I would run it by you before I said yes."

"Oh. You don't have to do that. I can take her."

"Have you ever taken a thirteen-year-old girl clothes shopping before?"

"No, but how hard can it be? I take her to the mall, she picks out a few things she likes, and we should be good, right?"

"In theory." He really is adorably clueless about the way girls work. I didn't even care all that much about fashion as a teenager but when a school dance rolled around, you better believe Holly and I were at the mall, spending whatever money our parents willingly handed over.

"You sound so ominous. It's just shopping, Kailyn."

"If you say so. But if you're okay with it, I'm more than happy to tag along." I realize I'm twirling my hair around my finger. This is why I wear it up in a bun so often. I pick up a pen and start doodling instead.

"I don't want to inconvenience you. I know you have a life, and I don't want you to feel like you have to do this because Emme asked."

"I want to come if you'd like me there." I tack on the last part to give him an out. The way my heart flutters is worrying.

"Yeah?" He sounds heart-wrenchingly hopeful.

"Yeah."

"She's been asking about you. She'll be excited that you can come. I'm glad she messaged you."

"Me, too. I'll let her know and we can iron out the details." I end the call and message Emme with the good news. I get about twenty excited GIFs in response, and we make a plan for Saturday. I head down the hall to the lounge to make myself a coffee.

"Someone's in a good mood," Beverly comments.

"Hmm?" I look up from my coffee mug.

"You're humming, and smiling."

I shrug. "Oh. Just a good day, I guess. Can I make you a coffee?"

"That would be lovely." She smiles and props her hip against the counter. "How are things with Daxton and his sister? Have you made any headway with him yet?"

My smile falters the tiniest bit. She's pushing this angle

hard, and I'm not so sure how I feel about any of it anymore. "He's concerned about making another big change right now. Having to interview, switch jobs, manage something new. It's a lot to take on for him but he sees the benefits. It's just going to take time."

"I'm sure you're keen to make partner. You'll figure out a way to convince him. What about the aunt? Do you think she's going to back down?"

"It's unlikely. She's looking to push the stability angle. Her age and her job are in her favor." I've done some research on her. There isn't much of a work history apart from her secretarial position at the school, which she's held for the past several years. She has been married three times, however, which leads to some questions about her ability to provide emotional stability.

Beverly nods, her lips pursed as she contemplates this for a moment. "Then you need to stress that we'd be flexible with hours here. Do you know what kind of salary they're paying him there?" She raps on the counter with her long, French-manicured nails. "Matching or exceeding his current salary will definitely be an enticement."

I regard her over the lip of my coffee cup, testing the sweetness. "That's a pretty personal question."

"You've been spending time with him, though, and he really does seem to trust you. I bet you could find out. Will you see him again this week?"

I'm not sure the time I've been spending with Dax, with

my tongue in his mouth, is the kind Beverly is referring to. "I will."

"Great. See what you get out of him."

A heavy feeling settles in my stomach as I hand Beverly her coffee and she saunters out of the lounge. I'm tipping the balance out of my favor, and I'm unsure who's going to get hurt in the fall.

⁓

On Saturday morning I meet Dax and Emme at the mall when it opens. Emme threads her arm through mine and leads me from store to store. Dax's job is to keep us hydrated and carry the bags. Two hours into the shopping extravaganza and he looks about done.

Emme disappears into a changing room with an armload of clothes, and Dax drops into a chair. "How long is this going to go on?"

"We could be at it all day." She's having a great time. While I'm typically dressed in suits from Monday to Friday, my weekend wardrobe consists mostly of jeans in a multitude of colors, T-shirts, and Toms.

Dax kicks at the toe of my llama-print shoes. "Your feet are tiny."

I wag my brows. "I can buy kids' shoes if I want."

"What about clothes?"

"I'm too curvy."

His eyes move over me in a slow sweep. "I like your curves."

Based on what I felt pressed up against my stomach the last time he kissed me, I believe him. I'm still not sure what to do about my feelings for him, if anything, but things have shifted between us, and it doesn't feel as if it's something I can control.

Emme throws open the changing room door. She's dressed in a pair of ripped, low-rise jeans, and a top that shows a good four inches of belly.

"What the—"

I kick his shin to shut him up. "I like the jeans."

Emme does a little spin. "Me, too! I don't know about the shirt, though."

"I don't think it fits the school dress code, does it? What if you wore a tank top under it?" I look around at the display close by and find a bright green tank. "Why don't you put this on. Layers are totally in right now."

"Good idea!" She nabs the tank and disappears back inside the changing room.

Dax groans under his breath. "Freaking belly tops?"

I pat his shoulder. "This is only the beginning."

"Did you wear belly tops?"

I lift a shoulder. "I had a couple."

He looks me over again, this time with a hint of something like disapproval. "Yeah, well, she's only thirteen. She needs to dress like the kid she is, not a miniature adult looking to go to the club."

"She's not walking around in booty shorts and bandeau bras, Dax."

"And she never will."

I laugh at his dark expression.

Emme comes out a minute later with the bright green tank under the shirt. "That's perfect! Isn't it, Dax?" I nudge him.

"Oh yeah, looks great." He gives Emme two thumbs-up.

We spend another half an hour in the store, Emme modeling outfits, Dax moaning about gray hair and committing murder and then balking at the five-hundred-dollar bill.

He trails behind us, laden down with bags, complaining about being hungry.

"Just one more store and we can break for something to eat," Emme calls over her shoulder.

She elbows me in the side and nods in the direction of a store. "I wanna go in there, but I don't really want Dax to come."

I follow her gaze to the teenage version of Victoria's Secret. "I'll take care of it. You go on ahead and I'll meet you in there."

"What are you going to say?"

"I'll just tell him this store is girls only."

"Okay." She hugs me—something I've come to expect these days—and then rushes on ahead, disappearing inside.

I turn, watching Dax's eyes go wide as he takes in the storefront. He makes flailing hand gestures. "I thought we were clothes shopping."

"Bras and underwear constitute as clothes."

"For fuck's sake. I'm going to need therapy after this."

I put a hand on his chest to stop him from following Emme into the store. "You're not invited to this part of the shopping experience."

He frowns and sighs. Then digs around in his pocket and pulls out his wallet. Flipping it open, he fishes out a few hundred dollars. "Will this be enough?"

"I should hope so."

He slips the money into my hand and then clasps it in both of mine. "Please just no thongs. I need her to be more little girl than teenager for a while longer. Then I can fool myself into believing boys aren't going to be a problem soon."

"No thongs, and nothing lacy or satin. I promise, only cotton."

"Thank you." He presses a soft kiss to my knuckle and his gaze lifts, along with the corner of his mouth. "Feel free to pick up something for yourself, too."

I roll my eyes. "I'll text when we're done."

I find Emme in the pajama section. "Thanks a lot for coming with us today. It would've been embarrassing to bring Dax in here."

"I'm more than happy to have an excuse to go shopping." I give her a side hug and we browse the pajamas.

"You know, Dax talks about you a lot."

"Oh?" I'm not sure what to say to that.

Emme chews on her ragged thumbnail. "He really likes you."

"Well, I like him, too. And I like you." I knock my shoulder against hers. I have a feeling I know where she's going with this, and I'd prefer to have a conversation with Dax, and maybe ask him exactly what he's said about me. "Oh! These are fun!" I hold up a pair of black pajama pants covered in glow-in-the-dark stars.

"Those are cool." She picks up the pair with a black skull and pink rose design. "But do you, like, like him like him, or just like him?"

I feign ignorance. "What do you mean?"

Emme shrugs. "I don't know. Are you guys just, like, friends and stuff?"

"We're friends like you and I are friends."

"Right. Yeah. That's what I thought." She looks disappointed, which makes me question exactly how Dax and I need to manage this moving forward. It's the reason I haven't committed to anything either way. I can manage a broken heart, but I can't deal with breaking Emme's if Dax and I don't work out.

Emme and I spend the next half hour picking out bras and underwear, a couple of new pairs of pajamas, and some athletic wear.

"These are fun!" Emme picks up a pair of hot-pink boy shorts covered in cherries. I don't think she gets what they mean yet. "Are you going to buy anything? You should get something, too."

I humor her and let her pick out a few pairs of underwear

for me. My personal favorite are the black and gold leopard-print ones that say *GO WILD!* over the crotch.

Dax is sitting on a bench, playing on his phone, when we come out of the store. He glances up, taking in Emme's bag and my own much smaller one. "Successful?"

I pass him the change—there isn't much. "Very."

His gaze goes to the bag hanging from my finger, his eyebrow raised in question. "What'd you get?"

"We picked out some fun underwear for Kailyn!" Emme says, rather loudly, while grinning.

"Did you, now?" Dax smirks while my face turns red.

"I don't know about either of you, but I'm starving! We should definitely find a place to eat." Based on Emme's smile, I have a feeling she might've invited me on this shopping trip with ulterior motives.

We end up at a sushi place and spend another two hours shopping after that. Dax is a trooper, giving his opinion when he sees something he likes. And of course I end up trying on a bunch of things, too, because Emme seems to think it's funny for us to wear the same outfits, seeing as I'm not much taller than she is. I imagine when she hits her growth spurt she'll shoot up.

The best part of the entire shopping experience is our stop in the kitschy little store that sells memorabilia inspired by TV shows and movies. "Let's see if they have *It's My Life* stuff!" I thread my arm through Emme's and drag her inside. I don't even check to see if Dax follows.

I head straight for the posters. They have lots of old movie ones but nothing from Dax's show, so I move on to the T-shirts, rummaging around in the last-chance rack, because sometimes they have great finds. "Oh my God!" I shriek when I find the one shirt I've been dying to own since forever, and it's on sale. "Look at this!" I hold up the *It's My Life* T-shirt and then hug it to my chest. It features Dax in a *Tiger Beat*-style pose, wearing his signature smirk with *#1 Dustin Fan* in bright yellow letters.

The teenager behind the cash register barely spares me a glance, and Emme looks at me like I've gone crazy. Dax is standing with his arms crossed over his chest, wearing pretty much the same expression as he is on the shirt. It's a small, but I'll squeeze my chest into it.

"This is a classic! Season two, episode seven. Best hair episode in the entire season, maybe the whole show! I'm so getting this! Oh! I wonder if they have anything else. Excuse me," I call to the kid at the register. "Do you have any more *It's My Life* stuff?"

He's busy texting, so it takes several seconds before he finds the will to lift his eyes from the screen and shrug. "Uh, maybe in the clearance section?"

"I'm sure anything you find in here will be in the basement at my house," Dax mutters.

"But this is way more fun than going through boxes in a basement!" I practically skip my way over to the clearance bin and rummage around while Emme tries on weird hats. I find a chipped mug with Dax on it that matches my new shirt, a bobblehead, and a keychain.

Impressed with my haul, I head for the checkout.

Dax gives me a look. "What're you doing?"

"Buying treasures." I dump my armload on the counter.

Dax picks up the mug. "Don't buy this. It's broken."

I grab it from him and hug it to my chest. "It's chipped, which is not the same. And it matches my new shirt, so I need it."

"Don't you already have a mug with my face on it?"

"That's my Monday mug. This can be my rest of the week mug." The truth is, I have a couple other mugs at home, but he doesn't need to know that. I only have the one at work. A backup is always a good idea.

By the time we're done shopping, it's after four.

"Can you come over for dinner? Dax, Kailyn should totally come for dinner, right? We can order takeout or something. Please?" Emme hangs off her brother's arm.

"We've monopolized Kailyn's entire day already. She might have plans tonight."

Emme frowns, as if the thought displeases her. "Do you have plans?"

I laugh, almost embarrassed that my social life is so lackluster. "Uh, no, no plans."

"So you can come have dinner with us. We can hang out in our new pajamas and play video games or watch a movie."

She looks so hopeful, and so does Dax.

How can I say no?

chapter fifteen

JUST DANCE

Dax

Emme insists that she ride with Kailyn on the way home, and the moment we're in the door, she drags her upstairs to change into the matching pajama pants from the store I wasn't allowed to go in. Not that I want to underwear shop with my sister. Kailyn on the other hand...

This thing with Kailyn is starting to feel a lot bigger than I intended, and pushing for more with her could backfire badly. But I'm selfish enough to try, because I want her in my life as much as Emme wants her in hers.

I pop the cap on a beer and take a long swig while I order pizza. I have bottles of root beer for Emme so she feels grown up, and I have options for Kailyn, depending on what she's in the mood for.

A few minutes later the sound of feminine giggles filters down the stairs. It's Emme's laugh mixed with Kailyn's. They appear in the doorway of the kitchen, both wearing black pajama pants with a cherry and pie cartoon print on them. I'm sure the innuendo is way over Emme's head, but it sure as hell isn't over mine. And Kailyn is wearing the *It's My Life* shirt. It's meant for a teenage body, so it conforms to all of her curves, which I don't mind at all.

While we wait for dinner to arrive, Kailyn and Emme have a *Just Dance* dance off. It's insanely entertaining, in part because Kailyn can dance, and watching her keep up with the moves is actually rather enthralling. Her laugh is infectious and Emme's smile is radiant. I think it's the happiest she's been in the weeks since our parents passed, and it gives me hope that eventually we'll both be okay.

When the pizza comes Emme is super obvious about making sure Kailyn and I sit next to each other. She picks a movie—a romantic comedy—which is the opposite of what she normally watches. Emme like films with action, more specifically anything to do with Harry Potter, or DC or Marvel Comics.

Halfway through the movie Emme yawns and stretches, making a big show of being tired. She gives Kailyn a hug, thanks her for coming shopping, and disappears upstairs, leaving us alone together.

"Well, that wasn't subtle at all."

Kailyn smiles. "Thirteen and subtle don't really go hand in hand, do they?"

"Apparently not." I've been waiting all day for some alone time, and now all I am is nervous, the weight of what I want and what it could change making my throat tight. "We don't have to watch this anymore." I turn off the movie as the on-screen kiss happens, ratcheting up the awkward a notch.

Kailyn smiles, but I can't read her expression. "I bet Emme knew that was coming and that's why she disappeared."

"I'm sorry about that." I motion to the ceiling, not needing to be any more explicit.

"You don't need to apologize. I think it's cute. The most important part is that she had a good time today and she's happy."

I adjust my position so I'm facing her, grateful that Emme forced me into the middle cushion so I'm already close. "I'm glad you could come. It was only good because of you."

I close my eyes, aware I've taken it from light to intense with one stupid admission.

Her fingertips brush along my knuckles, gentle, soft. "Don't sell yourself short, Dax. You're the reason Emme is happy."

"It wouldn't have been the same if it were only her and me." I flip my hand over, watching her fingers drag along the center of my palm. "I don't think I would've survived the underwear shopping, that's for sure."

Kailyn laughs. "Well, I'm reaping the benefits of that, aren't I?" She motions to her new pajama pants. "I'm not here out of empathy. You know that, right?"

"I come with a lot of baggage, though. I get that it makes this complicated." Shit. This is not how I meant for this conversation to go. I'm aware it's necessary since it's more than just me I'm putting at risk.

"It's not the baggage that scares me, Dax." Kailyn curls the ends of her fingers around mine. "My biggest concern is confusing Emme, so I think it's important that we present as platonic when we're with her."

"I understand." I try not to let the disappointment show. Maybe I don't live up to the idea she had of me, or it's too much to take on.

"But when she isn't." Kailyn bites her lip, and her throat bobs with a heavy swallow. "Maybe we could enjoy more of each other."

The heavy feeling in my gut eases up a little. *Is she saying what I think she is? Please let me be reading this situation right.* "Enjoy each other, as in..."

She gives me a look that's half-patronized, half-embarrassed. "I think you know where I'm going with this, Dax."

I arch a brow. "Are you giving me permission to get all up in your space for reasons other than being a confrontational dick?"

She laughs again, and the sound is as sweet as it is sexy. Kailyn is such an interesting contradiction of a woman. In her career she's driven, sure, and focused, but when we're close like this, she seems shy and uncertain. Her smile turns coy. "And if I was?"

"I'd take full advantage of that every single chance I got, starting now." I trace the edge of her jaw with a fingertip, aware there's more to this conversation, but for now it will have to wait.

Kailyn tips her chin up, eyes on mine as I lean in and touch my lips to hers. She lets me lead, our tongues tangling as I sweep her mouth, slowly at first, until gentleness dissolves into desire.

Kailyn's hands are in my hair and then ease down my neck to grip my shoulders as I rearrange us on the couch. I edge a knee between her legs and lay her back, stretching out over her. Soft, warm skin meets my palm when I find my way under the hem of her shirt.

She makes the silkiest sound, a hum and a moan fused together as we kiss and grope and grind, getting lost in the newness of each other. A thump from upstairs has us on opposite ends of the couch in a hot second.

Kailyn's eyes are wide but glassy, her fingers pressed against her kiss-swollen lips as we both look toward the stairs. Her hair is mussed and her cheeks are flushed. She's gorgeously disheveled. When Emme doesn't appear, and no subsequent thuds or noises follow, we both exhale in relief.

"I feel a bit like a teenager," Kailyn says on a breathy laugh.

"Maybe we should take this upstairs." I don't know how far she's willing to let this go, but I don't want it to end yet.

"What if Emme comes down and we're not here?"

"I could tell her we're going for a walk?"

Kailyn bites her lip, considering the lie. "We should hide our shoes, then?"

I grin. "Smart thinking."

Kailyn tosses our shoes in the hall closet while I knock on Emme's door. I find her stretched out on her bed with her earbuds in, writing in a journal. She pulls the buds out, a small frown pulling at the corner of her mouth. "Did Kailyn leave already?"

"No, she's still here. We're going for a walk." The lie feels odd, but necessary.

Her eyes light up. "Oh, okay. I can stay here, though, right?"

"Yeah, of course. Do you need anything?"

"Nope, I'm good. Have fun!" She's grinning as she pops the earbud back in and I close the door.

I feel a little ridiculous as I rush back down the stairs, treading heavily on the way. I hold up a finger to Kailyn, who's sitting on the couch with her hands curled over her knees. I pass through to the hallway, open and close the door with a loud bang, and lock it.

When I come back to the living room, her shoulders shake with suppressed laughter. I nod to the stairs and hold out my hand. "Wanna hang out in my room?"

She pushes up off the couch, and slips her fingers into my outstretched palm. I guide her up the stairs, peeking around the corner to make sure the coast is clear before ushering her down the hall. At least my bedroom is at the opposite end so we don't have to pass my sister's room, or worry too much about noise.

We slip inside and I close the door, locking it behind us. "We made it," I whisper.

Kailyn's giggle fades as she looks around the room, eyeing the king-size bed. My room is neat, no clothes lying on the floor, comforter smooth, pillows mostly straight. She runs her hands over her hips, the shyness returning.

I hope the interruption hasn't ruined the mood, or given Kailyn enough time to reconsider. "Are you okay with this?"

"It's just..." She bites her lip and takes a step closer, pressing her palms against my chest. "This is all a bit surreal."

"How do you mean?" I sweep my thumb along her bottom lip.

She looks down and gives her head a shake. "Never mind. It's silly and I'm going to embarrass myself."

I understand why her cheeks are suddenly flaming. "I wish I'd asked you out in law school when I had the chance."

"I probably would've fainted if you'd kissed me back then, which would've been so much worse than the fangirling."

She's still looking at my chest. I tip her chin up so I can see her eyes. "You're not at risk of fainting now, are you?"

As expected, she rolls those gorgeous green eyes.

"I'll take that as a no." I press my lips to hers.

Kailyn melts into me, parting her lips when I stroke the seam with my tongue. She's so much smaller than me, especially without her heels. I'd love to peel one of those sexy skirt suits off her curvy body, piece by piece. Hopefully we'll have other opportunities to make that happen.

I cup her face in my palms and pull back. "Should we get more comfortable?" I incline my head toward the bed.

"Comfortable as in vertical and naked?" She tugs on the back of my neck, pulling my mouth back to hers as we sidestep across the room.

"If that's what makes you comfortable, then definitely." I lift her onto the mattress and she shimmies over until she reaches the pillows, me following along after her. I grin at the silly pattern on her pajama pants as I edge my way between her legs and stretch out over her.

Kailyn's fingers dip under the hem of my shirt, nails skimming along my abs, making them jump under her light touch. "I can take this off?"

"You can take off whatever you want."

She grins and I help pull it over my head, then discard it on the floor. Kailyn's smile fades as she explores my chest with lazy fingertips.

Her eyes meet mine on a soft exhale. "I don't look like this under my clothes."

"Gotta say, I'm glad to hear that. Not sure how I'd feel about a chest hair competition."

Kailyn tucks her chin against her shoulder and laughs, embarrassed again. "That's not what I meant."

I nuzzle into her neck, kissing that sweet, sensitive space just below her ear. "If it wasn't already clear, I think you're gorgeous exactly the way you are. The cherry-print pajama pants and this shirt just make it better." Her vulnerability is humbling, and different than what I'm used to.

Behind that fierce exterior, Kailyn is soft curves and sweetness, and I can't wait to get my hands and mouth on every inch of her. We make out like teenagers, her leg hooked over my hip until it stops being enough.

I fold back on my knees and pull her shirt over her head, fanning her dark hair across my pillow. Her bra is simple, pale silvery-gray satin. I slip a hand under her, free the clasp, and drag the straps over her shoulders.

Her skin pebbles under my touch, nipples tightening as I expose them, and I dip down to take one in my mouth. Kailyn arches and gasps, fingers sliding into my hair, holding me to her.

When I come back to her mouth, our kisses grow deeper and needier, hands roam and caress until she's popping the button on my pants, fingers slipping inside my boxer briefs.

"Ah, fuck," I groan when her warm hand encases me. I push up on my arms, hovering over her as she strokes, pressure firm, thumb brushing the head with each pass.

Her gaze stays steady on mine as I ease a hand down her side, edging under the waistband of her pajama pants. "Can I take these off, then?"

"Yes, please."

She has to release me so I can drag them over her hips and down her thighs. I pause when her panties appear, and glance up, cocking a brow. Her grin widens and her nose wrinkles. These look new and very unlike something Kailyn would choose. They're black cotton with a gold cheetah print and the words *GO WILD!* over the crotch.

"These are interesting."

"I had help picking them out."

"Oh? Are there more?"

"Mmm. They had a great 'buy three, get two free' deal going."

"I look forward to taking each and every pair off your gorgeous, sexy body, then."

"Well, if you want that to happen, I guess you better impress me this time around." Her eyes glint with mischief.

I like this side of Kailyn. I expected soft and shy, but her playfulness is a pleasant surprise. I grin and drag a finger along the edge of her panties, from her hip to the juncture of her thighs. "I'll do my very best."

She nips at my bottom lip, but I don't give her more kisses. Instead I sit back on my heels, tuck my thumbs into the waistband, and lower her panties over her hips. Her impishness disappears as her fingers drift to her mouth. I lower my head to place a gentle kiss below her navel.

Kailyn drags in a tremulous breath, followed by a barely audible whimper when I suck the skin. I take my time removing her panties, heightening anticipation; hers and mine.

She presses her thighs together, that shyness returning. Tucking my fingers into that warm space at the bend of her knee, I ease her legs open a few inches. "I want to see you."

When she parts for me, I kiss the inside of her right knee, then move to the left. From one side to the other, I kiss a path up the inside of her thighs, toward the place I'm looking very forward to spending some time.

"Dax."

I lift my eyes, pausing to suck the skin. "Can I taste you?"

Kailyn's teeth sink into her bottom lip on a nod. A shaking hand glides down her stomach and stops just below her navel, but no words follow.

When I finally reach the apex of her thighs, I drag a single finger along her slit. Kailyn jolts, body bowing with her quiet cry of surprise.

"Is this okay?"

She nods, cheeks pink. "I didn't expect that."

"I'm going to touch you now, okay?" I warn with a grin. Parting her with my fingers, I brush my thumb over her clit. She exhales another unsteady breath.

"And now I'm going to kiss you." I drop my head and lick her, eyes on her face.

She covers her mouth with her palm, as if she's trying to hide her reaction. She bites her knuckle and turns her head to the side when I do it again. "God, you're really good at that."

"Would it be better if I fumbled around a bit, like we're in college and I don't know what I'm doing?" I tease.

She huffs a laugh, which turns into a sigh as I put my mouth on her again. Her sweet moans are quiet as I drag an orgasm out of her. Maybe because she's cautiously aware of how *not* alone we are in this house.

I kiss my way back up to her mouth. Kailyn's hands ease down my sides, and she pushes my pants and underwear over my hips. "You should be naked like me."

Once I am I reach for a condom from the nightstand.

Kailyn plucks the foil square from my fingers and pushes on my chest until I sit back. Tearing it open, she rolls it on, then pulls me over her again.

I drop my face into the crook of her neck, muttering a curse as I sink inside her, satin heat surrounding me. Kailyn's lips are at my temple, legs wrapped tight around my waist, the palm of her hand curving around the back of my neck.

I breathe through the tightness in the pit of my stomach, my body in overdrive, the sensation almost too much. This is different. It's far more intense than just physical need.

When I feel like I'm under control again, mostly, I kiss a path from her neck to her mouth.

Then I push up enough so I can see her face. "Hi."

She smiles, eyes soft and hazy. "Hey."

"You feel incredible."

"So do you." She tips her chin up. "Kiss me, please."

So I do. With our mouths fused I move over her, and despite wanting to take my time, to go slow and savor this, desire eventually wins out.

Gentle thrusts become more frantic as her quiet moans turn into pleas for me not to stop. I can't kiss her anymore, too intent to watch her unravel for me. My name is a whisper on her lips as she comes. Like a domino being pushed, I let go, chasing the high of the orgasm.

When the sensations finally abate, I unhook her leg and roll to the side so I don't crush her with my weight. We kiss for long minutes, hands still roaming each other's bodies.

When I finally pull back, I trace the edge of her jaw with my fingertip. This isn't like any other sex I've had before. I'm not sure if it's tied up in her connection to my past, or her being involved in my present, or somewhere between the two, but I know I want to keep this.

"Was that impressive enough?" It breaks the tension, and for a moment I wish I could take it back and say something else. Something better.

Emotions flit across her face, none of them lasting long enough for me to catch and hold them. She skims my lips with her fingertips, a small smile tipping the corner of her mouth. "Top-of-the-class impressive."

"I'll get to see the rest of your pretty new panties, then?"

She arches a brow. "I don't know about that."

"But I gave you orgasms, more than one."

"What if your performance next time isn't as impressive?"

"I promise that was just a warm-up. Next time will be even better."

I move to kiss her, but we both freeze at the slam of a door and the thump of footfalls coming down the hallway.

chapter sixteen

TREAD LIGHTLY

Kailyn

Panic sets in as I push on Dax's chest. His arm tightens around my waist, the steady, quick thump of his heart vibrating against my palm. Logically, I know we should be safe because the door is locked and Emme has no idea we're here, but the gravity of my decision hits me. What if Emme finds out?

Heavy feet tread down the stairs. I'm relieved for a moment before I realize she could be down there for a while.

"What if she doesn't come back up right away? What if she decides to watch TV?" I whisper.

Dax smooths my hair away from my face. "She's probably getting a snack."

I seriously hope that's all. I've never lost my head over a man like this. I can't believe we just snuck up to his bedroom to have sex without considering the worst-case scenario, which would be getting caught by his sister. It was pretty great sex, but still, this isn't the smartest thing I've ever done. It's actually right up there with walking through a Frisbee game with my eyes closed and that time I was watching reruns of *It's My Life* between classes but my earbuds weren't in properly and everyone could hear Daxton and the female lead sharing their first kiss. "I left my phone and my purse in the living room."

"Mine's in my pants." He smiles a little. "Don't worry. We can always climb down the trellis and run around the front of the house if we need to."

I imagine what that would look like, two adults climbing down the side of the house to hide the fact that we've had sex from a thirteen-year-old. His grin widens, possibly at my horrified expression. I am not a fan of heights. "It's not a joke, Dax!"

I push on his chest again. He's still inside me, half-hard based on how full I still am. "We should get dressed. I don't even know how long we've been up here."

Dax frowns but unlocks his arms. I roll to my back, breaking the physical connection. His body is amazing, long and lean with definition that speaks of time spent at the gym. I feel exposed as I reach across the bed for my flashy panties and pajama pants. Dax removes the condom and ties it off while I wiggle into my underwear. He presses a kiss to my shoulder before he picks up his boxers and throws his legs over the edge of the bed. I watch his incredible ass disappear into his boxer briefs, then he disappears into the bathroom to discard the spent condom.

I rush to grab my bra from the floor and slip my arms through the straps.

"Let me help." Dax sweeps my hair over my shoulder and

hooks the clasp, dropping another kiss at the base of my neck. I shiver at the tender contact, and again when he drags a single finger down my spine. He plucks my shirt from the edge of the bed and helps me into that as well, smoothing the fabric down my sides, his wide palms settled on my waist. "I would've liked some naked cuddle time."

I can't quite judge his mood, unsure if he's trying to defuse my panic or the sudden tension between us. This isn't some casual screw. There are consequences for our actions.

I laugh, but my anxiety comes through loud and clear in my high pitch and the way I'm unable to meet his gaze. "What if I'm not a cuddler?"

"You've never cuddled with me." He turns me around and lifts me by the waist, setting me on the edge of the bed. I'm sure he can sense my worry, and I'm certain he believes it has everything to do with Emme.

Part of me realizes that the sex shouldn't have happened, but the other part of me wants this connection because it's so much stronger than anything I've ever known before. And that terrifies me because I have so much wrapped up in both of them. The stakes are high, the potential losses great, and the possible damage frighteningly emotional.

"It's going to be fine," Dax says gently, his fingers slipping through my hair, maybe trying to tame it.

Despite the internal command to keep my hands to myself, I trail my fingers over his chest, following the contour of muscle. "It's a complicated situation."

"I know."

"We need to be careful, for Emme's sake," I whisper.

"I agree."

She's already attached to me, and I'm attached to her. I don't even want to consider how this might compromise my career, or my role as Emme's conservator on top of everything else. And if we don't work out, then what? I lose him, Emme, and the one thing I've been working all these years for? *What will I have then?*

I tense at the sound of footfalls coming up the stairs. The slam of a door follows and I blow out a relieved breath. "We should go back downstairs."

Dax nods, but he doesn't look all that happy as he dresses quickly. Before he opens the door, he takes my face in his hands, eyes searching mine before he tips my head up and kisses me. It's a slow tangle of tongues that makes my knees weak and my heart stutter. He pulls away on a deep inhale and caresses my bottom lip with his thumb. "Let me make sure the coast is clear."

He unlocks the door and opens it a crack, cringing as it creaks. "I'll WD-40 that for next time," he whispers, then peeks down the hall. "All clear."

My heart hammers in my chest as we tiptoe to the stairs and steal swiftly back to the living room.

I rush to the front hall and take our shoes out of the closet, then open and slam the door, maybe a little harder than I need to.

Dax leans against the doorjamb, looking ridiculously calm.

I poke his shoulder and he grabs my finger, pulling me to him. "You need to relax, Kailyn."

I exhale a deep breath. Maybe I'm overreacting, but then there's more going on here than two consenting adults having sex. "Sorry. I think we need to plan this better in the future." I'm talking like this is going to happen again, even though I've already told myself it shouldn't.

"I agree. I'd like a sleepover where I get to see what you look like with bed head, and we can have lazy morning sex."

I need his levity with everything going on in my head. "Pretty sure a sleepover is out of the question for the time being." I lift my chin, eyes on the ceiling.

"We'll figure something out." He links our pinkies. "Come sit with me for a while before you tell me you have to go home."

⸎

Two days later I'm in my office, files spread out over my desk, when my cell rings. It's Dax. Yesterday he sent me a very beautiful flower arrangement. I've never been much of a hearts and flowers girl, but the gerbera daisies in vibrant colors are particularly lovely, and coming from him they mean something special. Which is a problem. I'm more invested than I ever meant to be, and now not only do we have to try to hide this from Emme, I'm also supposed to convince him to work at Whitman. My head's a mess over this.

I pick up my phone and put some cheer in my voice. "Good morning, Mr. Hughes. How may I help you?"

"Are you at your desk right now? Can you check your email?"

"Yes, and yes. Why? Is there a problem?"

"No problem, this could actually be the opposite of a problem. I'll wait until you open the email before I ask more questions."

"Personal or professional?"

"Personal."

I grab my home laptop from my bag and access my emails, pulling up the one he forwarded. "This is about the alumni conference." Our law school is hosting a two-day conference featuring panels, speeches, and workshops led by some of the top lawyers to graduate from their program. I was offered an opportunity to lead a panel, but wasn't sure I could commit to it, or even wanted to.

"Are you going?"

I have to stop chewing on the end of my pen in order to answer. "I reserved a spot, but I wasn't sure if it made sense to attend. Why? Are you?"

"I'm speaking on a panel on Saturday."

"Oh." So much for seeing him this weekend. "Do you need me to watch Emme?"

He laughs. "No, Kailyn. I've made arrangements with one of her friends to have a sleepover."

"Have you talked to the parents? Will they be there? Does she know them well?"

"Yes, yes, and yes. She's been friends with Marnie since first grade and they've had plenty of sleepovers, so she'll be in good hands for the weekend."

"Well, that's good news." I'm a little bummed that he's going to be away all weekend. Maybe he'll have an evening free this week or something.

"Kailyn?"

"Yes?" I rearrange my mugs on my desk—the old and the new one with the chip. I think it's going to be my favorite now, because of the memory associated with the shopping trip and the events that followed.

"I have a hotel room booked for Friday and Saturday night." At my silence he presses on. "We could spend the entire weekend together. No pretending we're going for a walk, no hiding"— his voice drops—"and we can have lazy morning sex. What do you say? Are you in?"

I squeeze my thighs together. "Yes. I'm in."

His voice is smooth silk. "Are you thinking about lazy morning sex, Kailyn?"

"No." I'm sure lazy morning sex will be nice, but I'm looking forward to experiencing his other talents again.

He chuckles. "I think you're lying."

I smooth out my skirt, my body already responding to the endless possibilities that will come with an entire weekend together, uninterrupted by time constraints or the presence of a teenager. But I play it off as coy. "And why would you think that?"

"Because you're suddenly all breathy."

I can feel my face heating up. "I am not."

"You definitely are."

"It has nothing to do with lazy morning anything."

"Oh no? What does it have to do with, then?"

I check to make sure I have privacy before I drop my voice to a whisper. "That very talented tongue you have."

"Oh, really? Should I assume you're not referencing my stellar conversation skills?"

"You assume correctly, although I do appreciate your ability to keep me entertained, mind and body." My cheeks grow hot at the thought of having his head between my thighs again.

"Did you like it when I made you come with my mouth?"

I throw his words back at him. "You're good at reading people, aren't you? What do you think?"

"I think you liked it a lot. I might even go so far as to say you love my mouth on you."

"Is that right, Mr. Hughes?"

"It is. I enjoyed the taste of you very much, Miss Flowers, and I'm very much looking forward to repeating that experience multiple times."

"We should probably schedule that in, just to be sure you have enough time between panels to make that happen."

He laughs. "I'll get on that right away. Well, now that I'm highly uncomfortable and can't leave my desk without embarrassing myself, I should probably get back to work."

It's my turn to chuckle. "I hope you have a productive day, and it's not too hard."

"Interested in a quick lunch date?"

"Enticing, but I have meetings all day."

"That's unfortunate." Dax is silent for a moment, and his voice drops low. "Kailyn?"

"Yes, Dax."

"Pack all your fun panties for me, please."

I laugh. "Of course."

"Have a nice day, Miss Flowers."

"You, too, Mr. Hughes."

I end the call and exhale a long breath, considering all the ways in which I plan to enjoy this uninterrupted two-day span. But first I need to run it by Beverly as it means missing part of Friday. Something I should've done before I said yes to Dax, but I can't see her saying no.

I collect myself and review how I'm going to pitch this in my head on my way to Beverly's office. She's poring over documents when I knock.

"Kailyn, come on in." She motions to the chair across from her desk.

I take a seat. "I have a request I need to run by you."

"Oh?" She folds her hands in front of her. "Is everything okay?"

"Oh yes, fine. There's an alumni conference this Friday and Saturday. As you know, Daxton and I were in the same class, and he's attending as one of the speakers. I thought it might be a good idea for me to go as well. It could give me an opportunity to revisit the possibility of switching firms in a less formal environment." I'm laying the bullshit on thick, but the payoff will feel *oh so good*.

Beverly smiles. "That's a fantastic idea. How are things with his sister? What's happening with the aunt?"

"His sister is great, no more issues at school, so that's good news. The aunt is still pushing her angle." Linda has emailed me several times regarding the folder of information she passed over at the school all those weeks ago. I looked through it right away, but there was nothing that couldn't be found in a simple Google search. Most of the documents were gossip site articles about some of Daxton's unfortunate choices during his progression from teen heartthrob to top lawyer. There isn't anything particularly condemning in the past couple of years, but I see the picture she's trying to paint.

"That's perfect. Will Daxton be at the conference on Friday, or is he just attending Saturday?"

"He'll be there both days."

"Then I want you there, too."

"Great. I'll make sure to take care of everything before the end of the day on Thursday."

"Excellent. I look forward to hearing about the progress you make over the weekend. Do you think he'll want a gym membership? He's definitely in good shape. Maybe see what other perks might help pull him our way."

"Of course." I rise as Beverly turns her attention back to the papers on her desk.

"Kailyn?"

I pause halfway to the door. "Yes?"

"I can't wait to be able to make you a partner."

"Me, too." The excitement fades as I make my way back down the hall to my office. Dax coming over to Whitman would be so much better for him and obviously it means good things for my career, but the ramifications sit heavy with me. It feels like my gains no longer outweigh the potential losses.

e

Making partner isn't what I'm thinking about on Friday morning when I double-check my overnight bag for all my fun panties packed, and of course a selection of sexy ones.

Dax picks me up at ten. The drive to the hotel doesn't take long since it's during the day and traffic isn't terrible, but he's secured early check-in and a room on the penthouse floor, away from the conference goers so we have privacy.

As soon as we get to the room, we're a flurry of groping hands and busy mouths. It's nothing like the last time we had sex. After five days of messages back and forth discussing all the things we can't wait to do to each other, Dax is hell-bent on making every single one of those things happen in the first hour.

I'm a limp noodle by the time he finally comes—dear lord that man has incredible stamina. He rolls onto his back and arranges me so I'm lying on top of him, my chin resting on his chest. He sweeps my hair away from my face. "Do you know what's sexy?"

I reach across the bed and pick up the pair of hot-pink cheekies with *YOLO* written on the butt in huge block letters. "These?"

"They are pretty awesome, but no."

"Just wait until you see the other ones."

"I'm very excited to see what else you advertise on your ass this weekend." He grins and folds an arm behind his head, bicep flexing enticingly. "But seriously, do you know what I find incredibly sexy about you, apart from your excellent taste in underwear?"

I prop my chin on my fist. "Do tell."

"The way you come." He drags his tongue across his bottom lip.

I can't hold eye contact, it's just too intense. "What do you mean?"

"You're so fierce most of the time, but when you come, God, you're so sweet. It's fascinating to see you like that, just vulnerable and unguarded but still so . . . poised. Maybe that's not the right word. Whatever it is, it's my new addiction."

I duck my head and bury my face against his chest. "Now I'm going to be self-conscious."

"I don't want to make you self-conscious. You're phenomenal, Kailyn. Everything about you is incredible." He runs a finger from my temple to my jaw. "I love that I get to see this soft side of you. Whenever I think about how messed up everything is, I remember that out of all this bad came two good things. I have a very special relationship with my sister and now I have you. So as hard as all of this change has been, you make the difficult days easier."

The sweetness of the declaration is tainted by the things I'm keeping from him. Guilt tugs at my conscience and I consider for a moment telling him about the deal with Beverly. But I don't want to ruin this moment, and there's no guarantee he'll come over to Whitman, so instead I kiss his fingertips, my heart aching and swelling at the same time. "I'm glad I can do that for you, for both of you."

I stretch up to kiss him, and it quickly escalates until I'm underneath him again. He's sweet and slow this time, his eyes on mine as he brings me to the edge of bliss and tips me over into the heavenly abyss.

I'm in far too deep to get out unscathed. But I like this place we're in; it feels protected and safe for now, even though I know it isn't.

chapter seventeen

LITTLE LIES

Kailyn

Saturday does not include lazy morning sex because Dax is speaking at a panel. Instead we have a morning quickie, and an even faster shower before we head down for the continental breakfast. Dax is bombarded by people who want to offer condolences and talk shop. The women are something else, though. They simper and fawn. It's embarrassing and infuriating.

What I love about Dax is the way he's able to shift a conversation away from himself to include everyone around him. I don't have a problem holding my own, but people gravitate to him and he knows how to work a room.

I see firsthand how very different he is with me than he is with anyone else. When we're alone he lets his guard down, but around all of these people he puts on the actor mask, smiling, making conversation, and being generally charismatic.

He constantly pulls me into conversations with random fangirls, possibly to save him. He introduces me as a close friend from law school. Then he proceeds to tell whoever is currently in his orbit how incredible I am. He surprises me when he speaks at length about my willingness to take on pro bono cases and how we need more lawyers who exhibit such altruistic tendencies.

And of course no one wants to be rude, so they nod politely, voicing their agreement while he rambles on about how brilliant I was in law school. How I'm the only reason he pushed as hard as he did and ended up where he is. It's equal parts entertaining and humbling.

I realize, as he drives the conversation, that despite how difficult his life has been these past months, he's paid attention to me, to the things I want, what my goals are. And in a way, he's acknowledging the sacrifice he believes I'm making in taking on the role of conservator for Emme.

So often these events are about posturing, everyone talking about how awesome they are and how many hours they work, how they've made partner and their amazing beach house in who the hell cares where. I've always been personally proud of my choices, aware I'd make better money if I didn't take on pro bono cases. I could drive a better car, maybe have a nicer house, but Dax's praise is the affirmation I didn't realize I needed. And I fall a little bit more for him because of it.

Dax excuses himself twenty minutes before his panel, and I take the opportunity to freshen up in the ladies' room. It appears every single woman at the conference had the same idea and by the time I get to the panel every seat in the front half of the room is taken, again, mostly by women. I'm forced to take a seat close to the back of the room. With only a few minutes to go the space fills quickly. I smile at the man to my right, trying to place him.

It takes a moment, but I realize he's one of Dax's friends from law school, and from the pictures I've seen in Dax's house, I'm pretty sure he's Felix.

I give him a courtesy nod.

"Kailyn Fangirl." He cringes. "I mean Flowers. Hey. Hi. It's been a long time."

"Not long enough, apparently," I mutter.

"Felix McQueen." He holds out a hand, giving me no choice but to take it. "I thought I would've seen Dax downstairs at the bar last night, but it looks like you're keeping my boy busy."

I hate that I have to tip my head up to glare at him, but I do.

"He's a lot more relaxed this morning than I've seen him in a long time." He waggles his brows.

My face heats with embarrassment.

"It's a good thing, Kailyn."

A woman in the row behind us taps him on the shoulder and whispers something in his ear. He laughs and murmurs his own response before the moderator announces the panel is about to begin.

I don't have a great view from where I am thanks to the basketball player seated in front of me, but if I lean to the right

I can sort of see Daxton. He's eloquent and compelling, commanding the attention of the entire room, apart from the man sitting beside me.

Felix leans in close, the kind of close I would find uncomfortable if he wasn't Daxton's best friend. And maybe still do anyway. "I kinda owe you an apology."

"You're good. Dax already apologized on your behalf," I whisper, eyes still on Dax.

"Yeah, but he's pissed at me over it, so I figure it's better coming from me, yeah?"

He's not whispering, and a couple of people look over their shoulders at him, so I elbow him in the side. He lets out a loud *oomph*, drawing even more attention. Daxton catches the movement and cocks a brow, not at me, but Felix.

"McQueen, save it for the bar tonight," Dax says with a knowing smile.

That gets a round of chuckles from the group.

"Yes, sir. Sorry, sir." Felix salutes him, but he remains silent for the rest of the panel, mostly playing a game on his phone or texting. He pauses once to ask a completely irrelevant question.

When the panel ends, a horde of women rushes the front of the room.

"Come on, let's go get something to drink while he gets mobbed." Felix tips his head to the door.

I don't really want to leave Dax here with all the fangirls, but I'm also not interested in watching them fawn. "Okay."

Felix smirks. "Your enthusiasm is overwhelming."

"He'll be okay, right?"

"Yeah, he's used to this. You'll just have to deflate his ego later."

I chuckle and I gather my things, following him down the aisle. Felix is tall, taller than Dax even, so he waves, points at me, who I'm sure Dax can't see, and makes a drink motion. It's just shy of eleven, but the bar is already full of people taking early lunch and drinking pints like it's college all over again.

Felix and I find a seat at the bar. I order a latte and he orders scotch on the rocks. As soon as the bartender is gone he turns to me. "Sorry I was a dick in law school."

"Everyone was a dick, especially in law school."

He swirls the scotch in his glass. "Yeah, but I sort of screwed you over hard, so I feel bad about that."

"Why?"

"Why do I feel bad, or why did I screw you over?"

"Either? Both?"

"You and Dax were such rivals. It was...I don't know. He was so obsessed with beating you, and kinda obsessed with you in general, really. I figured, what was the big deal if your assignment was handed in late and his wasn't, you know? I didn't think it would mess with your GPA so much that it would skew anything. Except it did. So, yeah, sorry for being a dick."

"It was a long time ago. It doesn't really matter anymore. Besides, I'm exactly where I want to be."

"I still feel bad. We were real assholes, especially me, and I'm not sure I've changed all that much. Dax is different, though. He's a good guy in a bad situation, so I'm hoping we can wipe the slate clean since Dax and I are tight and he seems to like you."

"Consider it wiped." My phone buzzes on the bar top and I glance at the screen. It's Dax asking me to meet him in the room. "Looks like Dax is done with his fangirls. I'll leave you to deal with yours, then." I incline my head to a group of women standing not far away, two of which are looking in his direction.

"Being Dax's best friend is as much a blessing as a curse." He winks and downs his scotch, then raises the glass as the bartender passes.

When I get back to the room, I find Dax on the couch, shoeless with his feet propped on the coffee table, tie loose and the top buttons on his shirt undone. There's another panel this afternoon and a dinner we're supposed to attend tonight. Dax surprised me last night with a very stunning dress, and a pair of heels I tried on while we were shopping but decided were far too extravagant to purchase. Apparently he felt I needed them anyway. But based on how tired he looks, I'm not sure Dax is going to be up for leaving this room anytime soon.

"Is it too early to start drinking?" His cufflinks clink on the coffee table, and he drapes his shirt over the arm of the couch.

I check the time. "It's after eleven."

He drops his head back on the couch. "I should wait until at least noon."

It's been an emotional morning; the outpouring of empathy

over his loss is heartwarming but also painful and exhausting for him. "Don't we have a bottle of champagne that we never got around to opening last night? If we have orange juice, I can make you a mimosa, which I believe is completely acceptable before noon."

He holds out his hand. "Come here first."

I cross the room, still wearing my heels. A few of the girls I used to study with are here and want to meet up for drinks. I wasn't sure whether Dax would want time with his own friends or not. It seems he's far more interested in me over everyone else—although I'd attribute that in part to all of the condolences, and how it makes the loss feel fresh again.

As soon as I'm within reach, he takes my hand and tugs me closer. His eyes roam over me, his fatigue shifting to heat. He sits up, one leg on either side of mine, and runs his hands down the outside of my thighs. "You know what I need more?"

I thread my fingers through his thick, sandy hair. He really is absolutely gorgeous. It's no wonder his panel was 90 percent women.

It wouldn't have been difficult to convince people we're just friends this weekend since I don't quite fit the model type I'm sure most people would picture him with. And while he hasn't come out and said we're together, the implication is there in the way he speaks to me, and how attentive he's been despite the barrage of flirtatious women who constantly surround him.

He plays with the hem of my skirt. "Did you need to check out my panty situation?"

"Mmm. I think I do." He pushes the fabric up my thighs.

I'm wearing a pencil skirt, but the material has some stretch, so it slides easily, bunching at my waist. I'm wearing black hose with a lacy pattern that goes all the way to the waistband and obstructs the view of what's underneath.

He pulls at the hose. "Are these expensive?"

"Not terribly, no." I mean, they're not cheap, but I have a good twenty pairs at home.

"Do you have more of them here?"

"I have a pair of nude ones."

"No pattern?"

I shake my head.

"Hmm. I'll be careful, then."

I'm not sure how to gauge his mood. He's intense, which I don't mind in the least. It's been good to see him like this, in his element with his peers, engaged in something other than Emme. Not that his focus shouldn't be on her, just that his concern could be smothering if he's not careful. She's a teenager; they need privacy just like adults.

He removes my shoes and then the hose before slipping my feet back into the heels one at a time. He trails his fingers lightly up the outside of my legs and breathes out a groan. "You didn't buy these on your shopping trip with my sister, did you?"

"No. I made a special trip." My panties are sheer with black lace accents, and also a thong, which Dax soon discovers when he cups my ass.

His gaze flips up to mine, teeth sinking into his full bottom lip. "Turn around for me, baby."

I do as he asks and wait a few very long seconds before I peek over my shoulder. His expression makes my sometimes shaky body confidence soar. It's not always easy to be a short, curvy, dark-haired woman living in a Barbie world, but Dax has a way of making me feel beautiful.

"Fuck, Kailyn."

"You like them, then?"

I jump when his palms settle on my hips and his lips press against my right butt cheek, followed by his teeth when he bites down. "I love them."

He slips his finger under the thin strip of fabric connecting the waistband. A wave of goose bumps flashes over my skin as he drags his knuckle along the divide.

"Can I tell you something that might make me sound like a complete dick?"

"If you want to risk it, go ahead."

He chuckles and spins me around, resting his chin just below my navel. "When I came to your office to review the trust, I fantasized about shoving your skirt up just like this and fucking you on your desk."

Heat blossoms low in my tummy. "And was that the time you were checking for panty lines?"

"One of them. If it helps, I felt bad for objectifying you, especially when it was clear you weren't much of a fan."

"I was always a fan, Dax, I just thought you were a jerk."

"I can make up for that. I'll start my penance right here."
He kisses a path along the edge of my panties from my hip to
the apex of my thighs. Lifting his gaze, he parts his lips, tongue
pressing against me through the fabric.

I suck in a breath and latch on to his hair. A moment later
he slips one finger under the edge, barely brushing my clit. In
a smooth surge he rises, mouth suddenly on mine as he shifts
my panties to the side and slides two fingers into me. I grip his
shoulders, disoriented as he spins me around, and find myself
laid out on the couch.

"You know what else I need?" Dax kneels between my legs.

"To get me naked?"

"Definitely, but more than that I need to see you come. It
really is my favorite thing in the whole world."

"So no pressure or anything?" I laugh, but I'm actually nervous. Last night I was focused on the feel of him inside me
when I came. I don't think that's his plan now.

He doesn't answer, just drags my panties down my legs,
pulls me to the edge of the couch, and drops his head. I roll
my hips as his mouth moves against me, his deep groans and
the sweet sting of his teeth pushing me closer to the edge.

I press my palm to my lips, a moan caught in my throat.
Dax replaces his mouth with his fingers, thumb circling my
clit while he strokes the spot inside that sets my whole body
on fire.

"That's it, right there. That's the thing you do that drives
me insane." He rises up, hooking my leg under his arm,

spreading me wider as he braces his palm on the back of the couch.

"What thing?" I ask. Fingers still at my lips, I bite one, whimpering with his next curl inside me.

"What you're doing right now. When you cover your mouth or bite your knuckle. It's just so fucking sexy, like you're shocked you can feel this good and you're trying to stay in control."

"That's because I am," I whisper.

"Shocked or trying to stay in control?"

"Both."

"Why shocked?"

The next finger flutter is hard and fast. I swivel my hips and turn my face into my shoulder, my orgasm almost within reach.

"Look at me, Kailyn. Why?"

"Because no one's ever made me feel out of control except for you."

He crushes his mouth to mine as I come, waves of pleasure making my body jerk and tremble. He gets as far as unbuckling his belt and unzipping his pants when his phone rings. I cry out as he rubs the head of his erection over my sensitive clit.

The ringing doesn't stop, though, so I glance at the lit-up screen. "It's Emme."

"Fuck." Dax's head drops to my chest and he fists my bunched skirt with a shaking hand. "*Fuck*. I have to answer."

"I know. Get it before it goes to voicemail." I scramble to

right myself and grab the phone from the table, bringing it to his ear. He turns his head away and clears his throat into his shoulder before he speaks. "Hey, kiddo! How's it going?" He sits back on his knees, and his eyes roll up as he tucks himself into his pants. "Oh yeah? You're having a good time, then? You did what?" His eyebrows lift, and then he frowns as I push my skirt over my hips. "Oh, really? I'm glad to hear you wore a helmet. Yeah. She's actually here with me right now. Of course you can talk to her."

Dax holds out the phone, exhaling a deep breath as I take it from him. "Hey, Em, are you having fun this weekend?"

She tells me all about her zip-lining experience, and says they're going to see a movie later and that some boy named Clark has already asked if she'll hang out with him at the dance.

"How about you? Are you having fun?" Emme asks.

"It's a pretty boring conference." Dax rests his forehead on my knee and I run my fingers through his hair. "But at least I have Dax to keep me company."

"Yeah. He's fun sometimes. Okay, well, I should probably go, we're going out for lunch soon. Marnie's mom wants to talk to Dax for a minute. Will I see you soon?"

"Definitely, we'll make a plan."

"Awesome."

I pass the phone back to Dax, and he okays whatever plans they have before he ends the call and tosses the phone on the coffee table. "Is it bad that I'm enjoying not being a parent this weekend?"

I give him a sympathetic, reassuring smile. "It makes you human. You're allowed to miss your freedom, especially when it was taken from you so unexpectedly."

"That's exactly it, isn't it? It's a lot of responsibility, and the people who would normally help me through it are gone."

"You're handling it well."

"I don't want to talk about this right now. I only have another twenty-four hours with no responsibilities to get in the way." He picks me up and carries me to the bed, his mouth on mine, hard and demanding this time. The sex is the same.

Half an hour later I'm stretched out along Dax's side, one leg thrown over his, while his fingers trail gently up and down my arm. His phone rings from across the room and he sighs heavily.

"I can check to see who it is, if you want." I push up and roll off the bed, not waiting for his reply. We can't ignore phone calls when someone else is in charge of Emme's care.

The caller ID comes up as his work. "It's someone from your firm. Do you want to take it?"

"Yeah. I probably should."

I rush the phone over and he answers before it goes to voicemail. It's already four in the afternoon, we've missed the panel we were planning to attend, and I'm sure the opportunity for drinks with former classmates has passed. Dinner is in a couple of hours, and it might be good to go down to the hotel bar and be social for a while, even if the idea isn't all that appealing. And I don't want that gorgeous dress to go to waste.

Before I have a chance to make a move, Dax sits up and

grabs my wrist. At my questioning look he shakes his head and presses the phone to his chest. "Don't get dressed yet," he whispers.

I climb back up on the bed, still naked just like he is. The conversation lasts about ten minutes, during which time I grab his laptop so he can make notes about a case he needs to follow up on when he's in the office on Monday.

"Sorry about that," he says after he ends the call, tossing his phone on the nightstand. He closes the laptop and moves it as well. "I don't know what the point of that was. It could've waited until Monday."

"Is everything okay?"

"Yeah. Freeman is still getting used to the fact that I can't work ninety hours a week. He forgets that people have lives on the weekend and we don't all work twenty-four hours a day seven days a week."

I swallow down the lump in my throat. "Have you given any more thought to the possibility of switching firms?"

"It's starting to look a lot more desirable. I can't keep these hours up, and my priorities have changed. As much as I want partner, I think you're right about waiting on that, at least until Emme's more settled and so am I. And money isn't a driving force like it used to be."

"Well, I'm sure the salary would be comparable at Whitman. I think you have to do whatever is going to make life easier."

"It's obviously an excellent firm, since Beverly was smart

enough to snatch you up right out of law school." He grabs me by the waist and rolls on top of me, fitting himself between my thighs. "I'd get to see you every day if I switched to your firm, wouldn't I?"

"You would."

"I think I'd like that, a lot. But the pencil skirt uniform might create some embarrassing problems."

⌒

Dax drops me off at my place in the early afternoon on Sunday. He invites me for dinner but I blew off Holly this morning for our standing brunch date, so I'm making up for it with an early dinner. I also need an Epsom salt bath and a little space after such an intense weekend.

I squeeze in a short bath before I pick Holly up and drive us to the market. My thighs are tight, my calves ache, and even the arches of my feet are sore, possibly from all the toe curling.

"How was the conference?" Holly asks as we grab coffees and stroll along the promenade. The funky little shops remind me of my mom. When I was young we'd come to the market, or hit all the garage sales on the weekend in search of hidden treasures. My house is an eclectic mix of art pieces scavenged from various sales over the years. None of my plates and cups match, because they're more of the same, items purchased during adventures with Holly or my parents. My house is where I let my nostalgia hang out. Although I do keep useful memorabilia at work in the form of mugs.

"It was good. I ran into a few old classmates, caught up a bit."

"And how was Daxton?" Holly isn't much of one for beating around the bush, and I already told her he was going to be there. Until now I haven't mentioned the progression from enemies to friends to lovers, but I can't keep this to myself anymore.

"Kailyn?" she prompts when I don't answer right away. "What's going on between you two?"

"We slept together."

She comes to a halt in the middle of the street. "I'm sorry, can you repeat that? I swear you said you slept with him, but I must've heard that incorrectly."

A few people glance our way. "Keep it down!"

"None of these people know you, and I'm sure most of them would applaud you for sleeping with a hot former actor." Holly threads her arm through mine and leads me away from the thick crowd, down a side street. "I don't know what to say. Is this like a cathartic hate fuck, or what?"

"Uhh...I think it falls more into the 'or what' category."

Holly gives me a pensive look before she asks, "Is he any good?"

"Are sloths slow?"

"Want to rate him for me? Like on a scale of Jason Momoa to Ryan Reynolds, where would he be?"

"I had multiple orgasms."

She stops and grabs me by the shoulders, eyes wide. "No."

"Multiple orgasms, multiple times."

Holly hugs me. "My God. You need to keep him forever."

I laugh, but my stomach drops, because I have no idea where this thing is going with us, not just with Dax, but with everything surrounding him.

Holly steps back. "I need to know more, and I think we need alcohol."

Dax and I were like college kids with the sex and the drinking this weekend, but I might need a little something to calm my nerves. Confiding in Holly is necessary, but it also means I have to face the truth, and I'm not sure I'll like it.

We find a little pub and hole ourselves up in the back corner.

"So multiple multiples, huh?" Holly asks after we've ordered drinks and appetizers.

"Yup." I fiddle with my napkin, the flush in my cheeks echoed in other parts of my body.

"Is he like—" She makes some hand motions and I realize she's asking about size.

"Everything is very proportional."

"Nice."

The server drops off our drinks, and Holly waits until she's gone before she raises her glass. "To multiple multiples and being proportional."

I clink my glass against hers and chuckle. My phone buzzes on the table. It's Emme. "I need to check this."

It's a few pictures from the weekend. The last one is a selfie of Emme making a ridiculous face, thumbing over her shoulder. In the background is Dax, head tipped back, mouth hanging open, fast asleep on the couch. I message back that I'm out with a friend and that she should probably let her brother sleep.

"Sorry about that." I slip my phone into my purse.

Holly regards me with wary curiosity. "So apart from sleeping together this weekend, what's going on with you and Dax? Is this just a casual thing?"

I focus on my drink. "I don't know."

"Aren't you trying to get him to come over to your firm? How are you going to sleep with him and work with him?"

I bite my thumbnail. The nagging worries I've been hiding from since this entire thing started with Dax envelop me like a cold fog. "I haven't really figured that out yet."

"Well, don't you think you should?" Her voice is laced with concern. "What're you doing?"

"It just happened." I can't believe I just said those words to my childhood best friend.

She leans back in her chair and crosses her arms over her chest. "Oh no. Things don't *just* happen with you. You can't tell me you haven't thought about all of the potential repercussions before you fell into bed with him. Is it unethical for you to be sleeping with him?"

"Technically, no, since Dax isn't my client. I'm sleeping

with my client's brother, so maybe it's morally ambiguous, but it's not unethical."

"Is there a *but* in there somewhere that I missed?"

"There's no *but*. I just didn't expect to feel this way about him," I admit.

"And how do you feel about him?"

"I like him."

I get another raised eyebrow from her. "You like him?"

"A lot."

Holly sighs. "Do you mean you like the nostalgia of your teen crush?"

"The crush died at the end of law school. This isn't based on the past, Holls. I like him, who he is as a person, the things that make him who he is, the guy who calls me up on a Friday night for Aisle of Red advice and then walks around with a box of incontinence products because he doesn't know any better. The guy who sends me flowers and funky pens because he knows I like them. He's different."

Our appetizers arrive and we once again wait for the server to leave before we resume the conversation.

"I know it's a complicated situation," I admit.

"Does his sister know there's something going on between you two?"

I shake my head. "Of course not."

"So she thinks you're friends? Kailyn, this isn't just about liking some guy who's good in the sack. He comes with baggage, the heavy kind."

"I know that."

"He's suffered a huge trauma. You can't walk into this without weighing all of the consequences."

"I know that, too."

"Do you? Because it doesn't seem like you're considering very carefully what the fallout of this could be. Are you prepared to be a mother to a thirteen-year-old? Because that's exactly what you're signing on for with this."

Each point she makes feels like a stab of reality I don't want to acknowledge. "I can't replace Emme's mother."

"No, you can't, but she's going to be looking for someone to fill that role, and that's exactly what you'll be to her by getting involved with Dax. You're not even thirty, and you'll be taking on an orphaned teenager. It's not an easy road. You know this, Kay."

"Believe me, I get it better than anyone else. It's why we're keeping it just between me and Dax for now."

"Come on, Kay. It goes way beyond that, doesn't it? How long is the secrecy going to last? I get that you like this guy, but he's grieving, too. I'm worried about who's going to end up hurt in all of this. Does he even know why you're pushing to get him to come to your firm? How's he going to feel if he makes the switch and all of a sudden you make partner?"

I press my fingers to my lips, my panic turning into real fear. "I don't know if that's what I want anymore."

"I think you need to figure that out. More than one person's heart could end up broken here. Dax needs support, and

I'm concerned you're caught up in being his savoir. And if you end up working together, too, it adds another layer of complication."

I know all of this. I knew it before I spent the weekend with him, but hearing it from someone else makes it so much more real. And it's the reason I haven't said anything until now.

"It's the first time I've really connected with another person in a long time. It feels good to be needed by someone, to take care of someone else emotionally and feel like I'm being taken care of, too. Does that make any sense at all?"

"Of course it does. You took care of your mom when she was sick, you took care of your dad after she passed, and then he died, too, and you've put everything into being the best trust lawyer in the state. Maybe you want to save other families from struggling financially like you have when there's already emotional turmoil. And now you're taking on these pro bono custody cases for me. The security thing makes sense, and Dax...he's suffering and you're familiar with what that looks and feels like. He also represents so many good things from your childhood that you want to hold on to."

I rub my temples. "Are you going to charge me a hundred and fifty dollars for this session?"

"You can just get lunch." Holly laughs but reaches across the table and covers my hand with hers. "Am I wrong?"

I consider all the connections she's made and how I've started to put them together recently, too. Making partner has been the goal since my dad passed, a place to focus all my energy, but in doing that I've neglected forming new attachments and relationships, at least the kind that can end up hurting me, until now. "You're not wrong. But it's not just being a savior, or holding on to good things from my childhood. I care about Dax. And Emme."

Holly takes a different approach. "Okay, so what if things were different. What if making partner wasn't this thing you felt you needed to do? Would you still be working on trusts? What about family law? Would that be something you'd want to do beyond personal favors for me?"

"I consult for you because I want to, it's not just personal favors."

"But would you want to do it as a job?"

Five years ago I would've said no, definitely not. The grief of losing my mother lingered, and then after my dad passed, the idea of working on pro bono cases was untenable because I couldn't afford to. But now it's different. I have other things in my life to help ease those losses, and two of them are a very recent addition.

"Maybe?" I run my finger around the rim of my glass.

"Something to consider, isn't it? That way you could do what you love and have what you want, too."

It sounds so simple, but I know it's not.

chapter eighteen

THE BIRDS AND THE BEES

Dax

The week following the alumni conference is busy, and Kailyn and I don't have much of an opportunity for alone time. I pick her up for dinner one night—she's practically on the way home—but Emme monopolizes her for the most part. On the upside, picking her up means I also get to drive Kailyn home. We have frantic, intense sex in the middle of her front entryway, Kailyn pressed up against the wall, both of us mostly dressed.

It isn't until we're both sated and sweaty that I notice the hallway is lined with family photos chronicling her life with her mom and dad from childhood to college kid. She's incredibly sentimental. And her cats are clearly very reliant on her based on the way they rub themselves all over her ankles as I kiss her goodbye.

Tonight, Kailyn's taking Emme out for girl time. Apparently, going to a dance means Emme needs her nails done and stuff. It gives me the opportunity to spend some time with my friends, which I admittedly haven't done much of lately, too caught up in my sister and Kailyn.

I follow Felix's Porsche to a bar close to the office and we settle in, waiting for the rest of the guys to arrive. "So you and Fangirl, huh?"

"Don't call her that."

He gives me an arched brow. "She's out with Emme tonight?"

"They're getting their nails done, I think. Kailyn said it was girl stuff and I wasn't invited, which is fine by me." I relax in my chair. It's nice to be able to hang out after work and not worry about picking someone up for one lesson or another, or about making dinner that a thirteen-year-old won't turn her nose up at. I've mastered spaghetti and grilled cheese, and that's about it so far.

"So what exactly is going on there? She's a little stiff, yeah?"

I flip him the bird. "She's not stiff. You were a dick to her in school and she has a good memory. She also gets what I'm going through and she's good with Emme."

He frowns. "So that's what this is about? You two are friends and she's, what, like a stand-in mom?"

"It's not like that."

"Then what's it like? You were together the entire alumni weekend. You gotta be banging her, right? She not really your usual type."

"I don't have a usual type." I avoid the other question. Besides, I'm not banging Kailyn. I like Kailyn. Actually, I more than like her.

"If you say so."

A tall, leggy blonde with wide eyes and a smile to match sashays over, holding a pair of shots. "I'm sooooo sorry, but you're Daxton Hughes, right?"

I bite back a sigh and plaster a smile on my face. It's an automatic response, one I learned from acting and photo ops. The last thing I want is for someone to catch me mid–eye roll with a fan. I just want to have a conversation with my friend and not be hounded. I've gotten a lot more attention than usual since my parents passed. I thought I was over that, but the entire alumni conference showed me very clearly that's not the case. Thank God Kailyn was there to make it easier.

"That would be me."

She screeches and does a little excited dance. "I knew it! I brought you a shot! Can I get a selfie with you? My friends aren't going to believe I met you if I don't."

"Yeah, sure, we can take a picture." Hopefully she'll go away after that.

I shift to the edge of the booth so she doesn't get any ideas about climbing in with me. She takes about five thousand selfies in the span of thirty seconds, all of them complete with that duck lip thing girls do. Once she's done and decided she has at least fifty photos she likes, she hugs me, and I'm pretty sure she sniffs me. "Thank you!" She steps back and flails a little. "Oh! Let's do the shots!"

"Thanks, that's really nice of you, but I have to drive later." The last thing I want is to be roofied by a crazy fangirl. I smile, thinking about Kailyn's reaction when I tell her about this.

"You'll be fine after one shot." She gives me an exaggerated pout.

"My buddy here likes shots." I nod to Felix.

"Oh, hi!" She extends a hand. "Are you an actor, too? I don't recognize you from TV."

He shoots a look my way before he takes it. "I'm a lawyer."

She makes a face. "Oh. Well, wanna do a shot with me anyway?"

Thankfully the rest of the guys show up and displace my new friend. I slide over, making room for them in the booth and putting distance between me and the fangirl. She disappears eventually and we talk sports and eat wings while we watch the game on the big screen behind the bar.

It's loud, and the game isn't particularly exciting, so I check my phone. I have social media alerts, and new messages from both Kailyn and Emme. I check the messages first to make sure everything is okay. They've sent pictures of their painted toes and fingernails. Emme's are dark sparkly purple with little jewels or something stuck to the tip. I hope like hell she doesn't think this is going to become a regular thing.

Kailyn has a French manicure.

I send her a private message meant for her eyes only.

Dax: You know what those pretty fingers would look great wrapped around?

She responds with an eggplant emoji.

Dax: I was going to say a glass of wine, but that works, too.
Kailyn: Lies ;) Hope you're having fun.

More alerts come through for my social media so I check that, too, annoyed the fangirl has already posted the selfies she took on every single social media outlet she seems to have an account for, and of course I'm tagged in all of them. I untag myself where I can. It's not like this hasn't happened a million times before; it's just been a few years since it's been an issue.

I get home to find Kailyn and Emme sitting on the couch, heads nearly touching as they peer at my sister's phone. There's a mostly eaten bowl of Sour Patch Kids on the table, a treat I've started stocking up on since both Kailyn and Emme love them. "What's going on over there?"

"Nothing!" Emme shoves her phone in her pocket and giggles, giving Kailyn a look I can't decipher.

"We were just talking about the dance." Kailyn's smile tells me there's more to the conversation, but I'm not going to hear about it.

Emme whispers something to Kailyn and she raises her brow. "You'll have to ask him."

Emme gives her puppy dog eyes, the kind that make me fold all the damn time, but when Kailyn doesn't relent, Emme sighs and crosses her legs, knees bouncing as she looks to me. "So Ainsley Baker is having a sleepover after the dance."

"Okay." I wait for the rest.

"And I've been invited."

"Is Ainsley a girl?" It's a fairly androgynous name.

"Oh my gosh!" Emme flings her hands in the air and gives Kailyn her *seriously?* face.

"It's a legitimate question, Emme. It's both a girl and a boy name."

"I wouldn't ask to sleep over at a boy's house! Yes. Ainsley is a girl."

"How many friends will be at this sleepover?"

"Um, I think there are three of us, plus Ainsley."

"Her parents will be there?"

Emme nods fervently and glances at Kailyn.

"Why don't you give Dax her mom's number so he can call and get the details?"

"Oh yeah! I have that. Hold on." Emme pulls out her phone, and a few seconds later mine pings. "So can I go? Marnie is going and her parents already said yes."

I trust it's safe if Marnie's parents have already said yes, but I still want to make sure. "Let me call and get the details. I think as long as it's supervised and there are no older brothers, we should be fine."

"Ainsley is an only child."

"I still want to call."

"Can you do that now?"

"It's almost ten. I'll call tomorrow."

"In the morning? Her mom works from home."

"In the morning."

"Okay." She looks between me and Kailyn. "Well, I'm tired and I have to be up early, so I'm going to bed. Thanks for taking me out tonight, Kailyn, I had a great time!" She gives her a hug and then flits upstairs.

"She had fun?" I stay where I am until her door closes. It's a little less slam these days.

"We both did. You didn't have to pick up the tab for that, you know. I offered to take her. I was more than happy to pay for the nails and dinner."

"Taking care of my girls is the least I can do." I tip my chin up. "Let me see those pretty nails of yours."

She lifts her hands and vogues them in front of her face, smiling. She's wearing a pair of royal-blue skinny jeans and a very worn *It's My Life* T-shirt. Based on the way it fits, I'd say she's probably had it since high school and wearing it tonight was purposeful.

She looks gorgeous, and I haven't been inside her for more than five minutes in almost a week, which feels closer to forever. I stand in front of her and straddle her knees, leaning down so I can steal a kiss. It starts out chaste, but I've been thinking about her hand wrapped around my cock since she sent that eggplant emoji, so it escalates quickly.

"Dax," she mumbles around my tongue and pushes on my chest.

I back off a little. "Wanna come up to my room for a while?"

She glances at the stairs. "I don't know if that's such a good idea."

"She said she's going to bed."

Kailyn drags her nails down the back of my neck. "I think she suspects there's more going on here. We have to be careful. I don't want to set anyone up to get hurt here."

"I just want to get my hands on you."

She smirks. "I think it has more to do with getting my hands on you."

"That, too."

Emme's door closes again and I take a few steps back, bumping into the coffee table. I rearrange my hard-on so it's not obvious and make sure my shirt is covering the problem before I turn around. Emme appears at the top of the stairs. Her expectant grin falls a little.

"What's up? You need something?"

"Oh. Uh, I forgot to give you my phone!"

She rushes down, holding it out. "I already put it on Do Not Disturb so it won't beep."

"Thanks, kiddo."

"'Kay, night!" And up the stairs she goes again.

It's something she has to do every night, pass over her phone until the morning. Otherwise I'm sure there would be text messages coming at all hours. Usually I have to go up and knock to get it from her. I sigh at Kailyn's *I told you so* expression.

"When am I going to get some alone time with you?" I sound whiny. I'm hard and I have some fantasies in my head that I'd like fulfilled courtesy of Kailyn.

"This weekend, apparently, as long as you feel comfortable with Emme having a sleepover."

"That's days away."

Kailyn licks her lips, and the hint of a smile appears. "Didn't you say you had all sorts of memorabilia in the basement?"

For half a second I don't understand what the hell *It's My Life* memorabilia has to do with my hard-on. It just goes to show how single minded I am at the moment.

She stands up and does this little excited jumpy thing. It's fucking adorable. "Why don't you show me what you got?"

Half an hour later—okay, it's more like twenty minutes...fine, seventeen, but she came, too—she traipses up the stairs carrying an armload of *It's My Life* crap, and I'm a much more relaxed man.

❧

It's sleepover-dance night. My sheets are clean. I'm groomed, on my face and below the belt—and I'm stocked with condoms. I plan to get little in the way of sleep and lots in the way of Kailyn naked.

"Time to go, kiddo!" I call down the hall. It's already six thirty. The dance starts at seven and I've offered to drive. It's my way of sussing out the girls Emme will be spending the night with. I did the legwork, spoke to the parents, gave them my contact information, and went through the list of questions Kailyn sent me. There were many.

Everything should be good. Emme is excited and I get a night with Kailyn. It's a win for everyone.

"Okay! I'm ready!" Emme bounds down the stairs two at a time, backpack and overnight bag slung over her shoulder.

I do a double take. "Are you wearing makeup?"

Her cheeks flush, or maybe it's blush, I have no idea. "Just a little."

"Right." If she were auditioning to be a Kiss groupie, then maybe I'd say just a little, but Emme hasn't ever really worn makeup before, so it seems like a lot. Her eyes are rimmed with black liner and I'm pretty sure she's wearing mascara. And lipstick.

"Do I look okay?" she asks, suddenly self-conscious.

Her hair is perfectly straight and she's wearing a pair of patterned leggings, a poufy black skirt, and an off-the-shoulder shirt that shows an inch or two of midriff. I want to make her go back upstairs and change. "You look great!" I choke out. "Can I take a picture and send it to Kailyn?"

She waves me off. "I already sent her a selfie. She said I looked great, but she's a girl and she either dresses really formal but, like, pretty, but business-y, or she wears funky jeans and shirts from your show, so I wanted to make sure." She blows out a breath. "Can we go? I told the girls we'd be there before seven and we're kinda cutting it close, right?" She says this like it's my fault. I've been ready for the past fifteen minutes.

As soon as we're in the car, her phone starts going off. Boys' names flash across her screen: Clark, Liam, Jimmy.

I need to have the boy talk with my little sister. I remember being in eighth grade, not quite sure what to do with my hormones yet, or girls, but still a little interested. "What's going on there?"

Emme flips her phone over in her lap. "Oh, nothing."

"You have boys texting you now?"

She sighs, as if she's annoyed. "They all want to dance with me or something. I don't know, it's dumb. They stand on the other side of the gym and, like, wait for us to ask 'cause they're all too chicken or whatever."

"I just want to make sure you know that you can say no. Boys your age aren't very mature, and sometimes they might do things that make you uncomfortable—"

"Oh my God, Dax! You are not trying to have the sex talk with me, are you?"

"You're too young to have sex."

"Um, ew. I know! Look, you can save us both the awkwardness. I already know all the technical stuff from the human anatomy and health class, and Kailyn and I have already talked all about this stuff."

"Kailyn talked to you about sex?" When the hell did

that happen, and why didn't she ever say anything about it to me?

"Not like details or anything, just, like, the basics and how it's my body and it's special. Or something like that. She said it a lot better." Emme's cheeks are flaming and her eyes are on her lap.

I guess I'll have to thank Kailyn for having the conversation with her. "Huh" is my stellar reply.

"Anyway, you don't have to freak out, or worry, or anything. I'm not interested in, like, dating or anything. I've already had my first kiss and it was gross."

"You what?" I can almost feel hairs turning gray.

"It was at the beginning of the school year. Chris Becker asked me to go steady and I said yes even though I wasn't so sure I liked him like that. But then he kissed me and I was like no way 'cause he tried to put his tongue in my mouth."

I'm white knuckling the steering wheel, and I have to clear my throat before I ask the next question. "What did you do?"

"I pushed him and he fell into a mud puddle. I told him not to talk to me anymore. Boys are weird."

"Yes they are. I hope you feel like that about them until you're at least twenty-five."

"We're down from thirty, so that's an improvement," Emme mutters snarkily.

I have a feeling the next few years might give me an ulcer if this is just the beginning. I pull into the driveway of her friend's house. It's a nice place in a good neighborhood—I looked it up in advance.

There's a flurry of activity at the front door. Emme gets dragged upstairs to get rid of her bag but her backpack stays at the front door—I'm assuming makeup and hair stuff is in there. Lord knows she checked her reflection a million times on the way here. Her friends giggle and titter near the door, and Ainsley's mom, Adele, fawns over me in a slightly awkward way.

Ten minutes later I'm in a car with four very loud girls who smell like they took a swim in a lake of cheap perfume. Emme blasts the music in the front seat and they all try to scream over it to hear each other. When the chorus comes on, they sing together completely out of tune, except Emme—her voice is eerily on key. I have no idea how teachers manage a whole class full of this.

I pull up to the school and the girls' tittering grows louder. "Oh my God, Emme, look, Liam is waiting for you! Who's with him? Oh! Oh! That's Clark and Jackson and River."

"Who the hell named these kids?" I mutter.

"Your name is Daxton," Emme points out.

"But River? After the dead actor?"

"Who?" Emme asks. When I open my mouth to explain, she waves her hand around. "It doesn't matter. Okay! Thanks for the ride. I'll see you tomorrow!"

"Thanks for the ride, Mr. Hughes!" comes from the back seat as the doors open and the girls all pile out of the car.

Mr. Hughes? What the hell? The gaggle of girls meet up with the group of boys. They stand awkwardly with their hands shoved in their pockets, the girls looking over their shoulder at my car before they head into the school. I remind myself that it's a school dance, chaperoned by teachers, and nothing bad can happen.

I call Kailyn on speakerphone to let her know I'm on the way to pick her up.

"How was dance drop-off?"

"I have no idea how fathers do this. Between the makeup, the screeching, the perfume, and the boys, I'm surprised any parent survives this. And did you know Emme's already had her first kiss?"

Kailyn laughs. "You were probably the same age when you had your first kiss."

"My first kiss was on a set in front of a camera crew, and it was not awesome. My costar had just finished eating a Big Mac and didn't think brushing her teeth was necessary after extra onions." I slap the steering wheel. "That's what I should've done! I should've fed Emme garlic and onions for dinner."

"It'll be fine. It's a school dance. There's nowhere for them to hide and make out."

"I hope not, or I'm going to spend a few years in prison. Oh, and thanks for letting me know you'd had the sex talk with Emme."

"I told her she was special and all of her firsts should be with someone who cares about her."

"Oh, well, that was a lot better than what I would've said, and it's a little disturbing that you've already had that talk with her and she's only in eighth grade."

"There are a couple of girls in her class who have had sex already."

"Please don't tell me things like this when I've just left her in a gym full of hormonal boys."

"She's not interested. You're safe. For now."

"I hope you're right."

"I am. I'll have a beer waiting for you when you get here to offset the anxiety." I can hear the smile in her voice.

"I might need something stronger."

"I'll see what I can do."

Less than ten minutes later I pull into Kailyn's driveway. It's not too far from my place, but in a more modest subdivision. She lives in a bungalow with pretty flowers lining the front walk. Everything is neat and well maintained, as I'd expect from her. Her cats eye me suspiciously from the windowsill inside the house.

The anxiety over Emme and the dance is forgotten as soon as the door swings open. Kailyn is wearing a very sexy royal-blue dress that hugs every single one of her very lush, very hot curves. She's barefoot on the hardwood floor. She holds out a wineglass. "Sadly wine is the strongest thing I have."

"This right here is the ultimate in archaically sexist male fantasies." What I wouldn't give to be greeted every damn day of my life by this exact sight.

"I'm sorry?"

"Nothing. Thank you. You look incredible and I care about you and I think you're very special." I pluck the glass from her hand and set it on the side table so her hands are free and I can kiss her. "I also think it would be a very good idea to call the restaurant and push our reservation back so I can show you exactly how special I think you are."

Kailyn grins against my lips. "Don't think you can manage making it through dinner before you see what kind of panties I'm wearing?"

"Are they cheekies?"

She laces her fingers through mine. "Why don't you come upstairs and find out."

chapter nineteen

DINNER DATE DISASTER

Kailyn

Dax does a very thorough job of showing me exactly how special he thinks I am. We don't leave for the restaurant until almost nine. My hair is a little wild from his hands having been in it, but he's much more relaxed and I'm feeling pretty damn fantastic myself.

He takes me to a lovely, very exclusive restaurant that I would never be able to afford. We talk about my pro bono case and how excited I am that it looks like this little boy will have a permanent home soon. I love Dax's attentiveness and enthusiasm for the things I'm passionate about. He makes me feel like I'm the only person in the room when we're together like this. Despite the attention he sometimes gets, I never have to fight for his. As difficult as the road ahead of us may be, I can see a future unfolding with him.

We're halfway through our meal when he gets a call from Ainsley's mother. I assume it's to let him know they're home from the dance. At least until his expression becomes incredulous.

"They got caught with *what*? Where did they get it? Emme? Are you sure? We're on our way. No. No. I'm so sorry. We'll be there as soon as we can."

He throws his napkin on the table and shoves his chair back.

"What's wrong? Did something happen?"

"They got caught with alcohol at the dance."

"The girls?"

"Yes. We have to go. I need to settle the tab."

I put a hand on his arm. "You get the car, I'll settle the tab."

His phone rings again; this time it's the school. He purses his lips and nods, bringing the phone to his ear as he heads for the door. I quickly pay the bill, leaving our half-eaten dinner at the table, and meet him in front of the restaurant. If I hadn't been on my second glass of wine, I would offer to drive. I check my phone and find the school has also called me.

Dax grips the steering wheel. "I can't believe this. How is this happening? How the hell did I miss this?"

"What happened? Where did the girls get alcohol from in the first place?"

"All I know so far is that they found a bottle of vodka in Emme's backpack."

"That doesn't sound like something she would do."

Dax runs an anxious hand through his hair. "Where would she even get a bottle of vodka?"

"Do you have a liquor cabinet at home?"

"Yeah, but she doesn't go in it. At least I didn't think she did. Now I have to wonder what else I don't know." He hits the brakes when the light turns red and slams his palm against the steering wheel. "Fuck."

"I'm sure there's a reasonable explanation." I put a hand on his forearm but he shakes me off.

"What kind of reasonable explanation can she possibly have for stealing a bottle of vodka?"

"I don't know, Dax, but you need to calm down before you go in there. Otherwise it could make the problem a whole lot bigger."

He doesn't respond, just grips the steering wheel tighter. I don't want to interfere, but going in elevated isn't a good way to manage what will be a sensitive situation. He pulls into the parking lot and screeches into an empty space.

Before he can get out of the car, I curve my palm around the back of his neck. "Dax."

His jaw clenches but he turns his frustrated gaze on me. Dax has never been silent, and I don't like not knowing where he's gone in his head.

"I need you to take a breath. Emme is a good kid going through a rough time. You're a good brother learning how to be a dad. Find out all the facts before you react to the few you know."

He closes his eyes and exhales a slow breath. "I'm trying, Kailyn."

"I know you are."

"All I wanted was a night to be me."

There's so much more in that single admission. His guilt over wanting that time fills the space around him, and I'm certain he's already blaming himself for what's happened. "I'm sorry you couldn't have that."

His phone buzzes again. "I need to go in there and find out what's going on."

"I can come with you, if you want."

He nods and I look away, hiding my relief. I want to be there in case he loses his cool, which seems likely based on how edgy he is. We enter the school through the front doors. The lot is mostly empty and the school is fairly dark, apart from the front foyer.

We head for the office. A group of adults mill around the front desk, including a set of police officers, while four girls sit in the chairs, none of them talking.

"Dad!" Emme shoots up out of her chair and rushes over to Dax. Surprise registers when she realizes I'm with him. Her eyes are red rimmed and puffy, the makeup she put on while we were on video chat smudged.

She throws her arms around him and for a moment he just stands there, frozen. And then I realize why: She called him Dad, not Dax. It's an easy slip, especially in a state of duress. He hugs her back, his face tight and ashen.

"You're finally here. What took you so long, Daxton?" His aunt Linda steps out from behind one of the police officers. While I haven't seen her since the last school-related incident,

I still receive weekly emails inquiring about the safety of the trust and whether the funds are being allocated properly. We're still waiting on a date for the custody hearing, hoping Linda's going to drop it, although it seems unlikely at this point.

"I came as soon as I was called, which was only twenty minutes ago."

"You live minutes from the school," she points out.

He motions to his dress pants and tie. "I was out for dinner, not that it's any of your business. Why are you here?"

Linda presses her hand to her chest. "I volunteered to supervise the dance, and when they couldn't reach you at home, they asked me to step in."

"Let's go into my office where we can discuss the issue in private." Mr. Proctor motions to his open door.

There's a murmur of agreement and we file into the office. It feels claustrophobic with the solemn police officers and so many people stuffed into the room.

"Why don't you have a seat, Mr. Hughes." Mr. Proctor offers.

"I'm good standing, thanks."

I put a hand on his arm, a silent warning to keep his cool before I take a seat next to Emme. Dax stands behind her, a reassuring hand on her shoulder.

"I'd like an explanation for what's happened here," Dax says.

According to the principal, Linda was on door duty and noticed the girls going back and forth to the bathroom a number of times. Emme's locker is near the girls' bathroom and there's no locker access during the dance, which makes sense, but Emme went to hers twice, so they performed a locker search. "And this is what we found."

The principal withdraws a half-empty bottle of Grey Goose—expensive for thirteen-year-olds—from the backpack on his desk.

"I didn't steal that, Dax, and Ainsley and Marnie and Sasha said they don't know anything about it, either," Emme says.

Linda sighs from her seat next to the principal. "How did it get in your locker, then? Are you passing out your combination to your friends? You know we've talked about that."

"I didn't give my combination to anyone! I swear, Dax. I don't know how it got in my locker! I just went in there to get . . . girl stuff," Emme mumbles, cheeks turning red.

"Girl stuff?" Dax seems confused.

"Sasha got her period and didn't have anything with her. I wasn't trying to make trouble, I swear."

"It still doesn't explain how the alcohol got in your locker, Emme," Linda says.

"Does this bottle look familiar to you?" The principal gestures to the Grey Goose, looking tired and frustrated.

"I don't know. Maybe?" Dax runs a hand through his hair, faltering as he looks between Linda, Emme, and the bottle.

I silently will him to stop being Dax the brother/father and be Dax the lawyer, who would never incriminate himself this way.

"Do you keep alcohol in the house?" Linda asks.

"What kind of question is that? I'm an adult. I can drink responsibly."

"What about Emme? Do you let her drink at home?"

"What?"

She arches a knowing brow. "She might have mentioned that you let her try your beer, and that sometimes she's allowed to have wine at dinner."

Betrayal flashes across Dax's face and he looks to Emme. "A sip, not a glass, which has nothing to do with this."

"Maybe it does. It's possible your permissive parenting has led to this situation, Daxton."

"Permissive parenting?" His voice rises, and the officers observing from the corner straighten and frown. "Who the hell are you to talk? You have two kids who live on the other side of the country because they couldn't get away from you fast enough. And didn't Samantha get pregnant before she was even done with high school? Before you start dissecting my parenting skills, you might want to take a look at your own."

"Mr. Hughes, please lower your voice."

Dax turns his angry glare on the principal. "My sister is being accused of bringing alcohol to a dance and she said it wasn't hers, so I'd like to know how the hell it got there."

"Emme, could you please take a seat in the waiting room?" Mr. Proctor's smile is tight.

"Yes, sir," she mumbles. Her wide, scared eyes find mine before she leaves the office.

I put a hand on Dax's arm and nod to the seat next to me.

He gives me an unreadable look, but drops down beside me, knee bouncing with agitation.

"Mr. Hughes, I know things have been difficult for Emme, and I'm sure they've been equally difficult for you, but this isn't the first time we've had problems with Emme since she lost her parents. I realize she may be acting out, but the facts remain that the bottle was found in *her* backpack in *her* locker. It's difficult to argue with hard evidence."

"You may want to consider the impression drinking in front of Emme has on her, and how offering her alcohol may normalize it for her," Linda offers.

"What exactly are you trying to say, Linda?"

"I'm sure this new responsibility is stressful for you. You might want to look at exactly how much you're drinking." She cocks her head to the side. "Have you been drinking tonight? Is it even safe for Emme to ride home with you?"

Dax grips the arms of the chair as if he's about to push out of it. "Are you kidding me?"

I slip my fingers between his, hoping to help keep him in check. I've never seen Dax go off, but I have a feeling that if he's pushed much further, he will. "Dax had a single glass of wine with dinner. He's perfectly capable of driving. As for the bottle of vodka, he'll clearly talk to Emme about the origins. I think needling Dax is unnecessary, and it would be more helpful to discuss the consequences of Emme's actions. We have officers present, and I'm curious as to their role here."

"We're here to mediate, ma'am."

"Mediate?"

"Ms. Thrasher indicated there might be some hostility over her presence."

And of course Dax walked right into that trap.

His fingers clench around mine and I squeeze back, a silent message to keep his temper on lockdown.

"Well, based on the accusations here, I think there might be some legitimacy to that hostility." I motion to the people in the room. "Can we discuss the consequences for possession of alcohol?"

"She's facing a three-day suspension minimum."

"And there's an appeal process?" I ask.

"Yes, of course, but—"

I cut the principal off midsentence. "As the conservator, I speak for Emme, so I'd like to request that you forward that information to me and Daxton. In the meantime we'll take Emme home and see if we can't get to the bottom of this on our own."

"Is Daxton fit to drive? Are you?" Linda spits out.

"As I said, Daxton had one glass of wine with dinner." I am concerned about how agitated he is, though.

"Maybe a Breathalyzer test would be advisable, considering the circumstances." Linda looks to the officers with wide, imploring eyes. "I only want to keep Emme safe."

Daxton barks out a humorless laugh. "Of course you do." He looks to the officers. "Since Emme's safety is always my top priority, I'll gladly take a Breathalyzer test."

I'm relieved he doesn't put up a fight, and we follow the officers, with Emme in tow, to the police car. Dax passes the test. While they're at it, they test Emme as well, twice. It appears she hasn't consumed any alcohol, but it still doesn't explain where the vodka came from. Dax is fuming as we cross the parking lot, the situation having pushed him to the edge.

"Are you calm enough to drive?" I ask when we reach the car.

"I'm fine," he says through gritted teeth.

I open the door and slide the seat forward—Dax drove the Audi tonight, the non-family-friendly vehicle. Emme gives me an imploring, tearful look as she gets in.

"I'll sit in the back with Emme."

Dax wears an impassive expression as I awkwardly fold myself into the back seat, then closes the door.

"I really didn't steal the vodka. I don't even like the way it smells, Kailyn," Emme murmurs through her tears.

"We'll get it figured out." I squeeze her hand in reassurance, wanting to provide whatever comfort I can.

Dax climbs into the front seat, eyes flicking to the rearview mirror as he buckles himself in and starts the car. I note the nearly imperceptible shake in his hands as he grips the wheel.

We start out heading toward Dax's place, but when he makes a right a few blocks earlier than he should, Emme perks up anxiously. "Where are we going?"

"To drop off Kailyn," Dax says flatly.

"Can't she come home with us? Can't you come to our place?" Her eyes are watery, bottom lip trembling.

"Kailyn's already done enough tonight. We need to deal with this as a family, Emme."

The words feel like bricks dropping on my chest.

"But I didn't do anything wrong! I didn't take the vodka! Please, Dax. Someone must've put it in there when I was in the dance! You have to believe me. Why doesn't anyone believe me?"

Tears stream down her face, and I put a consoling arm around her. When we're stopped at a light, I try to catch Dax's gaze in the rearview mirror, but he's stone-faced, hands on the wheel, eyes fixed straight ahead.

"Can you think of anyone who might have your locker combination?" I ask quietly.

Emme sniffs, picks up her bag from the floor and rifles through it. "I keep my lock code in my agenda, maybe someone got it from there? Maybe I left it in one of my classes?" She looks so hopeful, but it disappears as soon as she finds her agenda in her backpack. Her frown deepens as she continues to rummage. "I'm missing a book. My journal isn't in here."

"A journal is the least of your worries, Emme. You got caught at a dance with stolen alcohol and you're thirteen. Do you have any idea how bad this looks?" Dax's anger flares.

"But I didn't do it!" Emme yells.

"Everyone needs to settle down." I'm worried about this escalating when I'm not present to mediate.

Dax pulls into my driveway a minute later. He gets out and rounds the hood, his door still wide open.

"Can I come with you?" Emme whispers.

"No, honey, you and Dax need to figure this out."

"I didn't do it. Do you believe me?"

"Of course, sweetie." From what I've witnessed of Emme, she's not a bad kid, and her tears seem genuine.

"Then why doesn't Dax?"

"He's confused right now." The passenger door opens and Dax slides the back seat forward, holding out a hand to help me out.

"You staying in the back or moving up front?" He's cold and detached as he regards his sister.

"Staying in the back," she replies, a bite in her tone to match his.

"Suit yourself." He slides the front seat into place and closes the door soundly.

"Dax." I skim the back of his hand but he shakes me off.

"This is my fault. I was too busy thinking about myself, not Emme, and look where it's gotten me."

"She could be telling the truth."

"Or she could be lying to get attention. Regardless, she has mine now. I need to get her home."

He's shutting down on me, closing me out because he feels responsible for this, and I can understand why. "Will you message me when you get there, please, to let me know you made it safely?"

"Yeah. I'll do that."

I don't ask if I should call him tomorrow, uncertain whether the answer will be one I like.

I glance toward the car, but the windows are tinted and I can't see Emme in the back seat. He doesn't bother to hug me, and the absence of that affection causes an ache in my chest as Dax rounds the hood. He waits while I unlock my door before he gets in his car and leaves.

Ten minutes later my phone pings with a text.

Dax: Home

I struggle with how to reply and finally settle on *thanks*. After an hour in which I get nothing further from Dax and no messages from Emme, I give up and finally head to bed. As I watch the numbers change on the clock, I worry about what this will mean for us.

What scares me the most is the possibility that I've lost not just Dax, but Emme, too, and the pain is divided equally.

I've fallen in love with them both.

chapter twenty

I HATE YOU

Dax

Emme is silent all the way home. I fire off a message to Kailyn as I pull in the driveway and shove my phone in my pocket. I'm so angry, at myself, at Emme for doing this, at my goddamn parents for dying and leaving me here to figure this shit out on my own.

I let Emme out of the car. She's still crying, little hiccupping sobs that make her shoulders shake. She hugs her bag to her chest, hair falling forward to cover her face as she follows me to the front door. I motion to the living room couch. "Have a seat."

Emme tosses her backpack on the floor, bottom lip trembling. "I don't want to have a seat. I want Kailyn, and you took her home!"

"Well, you've got me instead, so sit down and start explaining what the hell you were thinking."

"I wasn't thinking anything because I didn't do anything wrong!" she shouts.

"Really? Because the evidence is to the contrary." I'm fighting to stay in control, and losing the battle.

"I didn't steal the vodka!" Emme says, for what feels like the millionth time.

"Stop lying to me," I yell, anger finally winning out.

"I'm not lying!"

"How the hell did a bottle of fucking Grey Goose manage to get in your goddamn bag, then?"

"I don't know! Check your damn liquor cabinet." She dashes away more tears.

"You sure you want me to do that?"

"Yes!"

Emme crosses her arms over her chest as I wrench the door open, bottles clinking against each other. Front and center is the Grey Goose, still sealed because liquor has never really been my thing, except for the occasional glass of scotch at a special event.

"See! It's right there! I told you I didn't steal your stupid vodka!"

"Where did that bottle come from, then? Did one of you take it from your friend's house? And there's no point in lying, either, Emme, because I'll be calling to make sure all of their alcohol is in their liquor cabinets, too."

"I don't know where the fuck it came from!" she screams.

"Watch your goddamn language." I realize I'm being a hypocrite and that losing my cool is making this situation worse.

"You swear all the *goddamn* time!"

"You know what? You're grounded until further notice. Leave your phone on the coffee table. And there will be no laptop and no TV until you're honest about what happened tonight."

"Well, I guess I'll be grounded forever because I already told you the truth and you don't believe me." She slams her phone down on the coffee table.

"Stop covering for your friends, Emme. They're not going to help you out of this one."

"Fuck you! You're not my dad and you never will be, so stop pretending you are." She clenches her fists, eye wild and angry. "I wish I'd been in the car with them when they died. It would be better than living with you!"

Her words feel like punches to the heart. "Emme! Don't say that."

She pauses with her hand on the banister, tears streaming down her face. "Why not? You want me to be honest, right? Well, I hate everything about being here. I hate living with you! I hate you!"

My chest constricts with her admission, and I stumble back a step as if the words are a physical slap. Her eyes flare and she spins around, her sobs stilted as she rushes up the stairs. The door to her room slams.

I close my eyes and choke on my emotions. I want to force Emme to take her words back. I want to make sense of what happened tonight. But the reality is, if I'd been paying more attention to something other than my own needs, I might have seen it.

I cross over to the couch and sit down, pressing the heels of my palms against my eyes, as if it will stop the emotion from leaking out. I don't know what to do, or how to fix this.

I slip my phone out of my pocket. I have a message from Kailyn. Her response matches mine. One single word. A simple *thanks*.

God, I've screwed this up, too. My entire life is one giant clusterfuck. I want to ask Kailyn how to make this better, but maybe that's the problem. Maybe I've been relying too much on her when I should be trying to manage on my own.

I stare at the screen until it goes blank again. Then I sit on the couch, eyes fixed on nothing, wishing my life were different.

I've ruined everything. Every single thing I've done tonight has made this worse. Linda will undoubtedly use it against me, and maybe she has a right to.

I knock on Emme's door before I go to bed, but she doesn't answer. I peek inside and find her curled up under her comforter with her back to the door. "Em? I'm sorry I yelled at you."

She remains silent, even though I have a feeling she's still awake. I cross the room and put a hand on her shoulder.

She jerks away. "Leave me alone."

"Em."

"Just go away." Her body trembles as she fights another sob.

I don't want to leave, but I don't know what else to do for her without making this terrible situation even worse. I close the door and sit down in the hall, listening to her cry, wishing I knew how to be better at this.

⟳

The next morning I discover just how early in life the wrath of women begins. I figure after a night to cool off and some sleep, we'll be able to talk it out.

Emme's laptop is in the hallway when I wake up, which I take as a good sign. I assume it to mean she's willing to accept the consequences of her actions without a fight. I also stupidly believe it means a conversation without yelling is next.

Oh, how wrong I am. Emme won't come out of her room for anything. Not even food. By dinnertime on Saturday I'm fed up with the standoff. I open the door to her room and find her lying in her bed, facing the wall, exactly as she was last night. I have to wonder if she's moved at all. "You have to eat."

"I'm not hungry."

"I'm not leaving this room until you come downstairs and eat something."

"Fine. Stand there all night for all I care."

"You can be angry at me and hate me all you want, but you're not going to starve yourself." My voice breaks at the *hate me* part.

She stiffens but her shoulders deflate and she rolls over. "Fine."

Her hair is a wild mess, and she still has streaks of black eyeliner rimming her eyes, which are puffy and red. I'm pretty sure I look almost the same, minus the eyeliner. She stomps past me and I follow her to the kitchen.

"I ordered pizza."

"I'll have cereal, thanks."

She opens the fridge, pulls out the milk and a box of crappy sugary stuff, slamming it down on the table. I lean against the counter as she grabs a bowl and spoon and crosses over to the island. She doesn't bother to sit down. Instead, she pours herself a bowl and shovels it into her mouth, barely chewing. I imagine she's starving and this standoff is meant to torment me. Once she's inhaled the cereal, she puts everything away, staunchly avoiding eye contact.

"We can't fix this problem if you're not talking to me, Emme."

"Why should I bother? You don't believe anything I say, anyway."

"I need an answer that makes sense, Emme."

"Well, I don't have one, so I guess there's nothing to say." And with that she stomps back up to her room and slams her door. I've about had it with the damn door slamming.

Even though I'm not particularly hungry, I nab a slice of pizza and flop down on the couch. Emme's phone is still where I left it. The screen flashes with an incoming message.

She has loads of them from her friends from last night, one from that Jimmy kid and about fifteen from Clark.

After a conversation about privacy and me being responsible for her phone bills, she grudgingly gave me her password and free rein to check her messages. As I scroll, I note a message from Kailyn.

I key in the code and check the message. It was sent last night, probably around the same time I dropped Kailyn off. I was a complete asshole to her, and haven't heard from her at all today. I assume she's giving me space.

Usually when I go through messages Emme is here with me so it feels a lot less like I'm snooping. Guilt creeps up the back of my neck as I read through the last messages to Kailyn.

Emme: Is Dax mad at u cuz of me
Kailyn: No, honey, Dax is upset about the situation.
Emme: Cn u come over tmrw
Kailyn: I think you and Dax need to work this out.
Emme: Can I still msg u
Kailyn: You should ask Dax if that's okay.
Emme: k Im sry I ruined 2nite
Kailyn: you didn't ruin anything <3
Emme: almst home. Talk l8r

I read them over and over, trying to see inside them. What was I doing? What was Kailyn doing? All this time spent with Emme, and if we didn't work out, what happened then? Once the custody issue is finally resolved, Kailyn won't have a reason to be part of our lives. Would she stay in Emme's life anyway? Fuck. My head is everywhere right now. And Kailyn is really the last place it should be. I should be worried about Emme getting caught with booze and where or whom she got it from, and who else Emme is protecting.

Around ten Kailyn messages asking if I'm okay.

I send one back to let her know Emme is grounded and I've confiscated all of her electronics, and that I need to focus my energy and attention on her.

Twenty long minutes go by before she responds. This time I get two words.

Kailyn: I understand

I'm not sure why they're so painful when I'm the one pushing her away.

❧

Sunday is more of the same. Emme avoids me apart from coming down once to shove a giant bowl of cereal in her face, and then disappears back into her room. At this point it's a battle of wills.

After calling all the other parents, it's confirmed that no one is missing a bottle of vodka—so it means someone bought it for them. The question is who?

I check the messages from her friends, hoping to get the answers Emme refuses to provide. Mostly the messages are about getting yelled at, and how no one knows where the vodka came from. Ainsley asks if Emme actually brought it "cuz grounded 4ev."

None of her friends seem likely to encourage that kind of behavior, which leaves me with the same questions and no answer.

At four in the afternoon, Felix shows up with a six-pack. There's some irony in that, but I'm not going to say no considering the weekend I've had.

"You look like a bag of shit."

"Thanks."

"Where's the underage booze thief?"

I turn and smack his arm. "Shut up, asshole."

"Sorry. Shit." He looks around as if he's expecting to see her. "Is she down here?"

"She's in her room."

"So why are you telling me to shut up?"

"Let's go outside."

He follows me to the back patio and passes me a beer. "You look like you need this."

"It's been a hell of a weekend, that's for sure."

"I'm surprised your girlfriend isn't here."

I glance over at the door on reflex, just to make sure Emme isn't around to hear our conversation. "Kailyn isn't my girlfriend."

Felix lifts a brow as he tips his bottle back. "Really? Because I seem to recall you telling me you were looking forward to Friday night so you could get all up in that. Guess that plan went in the shitter, huh?"

"Yeah, well, if I hadn't been distracted by a nice rack and a sweet ass, I might not have missed what was going on with Emme." Even as I say it, I feel horrible; Kailyn isn't a piece of ass I'm tapping, and she never has been.

Felix gives me a hard look. "You sure about that? I mean, if you hadn't been with Kailyn, you would've been out with me passing off the wannabe groupies you can't be bothered with."

He has a point. But it's more than that. "Emme's too attached to her."

"And that's a bad thing? She seems pretty stable, and she spends time with Emme willingly, without you there."

Kailyn is stable. She's career driven, but she makes time for the people she cares about, and she's sure as hell made time for me and Emme. Maybe more than she should. "I'm too dependent on her, to the point where I feel like I can't do this without her. I mean, she's been involved since the funeral, and they made her conservator. I keep going to her, like I expect her to make things okay. What happens when the custody issue is resolved and she's not obligated to be part of this anymore? Is she gonna bail? Emme can't handle that, and I don't really know if I can, either. It's a mess. I gotta get out before I get in too deep."

"I hate to break it to you, but I think you're already there."

"Well, then I should cut out now. Make it just about the legal aspect. I don't have time to juggle a relationship and Emme and work. I can barely handle Emme and work as it is." And Kailyn has been picking up the slack for me in the Emme department when work gets in the way, which is another problem I'll have to resolve sooner rather than later. Jesus, what the hell is even in this for her? What do I bring to the table other than a shit ton of baggage?

"Maybe you're taking on too much. You were back to work a week after the funeral. Take some time off. It's not like you don't have vacation banked."

He's right. I have weeks of unused vacation time. "Yeah. I don't know. I've been thinking about that, too. Kailyn's mentioned a couple of times that her boss wants me on their team."

"Do you really want to start over when you're close to making partner, though? Who would I have to make fun of during meetings?"

I laugh a little, but it's flat. "You could always make fun of Gene."

"From the tax department? Too easy." I can feel his eyes on me. "You're seriously considering this, aren't you?"

"Here's the thing. No matter how close I am to partner, I can't go that route now. Not when I need flex hours. I'd be working ninety hours a week, and I'd be in the courtroom all the time. I need flexibility, and I've looked into that company's policies on family. It could work."

"Would you take a pay cut?"

"I don't know, but the paycheck isn't the priority anymore. Neither is the prestige of making partner."

"How're you gonna manage working there with Kailyn?"

"It wasn't like it was going on all that long. We can be professional."

"You sure about that?"

"I'll figure it out. I can't keep going the way I am." This train is going to derail eventually and I need to get off before that happens.

chapter twenty-one

WE ALL FALL

Dax

The drive to work on Monday is miserable. Not because the traffic is worse than usual or the weather is shitty, but because I have an angry thirteen-year-old girl in the passenger seat who still isn't talking to me. It's driving me insane. I don't know how people give each other the silent treatment. I would lose my ever-loving mind. In fact, if it goes on much longer, that may just happen.

"You can set yourself up over there and start on homework." I motion to the chair on the other side of my office.

Emme says nothing as she dumps her stuff beside the chair and pulls out her laptop—I had to revise my electronics ban since all of her homework is online. But she's not allowed to do it in her room. She has to work in the kitchen, which she hates. Along with me.

She quietly seethes while I check emails and go through my voicemails. Freeman pops his head in the door and glances at

Emme set up in the corner. "Do we have a new intern I don't know about?" He's smiling, but there's tension behind it.

"Hi, Mr. Freeman." Emme's voice is raspy from disuse.

"Emme's not feeling one hundred percent, so she'll be here for a couple of days." I also refuse to let her stay home on her own, aware she'll likely spend the entire day in front of the TV. It's what I'd do without supervision.

He taps on the doorframe, a sign of his agitation. "Can I see you in my office?"

"Of course." I push out of my chair. "I'll be back."

Emme nods, chewed-up nails already in her mouth as I follow my boss down the hall.

"Is this going to be a regular occurrence?" he asks once we're in his office.

"I'm sorry, I should've run it by you before I brought Emme here. She won't be a problem. She'll stay in my office and if I have meetings, I can send her down the street to the café."

"Is everything okay? I understand you're going through some personal difficulties, but you've been distracted a lot lately."

That the death of my parents and my guardianship of my sister is construed as *personal difficulties* is laughable. "There's been a lot of change. I've had to shift my priorities now that Emme is my responsibility."

He steeples his hands. "I'm sure it's put increased demands on your time outside of work. I hope that her being here isn't going to compromise that further."

"She won't be a distraction." I'm annoyed that this is the angle he's taking. At no point has he asked how I'm coping, how Emme's coping. His sole concern seems to be whether I can accomplish everything he needs me to in the time I have allocated.

He smiles. "That's good to hear. I know partner is on your radar and I'd hate for that to be compromised."

I consider whether I want to have this conversation, and decide it's better to get it out of the way. "Actually, I think we should talk about that. Now that I have these new responsibilities, I need to reevaluate my career plans, and that includes making partner. It's still definitely something I'd like to work toward, but I need my focus to be on Emme and her well-being. I think Felix would be equally as viable a candidate for partner."

He blinks a few times, the only sign I've shocked him. "You're sure this is what you want?"

"Emme's only going to need me for a few more years, and right now she needs me the most. She has to be my first priority."

He's silent for a few moments before he finally nods. "I understand. It's commendable that you're putting her needs ahead of your own."

It's about time, actually, but I don't say that. And as I sit across from him, I keep thinking about Whitman and what they might be able to offer me. Feelings for Kailyn aside, it would be better for Emme and possibly better for me. "I should get back to work."

My conversation with Freeman weighs heavy on my mind the rest of the morning. Emme comes with me to get lunch. We order to go and head back to the office instead of grabbing a table. The silence is choking me.

"Are you in trouble for having me at work?" Her voice is low and hoarse.

I glance at her, head bowed, fingers at her mouth. There are dark circles under her eyes. "No, I'm not in trouble."

"Mr. Freeman seemed mad."

"He always seems mad, especially in the morning."

She sighs. "I'm sorry."

"I wish you'd tell me what happened at the dance."

"I already did. I swear on Mom and Dad, Dax, I didn't steal the vodka. I don't know how it got in my locker, but I didn't put it there. We went to my locker twice, once to get stuff for Sasha and once to get Ainsley a hair tie, and that was it."

Her oath shocks me into stillness. She's serious. I can see it in her imploring gaze and the tremble of her chin.

"I'm sorry, kiddo." I pull her into me, hugging her hard. "I should've trusted that you were telling me the truth."

She clutches my jacket, face mashed into my chest. "You believe me?"

"I believe you."

We stand in the middle of the street, people shooting curious looks our way as her shoulders shake and her tears soak through my jacket. When she finally lets go, her eyes are rimmed with red and her face is blotchy. "Does this mean I can have my phone back?"

I bark out a laugh. "Yeah, you can have your phone back."

"Can I text Kailyn?" she asks meekly.

That it's her first question makes my chest tighten a little. I wonder how hard it's been for her to be without anyone these past few days. Another rookie parenting mistake on my part, taking everything away from a girl who's already lost so much.

"Yes. You can text Kailyn."

That spurs on another hug and a fresh round of tears, happy ones this time.

We take the elevator back to my office—where her phone is tucked away in my messenger bag. I feel lighter than I have the past few days, thanks to Emme's buoyant mood, but the question remains, if Emme and her friends didn't put the booze in her backpack, who did? And why?

The return of Emme's phone puts a massive smile on her face. She spends the next two hours thumb typing, and while I want to ask if she's talking to Kailyn, I manage to resist.

At two in the afternoon Trish, the custody lawyer, shows up and backhands my good mood in the face.

I glance at my calendar, checking to see if I somehow missed a scheduled appointment.

"Sorry to stop by unannounced, but I received some documentation this morning that I needed to share with you as soon as possible, and I was in the neighborhood." She gives me a strained smile, her eyes darting to the couch where my sister is stretched out, with her laptop. "Hi, Emme."

Emme lifts her hand in a wave. "Hi."

"Is there somewhere we can go to discuss this privately?" Trish asks.

"Em, you want to run down to the café and grab a snack or something?" There's a tightness in the pit of my stomach that I don't like.

"Sure. I can do that." Emme's gaze shifts from Trish to me and back again as she closes her laptop and crosses the room, taking the twenty I hold out to her. "You want anything?"

"I'm good. Grab yourself whatever you want."

As soon as the door closes behind her, Trish takes a seat opposite me. "I'm very sorry to drop in on you like this, but it looks like your aunt has been busy." She pulls a file from her bag and sets it on the table between us. "There are some pictures of you that look less than flattering in here."

"What kind of pictures?" Since college I've been incredibly careful about my public persona, aware that people are always watching and often taking photographs when I least expect it.

"You at a bar with some colleagues and a woman doing shots. There are time stamps that indicate it was after work hours." Trish opens the folder and spreads out a series of images.

There are half a dozen pictures of the crazy fangirl who tried to get me to do a shot with her when I'd been at that bar with Felix, the night Kailyn had taken Emme to get a manicure before the dance. I'd had one beer and I didn't touch the shot. "Those pictures have been taken out of context."

Trish taps the desk, her smile patient. "I understand that you want to have a life—"

"I went out for one beer with my colleagues."

"Which is reasonable. Unfortunately, with this most recent issue at the school and the underage drinking—"

"Emme wasn't drinking."

Trish gives me a sympathetic smile. "She was in possession of alcohol, though."

I scrub a hand over my face. "I know possession is a problem, but I'm still working on getting to the bottom of that. Emme says it wasn't hers, so I'm hoping there's a way to prove that."

"It's commendable that you want to have faith in what Emme tells you—"

I cut her off. "If she said it wasn't hers, I believe her."

"Well, then you need undeniable proof." She clears her throat. "The pictures aren't the only thing your aunt has up her sleeve, though."

Fuck. This just keeps getting worse. "What else could she have?"

"Did you know Emme kept a journal?"

She wanders around with a decorated notebook half the time. "Sure. That's kind of a typical girl thing, isn't it?"

"It can be. It appears that Emme shared some of her entries with your aunt."

"She shared them with Linda?" That seems odd. Poetry I can kind of understand, but journals are usually personal, or at least that's what I assume.

Trish gives me a pained look as she slides a stack of photocopies toward me. "These might be difficult to see, but please remember that these are Emme's private thoughts, and although she shared them with your aunt, I doubt she intended for you to see them."

"They're that bad?" I laugh a little, but sober quickly at her piteous expression.

With each entry I read, written in Emme's distinctive cursive, my heart shrivels and cracks. Phrases jump out on the page, ones in angry slashing caps, gone over again and again with ink until the paper threatened to tear under the pressure. The running ink and splotches on the page indicate she often cried while she wrote these. Each entry bears a date at the top right corner of the page.

One is dated around the time I started moving my stuff in and cleaning out our parents' room:

I HATE THIS. I hate that Dax is throwing out all this stuff and there's nothing I can do about it. He just comes in and takes over and changes everything. I wish he hadn't moved in here. I wish I could just take care of myself.

Another is from the time Emme punched out that Billy kid and I confiscated her phone:

DAX IS SO MEAN. I hate him so FUCKING much. FUCK FUCK FUCK!!!!! He took my phone for the whole weekend. Now I have no one to talk to. And he's such a hypocrite! One second he's saying he gets why I punched Billy and the next he's grounding me. He's such an ASSHOLE!

There are endless entries, all of them expressing Emme's frustration with living with me, my invading her privacy, trying to be her dad when I'm not. It's hard to read and even harder to understand why she would show any of this to Linda.

I swallow down the surge of emotion that threatens to embarrass me. I reach for the cold coffee on my desk, anything that will help ease the sudden dryness in my mouth.

"I know this is difficult, Dax," Trish says softly.

"I didn't realize she felt this way," I croak.

"I very much doubt she does. She's a grieving girl who's experienced a huge trauma and she's working through her emotions," Trish reasons.

"Even if Emme says she doesn't mean it, the prosecution is going to say she's being coerced to change her story."

"There's a strong possibility that they'll use that argument against you."

"Christ. Am I going to lose her?" I pinch the bridge of my nose and rub my eyes, on the brink of cracking. My sister has written countless entries about how much she can't stand me. "I don't even know if she wants me to fight for her anymore."

"I think you'll need to talk to her about that, as painful as it is."

I nod, my vision blurring. Everything I had seems to be slipping through my fingers. "I'll speak with her."

"Of course. Would you like to call me later?"

"Sure, yeah. That would be good."

Trish stands and I do the same, but my legs are unsteady and my palms are damp.

"Thank you for stopping by." I walk her to the door.

"Of course."

Emme's sitting in the waiting room with some blended drink—likely full of caffeine she doesn't need. "Come on in, kiddo." My voice breaks, the pain making the words jagged.

"Is everything okay?" She follows me into the office.

I motion to the couch. "I have to show you something and you need to be very honest with me about the truthfulness of it, okay?"

"Okay." Her sleeve is in her mouth, the edge already wet from her chewing on it. The skin around her fingers is red and torn. Her anxiety is making her unable to manage without some kind of self-soothing.

I push the papers toward her with a heavy swallow. Her brows come down before her eyes flare. "Where'd you get these?" She flips through the pages with shaky fingers.

"Aunt Linda said you shared them with her."

I watch her horrified expression change to confusion. "What?"

"These are photocopies. This is your writing."

"I didn't give them to her." She shakes her head vigorously.

"I would never show this to anyone. This is from my journal. I never let people read it 'cause it's what I write when I'm upset, or mad, or sad and just feeling bad about stuff. I don't know how Linda got this, Dax, and I-I don't mean it." She skims the painful words in black ink. "I don't hate you. I just—sometimes I get so mad 'cause nothing makes sense and I don't know how to handle all the things in my head. The counselor told me writing things down would help." Tears well and she wipes them away with the heel of her hand.

"It's like, we used to just have fun together. Before Mom and Dad died, you used to be fun Dax, but now you have to be another kind of Dax, too, and it's hard. Sometimes you still get to be fun Dax, but other times when you make rules and stuff it reminds me of Dad, and then I miss him and wish he was here and that it could be different. Does that make sense?"

I give her a small smile. "It makes perfect sense, Emme, but you have to understand how much this worries me, that you think these things, sometimes."

"I don't really wish I was with Mom and Dad, not like you think that means." She blows out a long breath. "Sometimes I really miss them and I wish I could be with them. And sometimes I just wish I could see them and make sure they didn't hurt when it happened."

"I understand exactly what you mean, but you can see how this wouldn't look good, right?"

"I didn't mean for Aunt Linda to see this. I don't know how

she got them." She looks up at me, panic stricken. "Does this mean she's going to take me away from you?"

"I'm going to fight to keep you with me, Emme, if that's where you want to be."

"I don't want to live with anyone else."

Just when things seemed like they were finally going to be okay, the bottom falls out again.

chapter twenty-two

DOWN, DOWN, DOWN

Dax

Less than twenty minutes later, I receive a call from Beverly asking if I'm able to stop by the Whitman office on my way home. She has some paperwork that needs to be signed. Normally Kailyn would be the one to manage that, but maybe she's still giving me space, or maybe she's realized I'm nothing but a headache she doesn't need.

Emme chews her nails until her fingers bleed on the way to the lawyer's office. This whole situation is a complete nightmare.

Beverly greets us with a friendly smile. "I appreciate you stopping in. Kailyn wants to file this tomorrow morning, so the deadline is a little tight."

"Is Kailyn here? Can I see her?" Emme asks, looking hopeful.

"I'm sorry, Emme, Kailyn's not in the office. She has court today," Beverly says softly.

Which is something I might've known if I hadn't stonewalled her all weekend.

"Oh." Her face crumples and I fear what will happen if Linda does get custody. I can't imagine she'd let Emme see Kailyn.

"This won't take long. You'll be in and out of the office in just a few minutes," Beverly assures Emme.

"Okay." She settles in one of the waiting room chairs, knee bouncing anxiously.

"Is everything okay?" Beverly asks as she guides me to the conference room, the same one I waited in when I first came to see Kailyn after my parents passed. God, how things have changed since then.

"It's been a rough day."

"I won't take much of your time, then. I'm sure you'd like to be home and so would Emme."

I nod as I take a seat, and Beverly places two sets of documents in front of me. It's a small amendment to the trust, making it easier to transfer funds. I sign the papers after Beverly reviews the changes.

"How are you handling everything?" Beverly asks as she slips my copy into an envelope.

"It's been . . . intense to say the least."

Beverly stands along with me. "I realize now is probably not an ideal time to bring it up, but I've mentioned before how much we'd love to have you on board here. We would most certainly be able to accommodate flex hours so you can put in the time necessary to support Emme in this very transitional stage. There's no pressure, but I hope it's something you'll consider."

"Kailyn has mentioned it recently. It's definitely something I'm looking at quite seriously."

She smiles as she walks me to the door. "That's great to hear. It'll mean wonderful things for Kailyn, having you on board."

"I'm sorry, I'm not sure I understand what you mean." Did she tell her boss about us?

"It'll help advance her career, and of course yours eventually, so it's a win for everyone, really. If that's what you decide. No interview would be necessary and your salary would be competitive. Of course, we can talk about this at a later date, once you're feeling more settled."

"Right. Of course." I don't hear much after that. I'm too busy mentally filtering through all the conversations Kailyn and I have had about switching firms. My throat tightens with the realization that she's been pushing for this the entire time.

Has she used me as a power play? It seems likely with how driven she is and how much she seems to want partner. Here I thought she was looking out for me and Emme, but really she was looking out for herself.

I pull at my tie. It feels too tight, like it's choking out the air in the room.

"Daxton? Are you all right?"

"Fine. Thank you. It's been a difficult day." All I can focus on is how the one person I thought was truly on my side has been playing me all along.

I step out into the hall and find Emme in the same place I left her. Beside her is Kailyn, dressed in one of her pencil skirts, legs encased in patterned hose, one red heel hanging off the end of her foot. Their heads are bent close, fingers laced together.

"I need to talk to you."

They both look up, smiles fading.

"Are you okay?" Kailyn asks.

"I'd like a moment with you in your office. I'm sorry, Emme. I promise I won't keep you waiting much longer."

"Did something else happen?" Emme asks, nervous again.

"I'll be back in a minute." I motion in the direction of Kailyn's office.

It's quiet in the building, well after hours now. Kailyn smooths her hands over her hips and follows me down the hall, quickening her pace to keep up with me. She puts a hand on my arm. "Emme told me what happened, we'll get it figured out."

I step away from her touch and wait until she's inside the office before I close the door and spin to face her. "What kind of game are you playing?"

"I'm sorry, what?"

"You know what, it doesn't even matter. You used me and my sister to further your career."

"What are y—"

I take a step forward, hands clenched, anger and devastation colliding. "Don't lie to me right now, Kailyn. Don't do it. I trusted you. I let you into my life, into my sister's life, and for what? What do you get if you bring me over to your firm?"

"It's not—"

"What do you get?" I yell.

"Whatever Beverly sa—"

"Save the bullshit," I snap. "You sure fucked me in lots of ways, didn't you?"

"It's not what you think, Dax. I care about you."

I ignore her imploring tone and push for the facts, because those are what I need right now. "What exactly were you offered to bring me on board here?" It all clicks together. "Partner? Is that it? You get a partnership?"

She sighs and closes her eyes. "Yes, but—"

"Stop. You don't get to throw a 'but' in there. So all the time you've been spending with me, with Emme, it's all been about you making partner." Jesus. I feel like I'm going to throw up.

"At first I wanted to make sure you weren't out to get Emme's money. She was my top priority. I didn't know you, didn't know your circumstances or what your motivation was."

"And after that it stopped being about Emme's trust being safe and it started being about you making partner. I get it."

"It's not that simple, and you know it."

"Isn't it? You could've told me what was going on. You didn't need to keep that from me if that's not what this was about." I motion between us and then reach for the door. "I hope you're happy with yourself. You've just broken a little girl's heart and it was already in pieces."

"Dax, please, you need to hear me out on this."

"No. I don't. What I need to do is make sure my bitch aunt doesn't get custody of my sister. And I need to start by cutting the people out of my life who are going to cause more damage than good."

chapter twenty-three

BAD JUDGMENT

Kailyn

Sometimes the biggest mistakes are made with the best of intentions. I want to follow Dax but I don't want to make an already terrible situation worse, and I also don't want to needlessly upset Emme more than she is.

So I let him leave. Because I have no other choice.

The irony is, I planned to speak with Beverly tomorrow morning about the partnership and that I'd prefer to make it on my own merit, not on my ability to persuade Daxton to come to Whitman. And now I'm too late.

I feel ill as I drop into my chair and splay my hands out on my desk. The high of winning yet another case where the right people are granted custody of a child for the right reasons this afternoon is crushed by the weight of my actions. Dax deserves to have Emme, and I feel like everything I've done recently compromises that. Dax needed someone and I came in to play savior, only I made an even bigger mess to clean up.

I take several deep breaths, hoping to calm the swell of emotions as they slam into me. I don't want to cry, not with Beverly still here. But judging by the pricking behind my eyes, I don't think I'm winning the battle.

A soft knock has me clearing my throat. I want it to be Dax returning to hear me out, but that's highly unlikely. "Come in."

Beverly peeks her head in and purses her lips. I have no idea what my expression is. I feel like I've come down with the flu. I'm pretty sure the last meal I had is going to come up before this night is over.

"You don't look very happy for someone who just won her second pro bono custody case."

"I am." I give her a weak smile. "I just have other things on my mind."

"Ah, you mean Daxton." She leans against the doorjamb and crosses her arms over her chest. "You should've told me how involved you are."

"I think that's past tense now." I start to laugh, but it dissolves into a terrible, broken sound. I've messed up so badly this time. Worse than I ever could've imagined, and not just with Dax but with Emme. What will he to say to her? How much is she going to hate me? I've put him in a terrible position, and all for what? A career move? One that no longer means what it once did. Not when it's going to cause so much unnecessary hurt.

"If I'd known, I would've approached my conversation with him differently."

"I was planning to talk to you about it in the morning. I didn't want to complicate an opportunity for him to work here." Which is true. More than the partnership, I worried that being involved with him could affect his chance at the firm. "I didn't mean for this to happen, Beverly."

She laughs. "No one ever means to fall in love."

Denying it seems pointless, as if I'm trying to support a position that doesn't require any defense. "I don't want my partnership contingent on whether Daxton accepts a job here. I can't have those two things tied together."

Beverly is silent for a few moments before she speaks. "I can understand that, considering the circumstances. Regardless of how you get there, Kailyn, you've put in the time and dedication for the partnership to be yours. Why don't we talk about this later, when you're thinking rationally and not with your heart. You should go home, try to get some rest. I don't think this aunt of his is going down without a fight based on the shit she's slinging, so it's going to be all hands on deck for the next little while." She moves to leave but pauses. "In case you weren't aware, in regards to the nonfraternization policy, already established relationships are reviewed on a case-by-case basis. Mostly it's to keep the lawyers from screwing their assistants or bosses. Just something to think about."

It would be if Dax didn't hate me.

I make it home before I have a complete breakdown. When I'm semicomposed, I call Holly. It's after nine on a Monday, we both have to work early, but my craggy voice and sniffles mean she drops everything to come over.

I'm not one for emotional outbursts. I cried when my mom passed and again when my dad went a few years later. I almost cried when I humiliated myself the first time I met Dax, but other than that, tears don't fall easily for me. I'm pragmatic most of the time. But not when it comes to Dax and Emme.

The possibility of losing them terrifies me.

Half an hour later Holly shows up at my door with an overnight bag. "What happened?"

"I messed up." My eyes start leaking again.

"Oh, peanut." She drops her bag and hugs me.

It takes less than fifteen minutes to spill the entire story once I'm composed enough to speak.

"I think the most important question is whether or not you see this thing with Dax as long term."

"I can."

Holly tips her head to the side and waits for me to continue.

"We understand each other."

"You're sure you're not just playing rescuer?"

It's a valid question. If I had more space, I'd probably have ten cats instead of two. Once I saved an entire litter when a feral mother gave birth under the back deck. I was so desperate to keep them I even suggested building them a house in the backyard because both of my parents were allergic. Despite my pleas, they insisted we give them up for adoption. I put up the ad and vetted those families like the lawyer I now am.

"It's not uncommon for people who have experienced similar losses to find comfort in each other."

Holly smiles. "That's true."

"I love him. And Emme."

"Enough to walk away from an opportunity to be partner?"

"Yes."

"You didn't even have to think about that."

"I was going to tell Beverly tomorrow morning that I didn't want my partnership to be based on Daxton coming to Whitman anyway. That I wanted it because I'd earned it. You know, for years I had this goal based on a bet with my dad, but he wouldn't want me to forfeit the chance to have something real and meaningful just to further my career. And honestly, Holls, trust law isn't what I want to do forever. I'd rather not make partner and shift gears than keep going in the same direction I am now."

"So then you shift gears."

"I want to move to family law. Help people who really need it. Like the Lipsons and the Wilsons and Dax and Emme."

"It's a great fit. I think until now it was just too close to your heart, and you didn't have enough of your own people to love to really take it on."

My chest aches as I recall just how upset Daxton was in my office earlier. "I might've lost two of those people tonight."

"He's hurt and he's dealing with more than is reasonable. The stress of what happened with his sister, the custody battle, all the uncertainty, he's been relying on you for a lot."

"And I let him down in the worst possible way, Holly. He thinks I did it all to make partner, not because I care."

"Do you really think he believes that?"

"You didn't see him today. He was so angry and hurt. I did a lot of damage."

"So how do you undo it?"

"I don't know. Find a way to help him keep custody of Emme, I guess?"

"You're resourceful, smart, and determined. You always find a way to make it happen if you want it bad enough."

There's no way Emme's aunt wants what's best for her. It's the trust she's after. Now I just need to find a way to prove it, and make Dax see it was never about the partnership for me when it came to him and Emme.

ᶜᵔ

Leading up to the final custody hearing, I only hear from Dax when it's absolutely necessary. He uses email and cc's his lawyer. Everything is polite and professional. He doesn't text, doesn't call, and avoids stopping by the office when he knows I'll be there. My heart aches on a daily basis. The only similar pain I can recall is the loss of my parents. But, no matter how much it hurts, I don't regret falling in love with Daxton, I just regret not telling him what I should have before I damaged what we had.

Heartache is the worst affliction. It robs a person of rationality, of logic, of forethought and patience. It makes everything good painfully bright and magnifies the bad with an intensity that's difficult to tolerate.

Thankfully, the one light in my darkness is the constant texts from Emme. Whatever Dax has said to her, it hasn't been enough to make her turn on me, too, which gives me hope.

So do the reports from Emme that Dax is sad, and whenever she brings me up he gets all cagey and dejected. While I wait out his silence, I dig into his aunt, dissecting the emails she sent me, looking for more in them. I seek out more information on her past jobs and her husbands, trying to make connections, but without input from Dax, it's difficult to make any progress.

Emme's still worried she's going to have to live with her aunt, but since the journal entries and the social media pictures—which were a stretch considering Emme was with me and I have the pictures and receipts to prove it, Linda hasn't made any more moves.

Regardless, I can't shake the feeling that she has more to do with the whole underage alcohol situation than we know. She was too smug, too all-knowing and just waiting for Dax to blow. And none of the girls had been drunk according to the police reports, since it turns out they'd all taken Breathalyzer tests. It doesn't make sense that a group of girls would steal alcohol and not bother to drink it.

A few weeks after the whole blowout at my office, Emme

texts about an assembly she's performing in and wants to know if I can come.

I'm not sure if Dax is aware Emme and I are still communicating on a regular basis. I don't ask about him, even though I want to. Although I certainly don't stop her when she wants to share. He's home every night. He's overly attentive. He's a terrible cook, but he's trying.

She misses me.

I miss them both.

I decide the conversation warrants a phone call. "Hey, sweetie, how's it going?"

"Okay, I guess. Do you think you'll be able to come?"

"Does Dax know you invited me?"

She's silent for a few seconds. "Everyone gets two tickets, so I can invite whoever I want."

I smile at her defiant tone. "You don't think it would be better to let him know instead of surprising him?"

"Why is he so upset with you? He won't tell me anything and he's, like, moody and stuff when I ask about you."

I sigh. "I made a mistake and I hurt him."

"Can't you say you're sorry?"

"Sometimes it's not that simple, Emme."

"He misses you, though, I know he does. You left a ring here and he's always sitting in front of the TV at night, playing with it."

Well, at least I know I didn't lose it. It's not particularly valuable, apart from sentimentality. "Hopefully with time Dax will be able to forgive me."

"Was it really bad? Your mistake?"

"It was."

"Oh." She's quiet for a few seconds. "Does that mean you won't come to the assembly?" I want to reach through the phone and hug away her sadness.

"Of course I'll come."

"Maybe you can try to tell him you're sorry again. I could tell him for you if you want?"

Her sweetness chokes me up, and I have to clear my throat before I answer. "It's probably better if it comes directly from me."

"Yeah. Probably. Okay. I'll text you the date and stuff. I can't wait to see you. I'm gonna give you a huge hug."

"I'm looking forward to it." I end the call and exhale a steadying breath, willing myself not to get my hopes up, but the heart doesn't always listen to the head.

chapter twenty-four

THE PIECES

Kailyn

I leave work early on the night of the assembly and change into a nice pair of normal black dress pants and a family-friendly blouse that's still a little sexy. Dax is going to be there, after all. I check my voicemail on the way into the school—I'm half an hour early, obviously hoping to run into Dax before the performance begins, and if the universe is on my side, possibly snag the seat beside him before one of the vulture-like single moms does. That's provided he'll speak to me.

I have a voicemail from Holly, but I can't hear it with the noise in the foyer, parents chattering excitedly as they wait for the auditorium doors to open.

I can't see Dax anywhere in the throng of waiting families, but I'm short, so my ability to see over all the heads is compromised. I navigate my way through the crowd, looking for a quiet room. I push through the first door that opens and step inside. I've found the library, and it appears to be empty.

I'm about to listen to the voicemail when someone else speaks. For a moment, I consider making my presence known, until I realize the voice is familiar.

Setting my phone to silent, I creep a little farther into the room. I can't see Linda, but I can certainly hear her.

"As soon as this custody business is wrapped up, we'll head to Vegas for the weekend, my treat this time."

There's silence for a moment, and I move toward the sound of her voice. How can Linda be planning a trip to Vegas when she's battling for custody of a thirteen-year old? I hit the Record button on my phone, hoping to catch what I'm overhearing on the off chance it's somehow incriminating.

I peek around a shelving unit and find her sitting in a chair, behind a desk on the other side of the room, the space made up to look like an office. She holds her phone in one hand, the other curved around a mouse, her attention divided between the call and whatever's on the laptop screen. She stops clicking and throws her head back as she laughs. "I'm not worried about that. Once I have custody I'll have lots of money to play with. We'll hit the blackjack table and double what we lost last time. By the time we get back, no one will even know it was missing."

She looks over her shoulder. "I don't think that's going to be a problem. She can stay with her brother on weekends. It'll make me look like I'm being accommodating and it'll get her out of my hair. Two birds, one stone, right?" She laughs again.

"It shouldn't be long before I get what should've been mine in the first place."

Before I can make my presence known or make a move to confront her, a buzz fills the room. "Linda, are you available? I need your assistance in the office, please."

"I have to go. I'll call you next week, but I figure it shouldn't be long before Emme's in my custody. That bottle of vodka was a genius idea, so thanks for that. Anyway, once I have access to that money, we'll plan a trip." She ends the call and closes the laptop, pushing out of her chair. I wait until a door closes on the other side of the room before I check to make sure she's gone.

Coast clear, I rush over to the laptop, flipping it open, crossing my fingers as the screen comes alive again. An online game of poker flashes across the screen. I glance over my shoulder to make sure I'm still alone as I click on the next tab, smiling when I find her email open. That's what you get for not logging out.

The conversation I recorded is damning enough, but I'll take any additional hard evidence that will nail her coffin closed. I scan the list of emails and note a starred one regarding a private school in San Francisco. I hope she's not thinking about moving. Clicking on it, I skim the email between Linda and an administrator inquiring about on-campus placement. Apparently she plans to send Emme to a boarding school should she get custody. I snap pictures and print out the email so I have a hard copy before I perform a search for any others that match the email address. I find a few more and print them as well.

I close the browser at the sound of voices drawing closer, flip the laptop shut, and leave the room the way I came in, hoping what I've gathered is going to be helpful in keeping Emme with Dax.

The hallway is empty but for a few parents straggling in. The assembly begins shortly, so I give the person at the box office my name and she passes me over the reserved ticket. Apparently it's assigned seating.

I'm surprised to find it's an actual theater, although I suppose this school has a fairly hefty tuition, and it's arts based, so it makes sense that they would have a real auditorium.

The usher shows me to my row, and of course I'm right in the middle, so everyone has to stand so I can get to my seat. The lights are already dimmed, making it difficult to see, but based on the profile, I'm beside Dax.

He shifts his attention from the person to his right to lift his jacket from the armrest—he's still dressed in a suit, presumably because he came directly from work. His eyes flare when they meet mine, brow furrowing as his mouth turns down and then lifts slightly in a wry, unimpressed grin. He might be angry with me, but it doesn't seem to affect the chemistry that pings between us as his eyes rove over me in a familiar, hot way.

I swallow past the lump in my throat and take the seat next to him.

He leans in close, warm minty breath caressing my cheek. "Emme invited you."

"I'm sorry."

He huffs humorlessly and shifts in his seat, dropping his elbow so it's no longer on the armrest, touching mine.

I hate the horrible churning in my stomach and the burn behind my eyes at his quick dismissal. "I know you're still upset with me, but I need to speak with you after the assembly."

"I'm not interested in a conversation."

I put a hand on his arm and he turns his head slowly, his glare directed at where I'm making physical contact. I want to erase his anger, make him understand that I didn't mean to hurt him. I move my hand to my lap. "It's not about us."

"Well, that's good since there is no us."

My heart feels like it's been punctured. Before I can say anything else, the lights go down and the curtains open. The stage is filled with students, all dressed in white shirts and black pants. Emme is front and center, scanning the audience.

Dax lifts his hand in a half wave when she finally spots him, and she smiles, her gaze shifting to me, and it widens even more. There's no way I'm going to make it through this without crying.

And then they start to sing. I've always known Emme has a beautiful voice. She sings in the car whenever she likes the song. She belts out the lyrics when we play *Just Dance*, and she hums a lot. But this is something completely different; this is the kind of music that reaches inside and touches your soul.

I can't hold back the tears when Emme steps forward for her solo. I recognize the song, vaguely. Her voice is hauntingly beautiful as she climbs the notes and dips down, taking us with her on an emotional journey. This is how she's dealing with this loss, I realize. She's found something to soothe the ache inside, maybe just a little.

I glance over at Dax, whose expression borders on tragic. I want to offer him some comfort, but I don't think it will be received well. Instead I root around in my purse for another tissue since the one I have is already soaked with tears. Thank God for waterproof mascara.

Dax leans over, lips at my ear. "Here." He hands me a fresh tissue.

I sniff and meet his eyes. "Thank you."

For a moment he holds my gaze and I see the same thing I'm feeling reflected in his eyes, deep sadness, regret, and longing.

When Emme's solo ends, the crowd rises to a standing ovation. Dax whistles and claps, maybe louder than anyone else in the room, and I hope like hell the information I've come across is going to be enough to end this battle with his aunt.

He picks up a huge bouquet of flowers and we wait as everyone files out of the auditorium. We're seated close to the front, so we're last to leave. I can feel Dax behind me, and I have the urge to reach back and find his fingers, to lace us together. I want to force him to listen to me and understand that what we have—had—was never about me making partner and everything about falling in love with him and Emme.

But I doubt he's going to give me airtime for that, and I have a much more pressing issue I need to alert him about.

"I really need to talk to you," I throw over my shoulder.

"I'm taking Emme out to celebrate. It's not a good time."

It's too loud and there are too many people around to find privacy. When we finally escape the auditorium, Emme's already waiting in the foyer, bouncing excitedly. She throws herself into my arms, wrapping me up in a huge hug with her skinny arms.

"You were amazing up there."

"I missed you," she mumbles into my hair.

"I missed you, too, sweetie, so much." I hold her tighter, fighting another wave of emotion and losing the battle.

When we finally let go, I have to brush away the fresh tears. Dax stands off to the side, his expression unreadable until his sister turns to him, and then his smile lights up a black sky like fireworks.

My chest aches, hollowness eating at me because I know they're not mine the way I want them to be, and I made it that way.

He holds out the bouquet, and her happy shriek is a sound I want to hear more of.

Emme turns to me. "We're going out for something to eat, can you come?"

I glance at Dax. His mouth flattens into a line. "I think Dax probably wants a little time with you."

Emme's smile falls. "But I haven't seen you in forever. Please, Kailyn? She can come, can't she, Dax?"

Emme sends an imploring look her brother's way. His cheek tics, but he forces a smile. "Of course Kailyn's welcome to join us. It's your night."

"Yay!" Emme throws her arms around me again. "Can I ride with Kailyn? Can we go to the diner down the street? I was too nervous to eat before the performance, and now I'm starving!"

Thank you, I mouth to Dax as she drags me toward the door.

He nods, but his smile has vanished again.

The diner is busy, full of other students and their parents who had the exact same idea we did. Emme sits beside me in the booth and chatters away. Once we've ordered she's dragged off to sit with a few of her friends. "I'll be back in a few minutes!"

"She seems like she's doing well."

"She has really good days. This is one of them." Dax arranges his silverware, but doesn't look at me. "You had something you needed to talk to me about."

I look around the diner. "It's about Linda." I reach into my purse and pull out the emails I printed off.

Dax leans back in his seat and crosses his arms over his chest, regarding me coldly. "What about her?"

"I overheard a conversation with someone before the assembly and it sounded rather suspect, so I recorded it. I also found this." I push the printed sheets toward him.

"What is this?"

"An email chain between Linda and a principal at a private school."

"What?" Dax skims it. "How'd you get this?"

"She left her email open on a laptop in the library." I set my phone on the table between us. "I haven't had a chance to listen to it, so I have no idea if I caught anything helpful or not."

"Helpful how?"

"In building your case to keep Emme with you."

"Emme keeps earbuds in the front pocket." Dax points to her backpack.

I unzip the compartment and smile when I find the little pouch I gave her to keep her girl supplies in when it's that time of the month. Tucked in beside them are earbuds. I slip the jack in and pass Dax one bud, pushing the other in my ear. He leans forward, forearms on the table, head down and inches from mine as I cue the recording. I turn the volume all the way up, cross my fingers, and hit Play.

It's not the clearest recording, and the noise in the diner makes it hard to hear. I pass Dax the other earbud and he listens again, and then again, eyes on mine as his expression hardens. He yanks them out. "What kind of person wants custody of a grieving teenage girl so they can cash in on her trust allowance?"

"Not a very good one."

He scrubs his face with his palm. "She can't get custody of Emme. There's no way."

I glance over my shoulder, checking on Emme, who's still engaged in conversation with her friends. She's actually sitting beside a boy who seems to be hanging on her every word. I wonder if that's Clark. Or Liam. Or Jimmy. She has quite the fan club.

"Come sit on this side." Dax slides over a few more inches and I move into the space beside him. I quickly pull the rest of the emails between the private school administrator and Linda. He stops at the one about boarding options. "She plans to send her to San Francisco? When has she had time to plan all this?"

I tap the time stamp. "It looks like she started as soon as she filed for custody."

"Can I keep this?"

"All of it is yours. I just want Emme to be safe and with someone who loves her and wants what's best for her. I didn't want to hurt her, or you. Whatever else I can do to help, I will."

He places his hand over mine and squeezes, eyes soft. "Thank you."

It's not forgiveness, but it's a step in the right direction.

chapter twenty-five

FORGIVENESS

Dax

Emme is beat when we get home, so she heads to her room, too tired for TV or anything else. Thankfully tomorrow is Friday, and I'm assuming the performance tonight will mean an easy day at school.

I'm hopped up on adrenaline, and my head is spinning, so once she's in bed, I grab a beer from the fridge and head down the hall to the office with the folder of printed emails Kailyn gave me.

I drop into the leather executive chair with a sigh. *Kailyn.* I don't know what to think. She seems to have gone to a lot of trouble to get this information for me, but why? Does she genuinely want to help? I hate not knowing what parts of our relationship were real and what was contrived to further her career. I don't think anyone can fake the kind of chemistry we have, but even that I can't be sure of. And now I'm questioning it all over again, because she came to the performance for Emme.

I massage the space between my eyes as I boot up my father's desktop. Since the funeral, I've put off dealing with the majority of the financial stuff that wasn't directly related to Emme. There are accounts that need to be managed, savings to be transferred, and bank statements to be reviewed. But none of it has seemed pressing since Linda sued for custody of Emme. While I wait, I rifle through the emails from Kailyn, organizing them by date. The first email to the private school was sent the day after Linda filed for custody. She is un-fucking-believable.

The screen on my father's desktop finally registers a login and I punch in his password, which is stuck to the corner of the display with a Post-it. I'm not sure what I'm looking for, other than something that will explain why Linda needs this money so badly, and why she feels it's rightly hers.

The folders with my father's documents are neatly labeled and organized, as was normal for my parents. I scroll through them, noting one with my name, one with Emme's, and lower down is Linda's, which would make sense as she was supposed to be Emme's legal guardian until about six months ago. I click on Linda's, and several subfolders pop up. I pause when I reach one labeled *Loans*. Clicking again I'm met with at least twenty separate documents, each individually dated, going as far back as fifteen years ago. I open the most recent, dated not long before my parents passed.

Apparently, Linda borrowed five thousand dollars from my parents. I open the next one down, dated several months earlier, and find yet another loan, this time for seven thousand dollars. Another one, dated a few months before my thirtieth birthday, is substantially larger, at fifteen thousand dollars.

There seems to be a lull, a period of two years in which no loans were issued, but before that my parents sporadically lent Linda money. Sometimes it was a few thousand dollars, but more than once they were in excess of ten thousand.

I'm sure if I went back through my parents' bank records I'd be able to track all the money they loaned her over the years, which is a lot.

Before I think too much about what I'm doing, I pick up my cell and call Kailyn. It doesn't even finish ringing once before she answers.

"Hey. Is everything all right? How are you?"

"I'm . . . okay." That's not really true right now, but it's an automatic response. "How are you?"

"Happy to hear your voice," she says softly.

Her honesty pulls my attention back to her. "What're you doing right now?"

"Uh, not a lot, how about you?"

"I found some stuff on my dad's computer." I hit Print on the loan documents. I'm sure there must be a folder in my parents' filing cabinets with signatures. The most recent are signed, scanned PDFs, but the older ones are drafts with no signatures.

"What kind of stuff?"

"Financial stuff connected to Linda that might explain why she wanted custody so badly . . ." I trail off as I note the time in the corner of the screen; I didn't realize it was almost midnight. "But it can wait."

"I'm not going to sleep anytime soon, if you want to talk it through."

"My parents loaned my aunt a lot of money."

"What constitutes a lot?"

"Tens of thousands over the past decade and a half. And that's just based on the documents in one folder. I have no idea if there's more that's unaccounted for." I rub my temple, the dull throb telling me a headache is on the way.

"I can come over." There's a short pause. "If you want help going through what you found. Or it can wait. I can shift my appointments around tomorrow morning, unless now is better."

"Now is better."

"I can be there in fifteen."

"Okay."

While I wait for her to arrive, I rifle through my parents' filing cabinets. At the back of one I find a thick folder with Linda's name on it, but before I can open it, Kailyn texts to signal her arrival. I find her on my front porch in a pair of black leggings and a ratty *It's My Life* hoodie, hair in a messy knot on top of her head, wearing her glasses, holding two takeout bags and a tray with coffees.

She smiles a little uncertainly. "I brought fuel."

"Good thinking." I take the coffees from her and step aside. "Come in."

We stand there for a protracted moment, staring at each other. Neither of us certain what to say, maybe. Tension lingers between us; unanswered questions hang in the air like thick fog. I've missed her, more than I wanted to admit.

"Want to show me what you found?" Kailyn asks.

"Yeah, follow me." I incline my head toward the office.

"Oh, wow," she murmurs as she takes in the papers lining the desk; the endless loan documents, the emails she printed out from the boarding school. She raps on the desk with her long, polished fingernails.

"And I just stumbled across this right before you got here, but I haven't had a chance to look through it." I offer her a chair and we pull up close to the desk as I flip the thick file folder open. Inside are printed copies of the loan documents, bank statements from my aunt with maxed-out lines of credits, credit cards with outrageous balances, and agreements between her and my parents that she would pay back the money.

I rub my temple as all the pieces finally click into place. "She has a gambling problem."

Kailyn stops biting the end of her pen so she can respond. "I was about to say the same thing. It would explain the trip to Vegas and the comment about doubling what they lost last time."

"It makes sense, doesn't it? Now I know why she's so desperate to make me into some kind of villain and take custody of Emme." I motion to the sea of papers spread out before us, still reeling. "This proves Linda's intentions were purely self-ish. She planted a bottle of vodka on a thirteen-year-old for Chrissake."

"There's no way she'll get custody now, not with all of this and that recording."

"I wouldn't have figured this out without you."

"You would've, it may have taken longer, but you would've found all of this eventually and put it together." She squeezes my forearm. "I just want Emme to be where she belongs, Dax, and that's with you."

She seems so sincere, but it's hard not to wonder how much of this is her wanting to help and her still working the partner angle. "Is that all you want?"

She regards me uncertainly. "What do you mean?"

"How much of this"—I tap the printed emails and glance down at her hand, still on my arm, keeping us connected, which I've missed over the weeks since I've seen her—"is to get you closer to your partnership? I don't know what's real and what's not with you, Kailyn. I don't know if I can trust your motivation for helping me."

Kailyn drops her hand to her lap and focuses there for a few seconds. "I know I broke your trust when you were in a vulnerable position and that earning it back won't be easy, but know that everything I'm doing right now is because I want what's best for you and Emme, and that's for you to have each other."

She takes a deep breath. "I admit that when Beverly presented me with the offer for partner, I took you on as a challenge. I had a very different opinion of who you were. I also wanted to make sure that Emme wasn't being taken advantage of. I had no idea what your reasons were, if you were just after Emme's money like Linda so clearly is." Kailyn meets my gaze with an imploring one of her own. "The first few years of my life weren't good, Dax. Thankfully, I don't have a lot of memories, but the ones I do have are the reason I'm here fighting for Emme to stay with you. I want you to know that the partnership stopped being a factor when I realized how hard you were trying to do what was best for Emme."

"And when was that, exactly?"

"When you called me from CVS." She smiles a little, maybe at the memory. "That's when I saw the real you."

chapter twenty-six

AMENDS

Kailyn

I will him to say something, anything that will let me know forgiveness is possible.

Confirmation comes in the form of his mouth crashing down on mine. For a moment I'm frozen and stunned, but my body seems to know exactly what to do even if my brain takes a few seconds to catch up.

Dax drags me out of my chair and pulls me up against his body, tongue stroking inside my mouth, arms wrapped around me. There's no place I feel safer than where I am right now. And I know that giving up the partnership was the right thing to do if it means I get to have this man instead.

We have the wherewithal to make it to the bedroom before we're frantically undressing. We collide with need and want, apologies given and accepted through touch. And when he's finally inside me again, the ache that's been weighing down my heart finally dissolves.

e~

"Dax! Are you up? I'm leaving for school in, like, fifteen, and the house doesn't smell like coffee!"

I bolt upright, the covers dropping to my waist. I mouth *shit* while Dax blinks blearily, confusion turning to heat as he takes in my bare breasts.

He clears his throat and calls out, "Be right down!"

A long silence follows before she finally replies, "'Kay." A few seconds later her bedroom door closes.

Dax gives my bare breast a squeeze. I smack his hand, my nipple already perking up from the attention. "What the hell am I going to do?"

"Uh, maybe there's still something of my mom's in the back of the closet? I know Emme missed a few things when we cleaned everything out. We can pretend like you showed up this morning?" It's more question than plan, but it's a whole hell of a lot better than the alternative.

I find a plain black dress that's about two decades old and close to my size. I guess it could be considered retro. I shimmy into it. It's tight at the hips, and the hem falls below my knees since his mom was several inches taller than me.

I finger comb my hair because Dax doesn't have a brush. I still have sleep lines on my face, but there's nothing I can do about that. I follow Dax to the kitchen. Thankfully, Emme is still in her room, so I'm able sit my ass down at the island and calm my breathing.

Dax is all smiles as he goes about making coffee. I don't know how he can be so calm when it feels like my heart is going to slam out of my chest. The bag of doughnuts I picked up on my way over last night helps make our charade look more authentic, minus the fact that there's no coffee to go with it. It's not that I have an issue with Emme knowing that Dax and I are talking again, it's her finding out because I've just walked out of Dax's bedroom with a serious case of post-sleepover sex hair.

Dax passes me a cup of coffee just as Emme appears. She shrieks and rushes over, throwing her arms around me. "Oh, hi! I didn't hear the doorbell ring!"

"Dax and I have a meeting this morning. We thought we'd go together."

She releases me and steps back, panicked gaze darting between Dax and me. "What kind of meeting?"

"The good kind, don't worry," Dax reassures her. At least we're hoping it's going to be the good kind.

"Oh. Okay. Can you drive me to school so I can hang out with Kailyn for a bit?"

"Sure."

Emme tells me all about her weekend plans, which include a sleepover at her friend Marnie's. I glance at Dax and he grins, clearly thinking the same thing I am. Dax runs upstairs to change into a suit before we drive Emme to school. We'll be coming back here as soon as we drop her off, but this keeps up the ruse.

Emme almost trips over a pair of shoes on the way down the hall. *Shit*. They're my llama-print Toms.

"You're wearing those to work?" Emme's nose crinkles.

Obviously there's more than one flaw in our half-assed plan. "I have heels at my office."

"Oh. Okay." She shrugs and slips her feet into her purple Chucks—I have the same ones—and shoulders her backpack.

"We can take my car," I offer.

Emme bounces down the driveway and puts her hand on the hood of my car. "What time did you get here this morning?"

"Just before you came downstairs."

"Huh."

"What?" I ask, suddenly nervous she's onto us, which is ridiculous.

"Oh, nothing. Let's go! Don't want to be late," she says with a big smile plastered on her face.

I meet Dax's WTF gaze over the hood before we get in. Emme sings along to the radio for a few minutes before she says, "Does this mean you two are back together?"

"What?" Dax and I ask in unison.

I catch her eye roll in the rearview mirror. "Oh, come on. I'm not dumb. I know you guys are, like, a thing, and then you wouldn't talk to Kailyn and now you are again. So that means you guys are back together, right?"

"Um…" I glance at Dax, because I have no idea what to say to that.

"Yeah. Kailyn and I are back together."

"So my plan worked." She has the same smirky smile as her brother.

"And what plan was that?" Dax asks, fighting his own grin.

"I invited Kailyn last night so you two would sit together and talk, and it worked. You're welcome."

I laugh as I pull into the student drop-off zone.

"Thanks for looking out for us, Em," Dax says.

Her head pops between the seats, and she gives us both a peck on the cheek. "Oh, and I totally heard Kailyn come over last night, so next time you don't like have to pretend like you didn't sleep over, 'cause it's totally okay. Oh! There's Marnie! See you after school."

The door slams, and Dax and I stare at each other slack jawed until the car behind us honks.

"Well, I guess we're not nearly as sly as we think we are, huh?" Dax laughs.

"Apparently not."

❧

After we drop Emme off at school, we go back to Dax's to collect all the evidence pointing to Linda's less-than-altruistic motives for wanting custody of Emme. Once we have it organized, we log into his mother's email account and filter through the ones between her and Linda—something we didn't think to do last night—and discover an endless stream back and forth between her and her sister asking for financial support. All fingers point to a gambling addiction that she battled on and off over the years and seems to have lost. It also seems to have been a significant part of the reason her most recent marriage failed.

We can only guess as to how much debt she's amassed, but it certainly explains why she's been so intent on discrediting Dax and seeking custody of Emme.

"Are you ready to take Linda down?" I ask once we're back in my car.

Dax drums on the armrest, surprisingly composed considering everything he's found out in less than twenty-four hours. "Sure am. Want to make the call?"

I pull out my phone, dial the school number, and wait for them to patch me through to reception. "Hi, Linda, it's Kailyn Flowers. Do you have a minute?"

I have her on speaker, so Dax is able to hear both sides of the conversation.

"Oh, hi, Kailyn, what can I do for you?"

"I have some new information that could impact the state of the trust and change how the custody hearing is managed."

"Oh?" I'm not sure if I imagine the nervousness in her voice or not.

"I know it's incredibly short notice, but I was hoping I could meet with you to discuss this in person. It's rather urgent."

Dax drums his fingers on his thigh, and we hold eye contact while we wait for her response.

"Isn't this something we can talk about over the phone?"

"I'm sorry, but it's rather time sensitive and would be best discussed in a private meeting."

There's silence for a few moments before she finally responds. "My lunch break is in half an hour. I could meet you at your office at eleven thirty?"

"That's perfect. Thank you so much, Linda. I'll see you then." I end the call, and Dax's smile mirrors mine. "She's never going to see this coming."

chapter twenty-seven

JUST DESSERTS

Daxton

Half an hour later—after a quick stop at Kailyn's so she can change and fix her hair—we're seated inside the same conference room where I first met Kailyn, the folders of evidence lined up on the table. Kailyn and I are both sipping coffee, although I feel like a scotch might be warranted once this meeting is over considering what we're about to do.

"She's going to drop the lawsuit, Dax. Everything will be fine." Kailyn squeezes my bouncing knee.

"I won't be able to relax until it's over."

A minute later there's a knock on Kailyn's door and her assistant appears. "Miss Flowers, Linda Thrasher is here to see you." She gives us both a conspiratorial smile.

"You can send her in." Neither Kailyn nor I stand to greet her as she enters the room and Cara closes the door behind her. Linda stumbles a bit when she sees me.

"I thought this was a private meeting."

"It is," Kailyn says evenly. "Private between the people who have a vested interest in Emme's future." She motions to the empty chair across from Kailyn and me. "Have a seat, Linda."

She pulls out her phone. "I'm calling my lawyer."

"I would reconsider that." Kailyn flips open the folder in front of her and reveals the email chain between Linda and the principal from the private school, and the pile of loan documents. "I feel it's in your best interest to hear us out first, Linda."

Face ashen, she sinks down in the booth. She looks between us. "What is this?"

"It's your come-to-Jesus moment. This is where you admit the only person's well-being you were concerned about was your own." Kailyn taps the pile of loan documents. "It seems you owed Evelyn and Craig a lot of money."

"I-I-I—"

"No need to qualify that with a response." Kailyn presents another set of emails between Linda and Evelyn chronicling her consistent requests for financial support over the years and Evelyn's pleas that she seek help.

"I ran into a bit of financial trouble—"

I cut her off. "A bit? You've been borrowing money from my parents for more than a decade, Linda. You know, it would've been one thing if you came to me asking for help, but to sue for custody so you could access money that isn't yours is morally reprehensible."

"Emme is better off with me. I've already raised children," she sputters meekly.

"Enough with the bullshit, Linda. Two days after you filed the custody lawsuit, you were already trying to find a way to get rid of her by sending her to boarding school. You planted the alcohol in her locker to build a case against me, for fuck's sake."

"T-that's absurd," Linda stammers.

"Is it? Kailyn overheard you talking about it yesterday."

She looks from me to Kailyn with wide-eyed panic. "Your plans to visit Vegas, how Dax would want Emme on weekends and you'd look good by giving him what he asked for."

Beads of sweat dot her brow and her upper lip. "You can't do this."

"Now would be a good time to drop the custody lawsuit against Daxton," Kailyn says flatly as she pushes her phone across the table and cues up the recording.

"You can't prove anything. So I've had some financial trouble. It's not like everyone has millions of dollars to play with—"

"It's all here. Documented proof that you're self-centered and opportunistic and, worse, you were going to use a grieving thirteen-year-old to your financial advantage." Kailyn hits Play, and Linda's voice filters through the office.

Linda's horror grows as her words are thrown back in her face. She raises a shaky hand. "I don't need to hear any more. I'll drop the lawsuit."

Kailyn stops the recording and smiles icily. "We thought you might say that."

We file away the documents while Linda wrings her hands

and gives me an imploring look. "Daxton, you have to under-stand—"

"Don't," I snap. "Don't try and justify any part of this to me. We'll be waiting for a call to let us know the lawsuit has been officially dropped."

Kailyn and I wait silently while Linda gathers her things and leaves the office in a rush. As soon as we're alone, I exhale a long breath.

Kailyn squeezes my hand. "Are you okay?"

"I think so?" I run my free hand through my hair. "It's just been months of uncertainty and chaos, so the possibility that this could be over is sort of...jarring."

"I can understand that."

"I'll feel a lot better when I get the call from Trish."

"I don't see her stalling. She knows if she doesn't, there's far more at stake than not having access to Emme's money. She planted alcohol in a student's locker—her own niece. She would lose her job if that comes out."

"She should lose her job," I agree.

"Let's wait until the suit is dropped before we blow another hole in her ship."

I nod absently. "Do you have other things you need to take care of today?"

"Only you."

I thread my fingers through hers and squeeze. "Good, be-cause I don't think I'll be able to accomplish anything else until we get that call."

"Why don't we leave all this stuff in my office and grab a drink while we wait?"

I help Kailyn carry the files back to her office, which is when Trish calls me with good news: Linda has officially dropped the lawsuit. I turn to Kailyn as soon as I end the call. "Well, that was fast."

"It's done?" she asks, eyes soft and hopeful.

I nod and pull her against me. Kailyn wraps her arms around my waist and settles her cheek against my chest. I drop my head, lips finding her crown as I breathe her in. It's only then that I notice the state of her office. It's practically empty, only a few boxes on her desk. I step back and motion to the space. "What's going on?"

"I'm moving offices."

"To a bigger one?" I hadn't accepted the offer Beverly put on the table a couple of weeks ago, yet, but I planned to, and soon. Two days ago she called and requested to meet at my earliest convenience, but the past twenty-four hours have been a roller-coaster ride, and I'm just finally catching my breath.

"Not bigger, just to the other side of the floor."

"But I—"

A knock at the door cuts me off. "Kailyn, I—oh! Daxton, hello!" Beverly smiles at me, then turns her attention to Kailyn and gestures to the nearly empty room. "Looks like you're almost there."

"Almost. I was just telling Dax that I'm moving to the other side of the floor."

"It's an exciting change for you." Beverly gives Kailyn a knowing smile and shifts her attention back to me. "Daxton, since you're here, do you have a moment to speak?"

"Uh, sure." I want to know more about this change.

"I'll be here when you get back," Kailyn says.

"Okay." I follow Beverly down the hall. I'd ask her what the change is, but I also feel like whatever the news is, it should come from Kailyn.

"How is everything with Emme?" Beverly asks as she motions me into her office.

It's stark white with a black desk and chair, very little in the way of accents or color. "Great, now that the custody lawsuit has finally been dropped."

"I just received a call from Trish. You must be relieved."

"I am. It means I can move forward, now that Emme's going to be safe and cared for, which is what I wanted."

"She's lucky to have you."

"She's a good kid. I'm lucky to have her."

She swivels in her chair. "I'm sure you want to celebrate the good news with Emme, so I'll cut right to the chase. I have a revised job offer for you to consider."

"Oh?" The original offer was already pretty sweet. It included a 15 percent pay increase, reduced hours, the option to work from home on some days, and a slew of other benefits.

She rests her elbows on the desk and steeples her hands. "I'd like to offer you partner."

It takes a few seconds for the words to sink in. "I'm sorry, can you repeat that?"

"With Kailyn moving into family law and not accepting the partner position, it's left an open position, and I felt you would be an excellent candidate. All of the terms from the original agreement still stand, there's a buy-in, of course, but we can negotiate that if you choose to accept."

"What about Kailyn?" I can't take that from her. I won't take that from her.

"I'm guessing from the look on your face she didn't have a chance to tell you. She turned the partnership down."

"Why would she do that?" She's worked so hard to get where she is.

"You can talk to her about that, but she's decided she wants to pursue other avenues in law, and I fully support her in that decision. Anyway, I don't expect you to make the decision immediately, but if you'd like to mull it over for a day or two before you get back to me, that would be understandable." Beverly is all business with a smile.

"This is an incredibly generous offer."

"Well, to be fair, I've been trying to get you on my team for the past five years. I'd like to make it impossible to say no."

I tap the arm of my chair. "What about your nonfraternization policy?"

Her grin widens. "It doesn't apply to already established relationships."

"And what if I don't accept the partnership? Does the offer still stand?"

"Of course."

"And it would mean there's still a partnership available."

Beverly nods. "It would."

"If you don't mind, I'd like a minute with Kailyn."

"Of course, take all the time you need."

I stand and shake Beverly's hand, still half in shock as I walk down the hall to Kailyn's office. I close the door behind me with a quiet click. "You can't give up the partnership."

She turns, her expression soft. "I want it to be mine because I earned it, not because I brought someone else on board."

"You have earned it." I cross the room to stand in front of her. "Why walk away from it?"

"Because you're more important than a partnership, Dax. You've worked hard to get where you are, too. Besides, I'm great at trusts, but it doesn't give me the sense of fulfillment I need. When I help a family work through an adoption, or negotiate terms for custody and parental rights, that fills my heart and my soul, and gives me pride and validation. It's where my passion is."

"But can't you switch departments and still be partner?"

She runs her hands over my chest and grips my lapels. "I want this security for you and Emme. I want you to be happy and I want to make sure you believe, without a doubt, that the partnership wasn't ever a factor when it came to you and me."

"This is an incredibly selfless thing to do, Kailyn." I cover her hands with mine.

She shakes her head and smiles. "It's probably the exact opposite of selfless. I love you, Dax. I want you to have this because it's what's best for you and Emme, which also happens to be what's best for me."

"I love everything about you." I dip my head and kiss her softly. "Especially your perfect heart. Which is why I'm not accepting the partnership. I'll come to Whitman, but that position is yours. Besides, I have a teenager to raise and a girl-friend I want time with, so partner can wait."

NUMBER 1 FANGIRL

Kailyn

Six Months Later

I'm in the middle of a Holly and Emme sandwich in the back of an Uber. "Where exactly are we going?"

Holly wears a passive smile. "It's a surprise. If we tell you, then it's not a surprise anymore, is it?"

I look to Emme, who's grinning so wide I can practically see her molars. "Come on, Em, give me a little hint. I'll take you shopping."

"I've already bribed Emme," Holly says, "with tickets to the Taylor Swift concert, so whatever you think you have up your sleeve, it's not going to top that."

"She got three tickets, so you can come, too, though."

Holly purses her lips and leans forward. "That was supposed to be a surprise, too."

Emme bounces in her seat. "Oops. Sorry. I'm excited."

Last month I moved in with Dax and Emme. I anticipated a transition period, but it's been surprisingly smooth. I suppose that might be due, in part, to the fact that I was already spending every weekend and usually one night a week at Dax's anyway.

I haven't given up my house yet, opting to rent it for the time being. It has a lot of memories attached to it, and letting it go completely isn't something I'm ready for.

Emme's come a long way in the past six months. After Linda dropped the custody lawsuit, her anxiety calmed, so much of it a result of Linda's interference.

Once the school found out about the planted bottle of vodka, she lost her job, and since has moved into an apartment. Last we heard she'd taken a job at a temp agency, and Dax, being the good man he is, hooked her up with a credit counselor when he found out she'd sought help for her addiction.

Emme finished the school year on a high with marks that were far more representative of "the regular Emme." While she has her bad days, she's certainly much more settled. I don't ever expect that she'll get over losing her parents, but Dax has taken on the role with grace and the typical father anxieties. And of course I'm part of all of it. Holly was right; by being involved with Dax, I've taken on the role of mom for Emme. And I'm happy to be a source of support and love for her, just as she and Dax are for me. In some ways I think I was wrong when I told Dax he would get used to the holes in his heart, that they couldn't be filled by other people. Having the two of them in my life has soothed my previous losses. They fill me with love and purpose in ways my job can't.

A few minutes later we pull up in front of my favorite restaurant. It's a little pub in West Hollywood that serves the best sweet potato fries with chipotle mayo. They also have the best burgers in the entire history of the universe. I may have written that in a review on Yelp and managed to get a few free burgers out of it.

It's normally pretty packed on a Friday night, so I'm surprised to see the empty booths near the window. Maybe we're just ahead of the rush.

Holly gets out first and I follow, waiting for Emme. She's wearing her typical hoodie-and-jeans ensemble, although she's retired the one with all the holes in the sleeves, for the most part. Holly has a cardigan on, despite the warm evening breeze. Although, to be fair, they like to blast the air-conditioning in this place.

As soon as she opens the door, I realize I've been duped. This isn't just a birthday dinner out with my best friend, my boyfriend, and Emme. There are balloons on every table with the number thirty on them, and a huge banner that reads *Happy 30th, Kailyn* is strung across the ceiling.

But that's not even the worst, or best, part. Everywhere I look there's *It's My Life* memorabilia. Posters hang on the walls and those freaking Dax Barbie dolls function as centerpieces. The hostess who greets us is wearing what looks like one of the *It's My Life* shirts I used to have with Dax's face on it.

"Kailyn Flowers?" The hostess grins. "Follow me, please."

I throw a look over my shoulder at Holly and Emme, who are both grinning stupidly. My parents always made such a big deal out of my birthday, probably in part because it wasn't acknowledged prior to my adoption. But also because they wanted to celebrate when I came into the world, and how it brought me into their lives. Since my dad passed, Holly has taken on the task of making my birthday special, so I'm sure whatever this surprise is, she has more than a small hand in it.

I brace for whatever is coming, but nothing can prepare me for what I walk into. I expect to see Dax, and he's definitely there, front and center. I'm not surprised to see a few friends and colleagues, but what I don't expect is to be swarmed by a mob of people screaming my name like I'm the one who starred in a wildly popular TV series instead of my boyfriend.

I'm enveloped in the biggest group hug ever for about ten very confusing seconds before the hug mob steps back and I realize exactly whom I've been hugged by.

"Oh my God!" And all of a sudden I lose complete control of my hands. They start flapping in the air in front of my face. "Oh my God!" I scream a second time as I fight with my body not to jump up and down, and lose the battle.

I slap a palm over my mouth, uncertain if I can contain another scream of excitement, or another bounce. My gaze snags on Dax as he pushes through the crowd, which comprises the entire cast of *It's My Life*. And they're smiling like loons, shouting my name and clapping like I've just put on the best performance in the world. I want to simultaneously melt into the floor and make every one of them sign something for me. I want to be twelve years old again so I can pin the poster to my wall and swoon over it every day.

It's only when Dax is a few feet away that I notice what's printed on the shirts. It's my face, with the text *Kailyn Flowers #1 Fangirl*. In fact, every single person in the room is wearing the exact same shirt. I look over my shoulder to see that Emme has lost her hoodie and Holly has taken off her cardigan to show off their own shirts. Holly's reads *Kailyn Flowers's Bestie*. Felix is behind her, hands jammed into his pockets, smiling along with everyone else.

"Happy birthday, beautiful," Dax says as he wraps me up in his arms.

"I can't believe you did this." I bury my face in his shirt. I'm sure my cheeks are a vibrant shade of red. "I hate you so much right now."

"No you don't." He tips my head back and smiles down at me. "You love me."

"This is crazy. How did you manage this?"

"We were due for a cast reunion, and I couldn't think of a better way to celebrate your birthday than with all the people who helped bring you into my life. I'd like to think without them you never would've fangirled on me all those years ago, and then I might not have had the chance to fall in love with you."

He drops a soft kiss on my lips. "Come on, let me introduce you to everyone."

I'm giddy and ridiculously excited as we make our way

through the room. Someone hands me a Sharpie and I'm forced to sign everyone's shirts.

Dax had one made for me that reads *Daxton Hughes Is My #1 Fan* with a picture of the two of us. He's wrapped around me, chin resting on the top of my head, his smile wide and warm and full of love.

It's hands down the most incredible birthday party I've ever had, thrown by an even more incredible man. My future with him might not be easy or conventional, but then nothing worth fighting for ever is.

Sometimes the darkest tragedies bring us the brightest lights. I'm lucky enough to have found not one, but two.

ACKNOWLEDGMENTS

As always, I have a boundless love for my husband and my daughter, who make this possible for me. Thank you for your patience and understanding and your hugs and positive encouragement.

To my family, thank you for your love and support and for helping mold me into the person I am today. I wouldn't be who I am without you.

Debra, salt without pepper is like Canada without maple syrup or hockey.

I have such an amazing group of friends and colleagues who help me take an idea and turn it into a book you can hold in your hands, and I couldn't do this without them. Kimberly, you're a unicorn and I'm so very glad I have you in my corner.

Sarah, you're an incredible human. Thank you, and the Hustlers, for holding my hand every time we do this.

Huge love to Leah and my team at Forever for making this so much fun!

Nina, you're a special brand of superhero; thank you for

all the years and the love. Jenn, you're amazing, and your positivity and insight make you a truly fabulous friend and colleague. Thank you for being on my team.

My Beaver Den book beavers, thank you for always sharing in my excitement over new books and projects. I love your enthusiasm for words and love stories.

I have so much love and pride for the incredible women in this community who are my friends, colleagues, teachers, and cheer-leaders: Deb, Leigh, Tijan, Teeny, Susi, Erika, Shalu, Kellie, Ruth, Kelly, Melanie, Kristy, Karen, Marty, Marnie, Julie, Jo, Laurie, Kathrine, Angela, my Pams, Filets, Nap girls, Holiday's, my Back-door Babes; Tara, Meghan, and Katherine (and Deb, again); thank you for being you and dealing with my crazy.

To my readers, the bloggers, bookstagrammers, and all the amazing people in this community who read and love and share: it's an honor to be one of you.

ABOUT THE AUTHOR

New York Times and *USA Today* bestselling author Helena Hunting lives outside of Toronto with her amazing family and her two awesome cats, who think the best place to sleep is on her keyboard. She writes all things romance—contemporary, romantic comedy, sports, and angsty new adult. Helena loves to bake cupcakes, has been known to listen to a song on repeat 1,512 times while writing a book, and, if she has to be away from her family, prefers to be in warm weather with her friends.